Roger McDonald was born in Australia in 1941 and grew up in country New South Wales and in Sydney. He is the author of three novels, *1915*, *Slipstream*, and *Rough Wallaby*, and of eight other books including poetry, essays, screenplays, and film-related novelisations. *Shearers' Motel*, his account of travels in the outback with New Zealand shearers, won the 1993 C.U.B. Banjo Award for non-fiction.

NO RETURN

Also by Roger McDonald in Picador

Slipstream
Shearers' Motel

WATER MAN

ROGER McDONALD

PICADOR
AUSTRALIA

This work was assisted by a writer's fellowship from the Australia Council, the Federal Government's arts funding and advisory body.

Acknowledgement is made to Faber and Faber for permission to quote lines from *The Elder Statesman*, T.S. Eliot, 1958.

Thanks to Craig Delaney for the thought behind the epigraph.

First published 1993 by Pan Macmillan Publishers Australia
a division of Pan Macmillan Australia Pty Limited
63–71 Balfour Street, Chippendale, Sydney
A.C.N. 001 184 014

National Library of Australia
cataloguing-in-publication data:

McDonald, Roger, 1941– .
Water man.

ISBN 0 330 27398 1.

I. Title.

A823.3

Typeset in 11/16 pt Palatino by Post Typesetters
Printed in Australia by McPherson's Printing Group

When bright things tarnish
he will truly be gone.

Then you will know him.

Contents

BOOK ONE

DEPARTURE

Snake Ring

1939

GUNNER FITCH ARRIVED AT CROPPDALE with his new wife and left her alone for the day, headed away from the road, across the dry river and up into the hills on foot, with only a limping black dog for company. He carried a canvas knapsack holding a long-handled tin torch, a Vest Pocket Kodak camera, corned beef sandwiches, a bottle of cold milky tea, wax matches, and a packet of gelignite and fuses.

His wife Rosan sat on the verandah of the men's quarters and watched him disappear into the sun with a tired wave. If only he wouldn't just dump her like this, then she wouldn't just drift.

He wouldn't return until nightfall; it was always the same. He needed a whole day to find what he could never see, but could feel in his nerves and stomach tension — fissures in rock under his boot-soles and lakes of underground water that would rise with a lapping rush through iron bore casing when he called in the drill. Sometimes he'd light dynamite sticks and drop them into cracks in the ground, put his ear to the earth after the blast, and listen for echoes. Rage was in him as much as patience. When he smiled, a prominent gold molar invited murder. His work exhausted him like a fever: his divining gave him fits, it struck so deep. When he returned at nightfall he would spread sheets of graph paper on the bonnet of the car, and while Rosan held the torch the Gunner would explain his findings to the land-owner. So much water here, so many feet under, at such a rate of flow. He would never be wrong. Rosan would have to do the driving afterwards while Gunner slumped in the passenger seat smoking roll-your-owns down to wet slugs and thinking his own thoughts.

On this occasion, though, something would be different. It would be her under attack, her arms trembling, her stomach in a knot, needing both hands to grip the big tin torch and shine it steady the way Gunner liked. Rosan looked around the bare dusty Croppdale compound and fanned herself nervously. What had she let herself in for, pledging herself to Gunner Fitch when she loved someone else?

THREE MONTHS PREVIOUSLY GUNNER FITCH had capped a bore at the Logan's Reef Jockey Club. Croppdale's owner, William D'Inglis, had performed the opening ceremony, turning a hefty brass valve as a cheer went up. Rosan had felt the impatience of the man as he met her eye. It had started something in her. Who was he to her that she would feel this bother? But it was exciting. They had turned away from each other — it was too much to account for; there was a touch of dread. A diesel engine pumped sprays that within a few weeks would turn a desolate home straight into a gentle green meadow, where on race days thoroughbreds with hooves like lacquered half-coconuts would chip the turf.

William D'Inglis was a handsome, burly, sandy-haired man with pale eyelashes and a bad temper, and women in Logan's Reef said he was a pig. It rankled the way he treated their men at the mill he owned (D'Inglis Self Raising). His workers hated him with a smouldering dependence, but that was all right, thought Rosan, inwardly taking his side though she had barely noticed him in her life before, everyone had their gripes, and D'Inglis Self Raising was a national name, they were stuck with it, it was them. Anyway, Rosan had just liked the way he looked at her, so she had been off and away, caught up in this, nervously biting her knuckles, hurrying along that day beside Gunner's lanky strides, pretending indifference.

After the opening ceremony Gunner had been approached by William D'Inglis to find underground water on his place, and had taken a thirty pound deposit because D'Inglis was desperate for water, and wanted it guaranteed. Gunner had issued him with a receipt stamped with the sign he had chosen for himself, a tubby little man in smudged indelible ink, striding out while holding a forked stick. The original was copied from an old book he'd found years before in a shelled church in Belgium. He'd cast a rough model of the figure and welded it to the radiator cap of his Diamond T truck. The sightless almond-shaped eyes were picked out in silver frost.

After the business with William D'Inglis had been completed and the deposit pocketed, Gunner had said it would be ten to twelve weeks before he could get out to Croppdale.

'After you've taken my money?' D'Inglis had grunted resentfully. 'I don't like that.'

'The money means I'll come,' asserted the Gunner. Rosan had nodded over his shoulder that indeed he would, *she* could vouch for him.

Gunner Fitch was in demand across a wide sweep of country. The Diamond T was high-slung and narrow-cabbed, with hard pneumatic tyres. With its cranelike derrick and load of scaly pipes chained on each side it stalked the landscape top-heavily. Gunner found water with gum sticks, willow sticks and, failing that, with lengths of old iron, twists of fencing wire, or just with his long lean fingers extended outwards. It didn't matter what. When he had first come calling on Rosan, who was half his age, and taken her dancing, it had been the same reaction. He'd become possessed, wrists extending from his coat, transforming himself from a silent, dark-suited collarless bloke with a felt hat jammed around his ears, into a jumping striding wonder who seemed to want to get out of his own skin in a hurry. Soon he was asking her along, supplying a picnic hamper with china plates. Stalking across gullies he kept his eyes closed. When he stopped and concentrated he became a thin twisted tree stump burnt down to charcoal.

While shadows had lengthened that evening of the Jockey Club inauguration and the long-necked empties grew in number under the trestled tables, William D'Inglis, boozy like the rest of them, had had a go at finding water. He couldn't get any reaction and it irritated him. He said Gunner Fitch was a con. He couldn't even get his thumbs on the stick properly, because he thought there had to be a right way and a wrong way, and Gunner kept saying, no, there wasn't any wrong way or right way. D'Inglis was an incommunicative man with the sulky Scottish good looks that went with money, and Rosan had put her arms around in front of him to guide his hands, mingling their beery breaths. It had made them know each other in a moment and understand there would be an assignation at some time. It was the feeling both had been waiting for, what their weighted, wary glances had signified, and why they'd been drinking, to give themselves courage.

MONTHS PASSED. ROSAN AND GUNNER had married. Gunner decided to buy a rickety corner store surrounded by a dirt verandah. It had a drooping peppercorn tree whose branches scraped the roof-iron, and a horse trough in the shade. He put the deeds in Rosan's name and said that when he died it would keep her.

Sometimes Rosan would see William D'Inglis driving past in his gold Pontiac, a light linen jacket draped over the empty passenger seat beside him, his two small sons, Kelvin and Jim, firing cap guns through the windows. His wife Peg was never with him. People said she was too good for the town. Both of them were married now, though, and so they were equals, Rosan believed. It was what she thought about all the time.

And she cunningly nursed a small resentment against Gunner to balance the equation further her way. It was what Gunner had told her about the history of two men and that other woman from years before — that Peg D'Inglis, either before she was married, or after — he did not say — had betrayed D'Inglis with another man. Rosan knew by the thinness of his smile that the other man had been Gunner.

Over the winter Gunner Fitch circled the map creating a spiral of properties with located water until Croppdale reached the top of his list and he had to go there. It was months after the wedding. There were many times when Gunner's work made him ill, when all he wanted was to lie in a darkened room with a damp towel over his face, and times when he wanted to shoot himself. This going to Croppdale was one of them. While packing the picnic hamper in the car Gunner betrayed in the shake of his limbs the flow of feeling that captured him when he found water. Only it wasn't water now. The china almost shattered while Rosan sat in the front, staring ahead, biting her full lower lip with her even white teeth. People didn't always know when they connected with the deepest part of another, or what the consequences would be. But Gunner knew. There was no point appeasing him.

WILLIAM D'INGLIS WALKED OVER THE wide bare dusty space between the Croppdale homestead and the men's quarters, taking his time to reach her. It was their moment, but they couldn't look at each other. He hung his thumbs in his belt, told her, while studying a cloud, that if she needed anything she was to go up to the main house. She said she would, if she needed to, but would have no need, being supplied for the day with a picnic and a book, while thinking his mouth looked sour, who'd want to kiss him?

He couldn't take his eyes from her stockinged

shins under her thin skirt. His voice thickened when he spoke. Men like William D'Inglis thought women like Rosan Fitch, formerly Logan, were small-town tarts and remembered special drinks to get them started, except they couldn't be tried now, they weren't suited to a daylight situation.

'If you need anything, just ask the woman at the house.'

'You just said that.'

'So I did.' He touched the brim of his brown hat, smiled, and went away. She liked that smile. It had quickness like a boning knife. It brought him to her through the thickets of her vows.

He hadn't referred to the woman at the house as his wife though, thought Rosan, and she believed that that was unfeeling. (But then the woman wasn't his wife at all, Rosan soon learned. His wife had left him some time ago. He'd kept it quiet; she had gone to Bowral to be alone, and was preparing to depart for England. Whoever that woman in the house was, raising a window, airing the bedding, and being ignored all day by Rosan and ignoring her, she was just a governess, an employee, no better than Rosan herself.)

She went inside the dusty men's quarters to get out of the glare. All this excitement was a mistake, and her life was plainly before her. The Gunner, like

William D'Inglis, was much older than her — he'd
been in the Great War as a youth; half his converse
was with the dead, nightmares full of confused
shouting since they'd begun sharing a bed, as if
hordes of mates and rampant bayoneters were coming between them. At forty-four he was amazing —
playing fullback for the Reef in Group Nine League: a
suicidal sprinter, colliding with a goalpost full stick,
flattened under a collapsed scrum, then raising himself on his knuckles, shaking off men, staggering on
spindly legs, seeing stars, getting back into it. The
word was that he played dirty, though. A nickname
that followed him from the war was Gunner Filth.
After games Rosan bandaged his cuts, bathed his
bruises, and attended his swollen joints with goanna
balm. She was lucky to get him, people said, lucky
he'd gone into debt for her to buy the shabby corner
shop in Logan's Reef and put the title in her name.

Looking around, Rosan despaired that her life was
to involve her in a kitchen like this one, painting
stoveblack onto cast-iron ranges, mopping bare
boards, serving food on china plates on special occasions, but otherwise using chipped enamel plates
from the outdoor camps and rough huts that Gunner
operated. She found a broom and swept along the
skirting boards, driving before her a pile of feathers,
dry leaves, fine dirt, burrs, and hairballs.

Down in the corner of the mess room was a pile of toys and books, tin boxes and wooden guns left by the children of the place. One of the books had a thick cardboard cover. It was called *A Boy's Adventures With Gods and Heroes*. Rosan rested her broom, lifting an armload to the table. A box lid fell open, spilling everything out. She was curious about those boys, Kelvin and Jim. Perhaps they would like her — who knew? Her whole life would be secret now, kept in darkness like Gunner's water. On a galvanised tray, on a bed of dry moss, were bits of old bottle glass, a tarnished necklace and a crusty ring. They were like little bower birds, those two, it seemed, and she hoped that they would come and play with her. She thought she might see in them aspects of William D'Inglis, who was closed off to her except in his lust. Gunner said he wanted children — two boys. He gave them names, Mal and Josh. (They were ex-Logan's Reef fellows who had died in his battery.) He often talked about them, making them seem more real than his time with Rosan. Gunner was a sixth son, the only survivor of a family of boys. All his brothers had died at birth or soon after.

Rosan carried the small treasures across to the washing-up tub. If the boys came in she would surprise them with the beauty of neglected things restored to their original glory. It was how she felt about herself in love. The ring attracted her most. It was so bound in green chemical crust that she had to hit it with the flat of a scrubbing brush. The crust came flicking off. The ring flew up with a life of its own, spinning in the air. Rings were in her thoughts a lot lately: the engagement ring that Gunner had travelled to Sydney to fetch, six diamonds in an arrangement of the Southern Cross, an expensive line of Prouds, made of platinum — nothing that a woman would naturally like but an argument for a man's wallet, really, especially a man like Gunner — and the wedding ring he had slid onto her finger in a small ceremony, a pure continuous seamless line without interruption that spelled a future for her, and made her say to herself, *damn!* and start to cry.

Rosan worked at the old ring with a nailbrush and a saucer of caustic soda. While her fingertips burned she saw how it shone back at her. Something was emerging there. It was gold. She was amazed — it was thick, sturdy old metal fashioned in the shape of two snakes twisted together. It was beautiful. It was uncanny, too, because soon after their marriage Gunner had shot a pair of tiger snakes mating — they'd been rolling and slithering through grass near an old Canary Island pine without a chink of daylight between them. They looked like these. Against her cries Gunner strode out after them, the gun cradled and kicking. An angry eye she had never seen before gleamed down the sights. He came back with clots of dead snake on his leggings making her sick. She withdrew, horrified: 'Don't touch me.' This was the man who had courted her with melancholy mouth-organ solos, with lilies and wildflowers gathered from roadside lagoons, who'd sung 'Danny Boy' at their marriage breakfast in a rippling tenor.

She breathed on the ring, and the snakes seemed to writhe in the warm fog of her breath. Shade came and went in the old weatherboard room as she examined the reptiles. Her loosened, long yellow hair dappled the light. The creatures were intent on the business of passion through eternity, their beautiful backs notched with tiny, perfect scales. They knew love, thought Rosan.

Then the shade deepened, and William D'Inglis stood in the room. 'I'm sorry,' he said, assuming he was intruding. But she glanced up and smiled back gladly. 'Of course not, don't be,' briefly touching her hair. 'Come over here. Look at this.' He closed the space between them, their hands brushed, and she bent to his side as they studied the ring.

'Rosan,' he spoke her name, a harshness catching, 'you went and married!'

She couldn't say anything to this. She had. What had he ever offered her?

There was no space between the snakes; each had the tail of the other in its mouth — two immaculate reptiles as close as anything living could get. She slid the ring onto the fourth finger of William D'Inglis's left hand.

'It's taken from your sons' playbox,' she whispered.

'They won't miss it.'

Then William D'Inglis showed her to one of the dusty men's quarters' rooms that contained twin wire-framed beds and rolled-up bedding. 'We'll be safe here.' He whipped a mattress to the floor, pushing the door shut with his back and wedging it against intruders with a bedside table, while Rosan sat on a rickety chair and unrolled her stockings.

GUNNER FITCH HEAVED BOULDERS INTO a cleft of gully and struck sparks down in the shadows where the sun never reached. He raised his arms back over his head until he almost unbalanced and hurled them down. He rolled back his sleeves and collected rocks, pelting them at targets on the opposite rockface of crumbling shafts, dislodging swallows' nests and striking anything that moved. His rage found fireflies in the damp ferny dark below and smeared them to blackness. Only Chinese miners had ever been into those depths before; no white man had dared in these rotting ridges. His dog danced around his ankles. Gunner stood, seeking water, his fists clenched at the level of his crotch like an agonised supplicant. How long he stood with the breeze ruffling his thinning black hair and the sun burning his bald patch was anybody's guess. His dog lay in the shade, watching. If only his boys could march again, thought Gunner Fitch, the gullies would sound to their songs, a Jew's harp would twang, Josh and Mal would leap and grin. The bump of their rifles, the grind of their heavy axle-trees and the bloodiness of their guns would be truly lost, and they would repossess life. They would dance on creekflats and be drunk under the moon, plough between rocks with their rickety mares and ascend finally from earthbound existence at a moment of their own sincere choosing.

Thinking such thoughts, Gunner Fitch always found water.

Around the countryside he went, locating wells, broaching springs, piercing dry hillsides. He kept bumping into mothers, brothers, and old uneasy sweethearts, offended survivors hobbled with mementos — a lettercard, a badge, a French coin. Gunner wanted to say, 'There's a time they will return, know it and die'. Only then would these lettercards gather mould, the badges dull, the coins turn quaint, the memories dissolve back into life, easing over.

Down on the other side of the ridge Gunner Fitch saw the whole of Croppdale laid out. Sweet silence filled the homestead valley under his feet, the wide-verandahed house under a cliff, its stands of poplars, unleafed as yet, and its dusty white track humping in, enlarging from the direction of Logan's Reef. Emptiness prevailed where earlier Gunner had seen the tiny floral imprint of Rosan on the verandah, before she disappeared inside. He wanted to yell, *Listen. Wait. Do this differently.* But there were rules of the dead. He saw William D'Inglis setting free his horses down at the yards, and felt his jumpy eye scanning the hills, seeking a glimpse of him before going over to the huts. Gunner sank from sight.

GUNNER KNELT AT THE BASE of a granite boulder the size of a bloated heifer. His dog Nell kept her distance. There was work to be done here. The rock weighed two tons or more. It overlooked a small hut and an orchard area to the east of the main compound. Away from that hut, set in an avenue of boulders, was a well. It glinted up at him like an eye. He made a calculation involving rate of roll, absence of wind, obstacles in the path. His aim was to shoot the boulder down the hill and drop it in the well. He'd scored harder shots in his time, hitting moving trains below the horizon, copping the mouths of dugouts disguised as primal mud, all the same everywhere, erupting. He had the sickening certainty he based his living on, a feeling like blue porridge in the guts, a desperate uselessness, fatal, unerring. He saw what would happen, and then it did.

He couldn't shift the boulder forward with his shoulder, only slightly backwards, so he took two red detonator caps from his knapsack and set them at angles to the fulcrum point where the boulder rested. His dog went skedaddling away and disappeared into a crevice of rock hidden by a hawthorn bush. Gunner, sweating, was able to rock the boulder back on the caps and set them off — he was banged aside as an ear-splitting crack rang out and the boulder toppled and rumbled down the grassy steepness to the tiny target a half-mile below. It was easy as a dream. The well stayed the same size, the boulder shrank, deflected, then returned to its true course. Finally it hovered appropriately in the air while Gunner counted two, three, four, and then it was gulped, gone, with just a muddy splash betraying where it had lodged.

Gunner Fitch closed his eyes and felt ice in his veins, bottle-green, sharp. He heard the faint yaps of his dog away in the mountain. He shivered. Under his feet, Gunner divined, was a cavern with a roof like a high mooning mouth. Things glowed there eerily bright, phosphorescent red, as if a torch had been shone up a nose. He saw water as a tongue lapping, murmuring, clucking.

The jolt from the boulder jamming in the well rang up through subterranean arteries until it rippled into Gunner Fitch's bones, and he felt himself vibrating mournfully in the gold fillings of his teeth. Not the air 'Danny Boy' this time, ah no, it would never be that again, but a marching song taking Gunner off to another war, releasing him from the poison of time. Gunner had already been in touch with his former commander. There was a place for him in the old brigade.

He called for his dog but she had gone to ground. All afternoon he heard Nell barking under the ridges. Finally the sound faded — she was deeper in, winding down, tracking old water races and forgotten Chinese shafts until she stood guardian on the shores of a lake in the mountain fed by a rolling unseen river.

DOWN IN THE HUTS WILLIAM D'Inglis rested on an elbow, smiling at Rosan Fitch. She traced the line of his lips with a tender fingertip and tears ran down her cheeks. Once more they moved together. Across the dusty mattress they rolled, seeking each other, head to toe, eye to eye. The salt of a tear, the darting of a red tongue-tip, the stretch of a white belly, the circle of love was endless in that day. They were in it.

IT WAS AFTER DARK WHEN a cone of torchlight moved down the slope on the far side of the river, and a man's boots could be heard disturbing river stones as he waded through the droughty shallows. No dog with him. A mood of menacing anticipation, broken only by the clinking of rocks. Then the lonely hiss of boots as he crossed the sand.

William D'Inglis had beers ready on the bonnet of the car, bottles already open. He and Rosan had already made a start — small wonder after their day — using shapely Pilsener glasses that D'Inglis had brought down from the house.

'There's a dog out there,' said Gunner, nodding his thanks and draining the glass he was handed. 'She disappeared on me.'

'Is she a sheep killer?' asked William D'Inglis.

'You might hear her some nights,' said Gunner, 'so do what you have to do, if you're bothered.'

'I'll take a gun.'

'Yeah, you should,' Gunner said, knowing that one day D'Inglis would go into the ground, fall or be pushed, and find what was under a life besides mine shafts and sink holes. If he didn't, this day was wasted.

Rosan held the torch over Gunner's shoulder while he explained what he reckoned was there, away above the Cropp River at an elevation suitable for gravity feed, an opportunity for sending water down to the homestead area at a tremendous rate, a drought-proofing of D'Inglis's money-hungry operations, around twenty-three thousand gallons a minute, he estimated.

'Hold on there, Fitch,' D'Inglis was disbelieving, 'the Chinks tapped creeks, but that sounds like a bloody great river you're talking about.'

'What I found,' said Gunner Fitch in his steady, soft voice, 'was a bloody great lake. There's a river inside your mountain feeding the lake that will flow for a thousand years.'

'You're very sure of yourself,' challenged D'Inglis.

'I have my days,' responded the Gunner softly.

He looked down to where William D'Inglis's pale

flour miller's hand was splayed on the bonnet of the car. Rosan couldn't help following his gaze, and she lowered the torch as if inadvertently, to display the shine of the ring. The light played on the importance of the gold.

Over the years that Gunner had known Bill D'Inglis he had never worn anything as fancy as this. The purity of the metal was unblemished. Under the clean gold Gunner saw snakes writhing with a life of their own, crusted with treacherous filth as they bucked through the earth.

'I won't be able to do the job, though.' Gunner threw his head back with a snap.

'Why the devil not?' D'Inglis challenged.

'It ain't the right time, Bill, that's all. She'll just have to wait. You've been hearing the news.'

'I'll have my deposit back, then,' answered D'Inglis.

Gunner said nothing.

They stared at each other. Rosan thought they were going to fight. She went around to the passenger side of the car and got in, then sat waiting with a rug on her knees and a cardigan around her shoulders in the upland chill.

Gunner Fitch cursed William D'Inglis in a whisper: 'I promise I'll bring them snakes right out of you, mate. So you look them in the eye or you won't have no peace, let me tell you.'

With a swift grab, he slammed his left hand on William D'Inglis's wrist, and with his powerful right grabbed D'Inglis's finger and tried to wrench the ring off. It wouldn't come. 'You'll keep,' he muttered, pushing the big man back easily, both hands to his chest. He threw his gear in the back of the car, climbed in and drove off, bottles and glasses scattering, leaving William D'Inglis wordless in the dark and Rosan trapped hopelessly in the passenger seat all the long drive back to Logan's Reef.

IT WAS THREE IN the morning when Gunner Fitch reached Croppdale again, gliding past homesteads with his headlights switched off, and taking a wrong turn among the twists and curves above the river where he ran out of gasoline, spilling it over himself while refilling the tank. He parked behind a rock a mile from the house, pumped a grease gun into a handkerchief and folded the corners over, stuffing it into his pocket.

Gunner Fitch walked through the farm compound, quietening the dogs, then stood on the flagstoned verandah above the river, sensing the many rooms of the sleeping house. William D'Inglis was up in the attic, a lamp burning. Gunner held the man steady in the sights of his consideration, starlight drenching him in phosphorescence, leaving traces on the doorknob when he moved, shiny thumb-prints on the old engraved window-glass, a comet's tail of static tracking his boots on the worn hall carpet. Through into the living room, photographs and silverware catching what little light there was, things in there Gunner might load in a sack and depart with if he chose, making himself rich. Dull ancestral plate. Murky crystal. Gold butter knives. He saw framed photos of horse-drawn wheat wagons queued at the D'Inglis's silos at Logan's Reef, pictures he had taken himself, signed R.C. Fitch in white ink. He came to an oil painting of the late Sir Manfred (Dusty) D'Inglis wearing Masonic Lodge insignia. And then he found a portrait of the haughty Peg MacPriam. He knew this one well, having taken it at the Royal Easter Show when Bill D'Inglis was courting her. She was a dab hand at tying sheaves for the district tableau. She was in jodhpurs, sitting on a hay bale against a mock post and rail fence, the woman who later deserted them, mother of Kelvin and Jim. Who was chasing down Peg MacPriam's particular river now? Why wasn't it him? He did not know. He was a simple irascible bloke with a skill at the base of his brain. All water diviners were dull, Peg had said, they were dim, but Gunner knew how to find things — he'd found her, hadn't he? They'd had their roll in the hay at the Royal Easter Show. It unsettled people, the way Gunner came at them, making them search in themselves, though they never knew it, and find what they really wanted. Look at the way he'd found Rosan, the way he'd divined love in her, driven her to find its match. That was the quality of his skill. It gave him the shits living it out.

Up to the top of the last narrow stair, then, Gunner Fitch went, reeking of gasoline, his heavy boots causing a board to creak with a sound like rifleshot, knowing that Bill D'Inglis would be wide awake, waiting for him. Gunner stood flattened against the wall outside the attic door. He could hear strained breathing. Such returned soldiers as Bill D'Inglis (Supplies) found if they kept a night-light on they could stave off their horrors. Gunner Fitch was a deeper initiate of nightmare, though: he spanned separations, lived in the deepest dark, divined himself to the pits of hell. It was why they'd called him Filth. Bill D'Inglis had seen pack mules mounting each other in terror on the old Flers–Gueudecourt–Beaulencourt road while starshells scribbled the sky and his Indian labourers went gaga, their guts dribbling out. But that was routine in the experience of the Gunner. At Bernafay Wood R.C. Fitch drank water from under ice where a mate's face was frozen. He made it a winter's-long sacrament and lived. He hadn't kept his sanity on the Western Front, ah, no, he'd given it its head. The boys were in there, Mal and Josh, lanky as saplings, gloating and giggling and cruel, braying like donkeys as the enemy overran them, their buck teeth sticking through their grins like cricket bats.

The Gunner slid a dirty hand along the wall and twisted the lampwick down, extinguishing it with a *phut.*

Bill D'Inglis was instantly up and fighting. Possums bursting into rooms made commotions like this, smashing hand basins, disturbing papers. Except for one introspective witness, a small boy, the rest of the household stayed sleeping as Gunner moved economically, fending off blows, just wanting the ring, nothing else, concentrating on that, and conveying this to the other by stamping on his windpipe, holding his left wrist down under the heel of a boot, shaking out grease from the handkerchief, smearing it over the finger, slipping the ring away easily, pocketing the thing. It was then that Gunner was inattentive and a punch from D'Inglis connected.

With a vomiting sound, Gunner spat a tooth onto

the bare boards of the attic stairs. Down on the verandah flagstones he staggered, drooling blood. The white
face of a small boy watched him from a downstairs
doorway in the pearly pre-dawn light. It was Kel, the
halfwit, Gunner noted from the corner of his eye. The
skinny pyjama-clad figure ran after him, trying to see
his face. In the farm compound, a place of shiny tin
sheds and white-painted yards, Gunner hesitated,
then leapt a fence. He ran under the cliffs before
negotiating his way upwards, finding a goat-path of
sorts, and finally scrambling vertically, hand over
hand, gripping tree roots and crumbly knobs of limestone. Halfway to the sky he stood outlined in full sight
of the white-faced remembering child. The whole of
Croppdale was under him in this light. Gunner Fitch
bellowed a question: 'See?', then repeated it and made it
a command — 'See' — putting his hands to the sides of
his head, ducking under a gnarled banksia root on the
goat track there, twisting his head off in the shadows,
leaving his head like a lump of coal in the cliff, charred
and immobile and staring back the way he'd come.

ON THE ROAD BACK TO the Reef, Gunner Fitch began
shaking, trembling at the wheel from more than

rough surfaces as his car jolted the corrugations and he swallowed more blood. He needed a fire. So he stopped on a lonely stretch of track, and huddled at the roadside, feeding flames with gum twigs, unable to heat himself through, putting his overcoat flaps around the flame to direct the heat upwards like a chimney. His tongue explored the hole in his jawline where his gold tooth had once been. It had cost him good money in Macquarie Street. The ring in his pocket felt rough and heavy, a poor exchange — it had grit and fluff stuck all over it, and was no good like this. He wanted it mirror-bright to shove in front of Bill D'Inglis's face sometime. Then they would both understand.

Prosperity

1992

IT WAS A BLUSTERY WINTER afternoon when a woman found a seat in a darkened, almost empty rehearsal hall. She left her umbrella dripping in the aisle and her sodden raincoat draped over an armrest. She jammed her boots on the back of the seat in front, and tucked her knees up under her chin. Thankful that nobody could see her from the stage, she stared ahead with angry attentiveness. She appeared calm, but her stomach rumbled, her hands trembled, her legs shook. Her hands clutched her knees, the knuckles showing white in the dark.

Minutes stretched out. She knew she was unwelcome here, but consoled herself by thinking that things would have been worse had she not come at all. The activity on the stage was haphazard, with lights dimming at erratic intervals, and shouts of warning as heavy items were dropped. Swearing was heard, and scattered laughter. Stale dust filled the air.

Her professional name was Storm Wilde — she had recently let it be known that she was dropping it. Her real name was Ida D'Inglis. She had chosen the stage name some twenty years before. Now she was not sure what she knew. She was frightened by what she had done, by writing this play, *Prosperity*, making a solid structure from youthful pretensions, branding herself a serious person rather late in life, she thought.

Actors were gathered in the front row, drinking coffee and talking. She was an actor herself, or had been until a spate of renunciations. She could have had the part of Midge, if she had wanted it, the female lead — young and lovely, with masses of fiery hair piled high, eyes flashing, petticoats foaming, bare feet dancing across the boards. She'd had the chance. Storm Wilde had the voice, the energy, the name, and she aged down spectacularly. (She would have had to.) But she was out of that shell.

Nobody else working on *Prosperity* had Ida's qualms. The actors kept lifting their eyes to the stage where Mal Fitch, pockmarked, nuggety, and wearing a black rollneck sweater like a sea captain, glowered down at them. He was the one on whom they depended for their sense of reality. He raged, sulked, demanded — until he found things in them they didn't know they had. Behind his back they said *Prosperity* was make or break for Mal, because Whale Belly Players had meant children's theatre till now, had for years. Mal Fitch himself thought differently despite the obvious. His theatre had never been for kids. They were just the ones who came in their hordes and gave it a name. His theatre had been for himself. Inescapably.

He called for quiet. Light flooded across the nondescript floor and over the flimsy arch that the designer had transformed into something unearthly. The scenery represented places that Ida D'Inglis and Mal Fitch both knew by heart, thistle-strewn landscapes, homesteads in steep gullies, narrow, rocky wheatfields, and a flour mill three storeys high. She knew the countryside and its quirks, Mal knew the town. Mal had suggested the title: 'Prosperity is like a tender mother, but blind, who spoils her children'. It was irresistible, though barbed. It wasn't what Ida had meant. What she had been after was a feeling of reconciliation. She had thought she could do it on the page, but the more solid everything became the less it was hers. The play became more Mal's than anyone's. He had never been to Croppdale, but the power of the place was at his disposal.

Mal shaded his eyes, glared into the stalls, and Ida knew she'd been spotted. He tramped about showing irritation, then descended from the stage, making his way to a seat near the front, where he pointedly slumped from view. Mal's attitude was that having declined a part, she had no purpose left in the enterprise beyond collecting royalties, if any. She tried not to take it personally, because he was the same with everyone.

Exposing her imagination to the man made her feel childish, as though she was confessing to an illicit love affair that had never happened, that was all one-sided, choked with enlarged, irrelevant emotion. Passion without connection — that summarised the lonely task of writing. Knowing her from stage and television, who would think that writing *Prosperity* had given cool, unflappable, wisecracking Storm Wilde cramps and nausea, vomiting and sleeplessness as those Ida D'Inglis characters came charging out, singing and rhyming? During the writing nothing showed: she met friends, went over to Mal's cramped untidy house in Darlinghurst, went to dinners and parties. But all the time, in bed, at breakfast, riding in taxis, at rehearsals, at the pub, writing anywhere she could, she existed inside a spiral-bound Flipback Shorthand Notebook, where she made her clumsy, block-lettered, badly-spelt pencillings.

Tremblingly, she had delivered the result. 'I don't know what this is, whether it's anything at all.' Ida's vulnerability was something shameful to her, a spasm, a regret. It was nothing new. To overcome its stranglehold she had become an actress.

Production was a formal kind of contempt. Mal broke a silence: 'There's a lot to be done with this.' She'd watched him sitting at his chart-table under the stairs, half-moon glasses on the tip of his nose, fingers grinding through chin-stubble, head down, sorting the pages as he shaped her longings into incidents. There had been a time when she had liked nothing better than to sit watching as he studied a book or made meticulous sketches for reinterpretation by James, the designer. His concentration was fabulous. No man had ever let her be in this way. He disappeared into the tunnel of himself and a thankful silence fell. As he read he chewed Marine Lifesaving Rations consisting of Allen's light butterscotch wrapped in heavy foil.

If he hadn't been a director he would have been a

junk dealer. He picked things up when he went prop buying in Whale Belly's Econovan. If he saw something on or in another vehicle as he drove along, he'd hold a card on the window: YOU SELL? Amazing what people would let go on impulse. Crammed in his room were a rusting bicycle, original watercolours, fishing rods, a portable gas barbecue, theatrical masks and wicker baskets with red chairs upended in them, rolls of pale blue linen and a car roofrack. When he was finished he'd throw up his arms — 'Let's get pissed!' — keeping habits from a time when half his life was lived in Push pubs at the bottom of the city, the United States and the Royal George, which, he said, had been his university when he arrived from the bush, bars full of paranoid unpublished poets and narrow-minded free thinkers. It was strange for Ida to reflect that he had known her all her life; that he remembered her as a baby; that he had loved her even then.

Ida had needed to smash a picture of herself. A raucous collage was the only way she could describe what had come tumbling through — bits of family history transposed, details from the gossip of her parents' social circle, or rather class, as Mal insistently called it, historical colour, the life of colonial bush roads and inns, snatches of Shakespeare, Greek myths, squatting-era ballads, *Such Is Life*, and invasions from dreams that were hers, but were also Mal's — this last being finally disturbing, as if she were being used as a vessel of processing while he lazily, imperiously, awaited a result, and she had only resentment to carry forward while he came stealing around her.

THERE WAS THIS LIFELONG IMPORTANCE of her to him. But she couldn't recall ever noticing Mal Fitch of Logan's Reef until an event when she was ten or eleven.

He'd been working as a dispatch clerk in her family's flour mill. She had the run of the place. She'd come speeding down a tin-lined loading chute, using it as a slippery slide, and he'd caught her at the bottom, plucking her free as a two-hundred-pound bag of flour came thundering down behind her. To get away from him she'd kicked him in the shins and — she had a distinct memory of this — he'd twisted her ear with vicious intent.

As a director, Mal Fitch had a saying: 'The script is an urgent telegram sent to the director'. She had obeyed this dictum. Reading her play, Mal kept holding sheets out to one side, then sliding them back into the pile in different positions. The whole reading job, from start to finish, took twenty minutes.

'What do you think?'

'I'm thinking.' He tapped a pencil on his teeth.

'Terrific, Mal,' she said throatily. She was tearful and hiding it.

She made them both a drink, a MacPriam's Tablelands Malt. Between them they had cases of the stuff.

Mal raised his whisky in a toast, still keeping her waiting. 'To that family of yours.'

She pleaded, 'I want your honest opinion, Mal, for Christ's sake'.

'All right. Calm down. I love every misspelt word and it's alive as a box of centipedes. Move over.'

Ida made room for him on the old couch. It might have been any one of the many times since they had first become lovers. With an arm round her waist, Mal eyed the bedroom door as he gulped his whisky. They would go in there shortly, get between the musty bedsheets.

'Just one thing,' said Mal expansively. 'You've jammed the ending in the middle. Somebody enters at the denouement who isn't in the dramatis personae.' He flicked through the pages for emphasis. 'Lachlan Strong, the drover.'

Ida looked into the bottom of her glass. 'Isn't that just life?'

'Strong's not much of a name,' said Mal. 'It's in the same category as "Storm Wilde".'

'Oh?'

They glared at each other.

'I know who's bugging you in this character. It's that old boyfriend of yours, Alec Hooper.'

'You know too much, that's your trouble, Mal.'

'Don't I just. Small towns are full of walking ghosts. The trick is to stare them down. You've never done that with old Al.'

It was true. Ida had not spoken to Alec Hooper, met his eye, or even looked in his direction for years. There were plenty of people like that in Logan's Reef who were treated that way by D'Inglises. (Mal said Ida was the only one forgiven for it — half the town was soft on her, like he was.) She would rather not think about Alec Hooper at all. It annoyed her that Mal could divine the strength of him in her. She'd never told Mal the whole story either, not by any means. His intuition was uncanny. His damnable gift was to make people deliver up their lives — though she could say, if she chose, that his own life was stuck.

Ida rose from the couch, went through to the kitchen and rinsed her glass, upending it on the draining board. Exasperated by Mal's jealousy and needling, she grabbed her bag, let herself out the door, and was on the road hailing a cab before Mal knew anything.

At fourteen, Ida had devotedly followed Alec Hooper (who was seventeen) down the sandy, casuarina-shaded reaches of the Cropp River. Alec was a stockrider employed by her grandfather, William D'Inglis, to clear the gullies of stray cattle. She galloped after him through every twist and swerve of his ride. They swam their horses in a deep pool. Then it was the two of them reclining on the sand, their saddles making big sweaty armchairs. They told each other about their lives. When their toes touched, bare, gritty with sand, they turned away, shocked into recognition of love. There had never been a more beautiful boy than Alec Hooper. That was all — and all Mal knew — except that on the ride home Alec had found an old collie lying in the mouth of a wombat hole and carried her all the way back to the homestead. Her fur was silvery-white, her eyeballs pale, blind, and weeping. They tended her in the kennels. Then they went and told William D'Inglis, Ida's grandfather, and he wasn't pleased. It was why all this was serious to Ida — the aftermath. William D'Inglis took his gun and destroyed the dog, and then turned on Ida in front of the boy and slapped her across the face. 'Where have you been all this time? What have you been up to?' Then, full of indignation, he had kicked Alec Hooper in the backside and told him to get off his land.

Remembering it all in the taxi, Ida wept.

That night, of course, he waits for her. She is with a group of relations on the banks of the Cropp River. Alec Hooper stands with the horses on the other side. Ida wades across. The light is golden with wattle bloom on the tea-coloured water. She goes to Alec on a sandbank and leans against him, looking straight at him for once. His eyes are astonishing. They are like a curve of the world seen from above, with inlaid patterns of gold and silver. She cannot turn away from them. There are layers like removed sections, or terraces, with beautiful floating gold stars on the surfaces. Ida is filled with longing. His eyes are so deep that she wants to sink into this gold and white unfolding beauty for all time. But then the vision goes, it is normal contact again, they are in an uncomfortable sandy crouch kissing (which they had never been in, in fact), and her relations are calling out, wading over the shallow Cropp, and Ida wakes in a cold sweat asking herself, *Where have I been in my life?*

THERE WAS SOMETHING MORE TROUBLESOME still that Ida felt would never be redeemed in life's chain of consequence, and which later came out in the action of *Prosperity*. One time when her father Kelvin was away in Kenmore hospital getting ECT, William D'Inglis came back from retirement to supervise the workers. The workers routinely hated him. But Ida knew who it was who dislodged a two-hundred-pound bag of flour from a loading platform that struck the old man from behind and put him in a wheelchair for seventy-two months.

AMONG FRIENDS OF IDA D'INGLIS the word went round that, for her, artistic achievement was a breeze. Mal helped with that idea. She couldn't believe it — the way people made her agony, her grab for truth, into a fleeting topic of conversation. Mal infected the air with the idea that Ida had just dashed the thing off. It was the way he always talked about writers. Why should he change just because it was her? Mal's part would be the hard grind. He would have a battle boiling this one down to belly laughs.

Others had plays in them as good as hers — people said — if only they'd had her advantages. Storm Wilde was known to lead a charmed life, with such fetchingly fading beauty, talent, brains, and wealthy family backing. She was a familiar face countrywide, thanks to the commercials she and Mal had done for MacPriam's Tablelands Malt, the all-Australian whisky that connoisseurs said tasted like wet sacking.

Nothing was ever easy, though. At the end of childhood Ida D'Inglis had been diagnosed with leukaemia. She had lived with death. A year had gone by while she skipped, sang, gave cheek and tried to understand what life was. Blood transfusions kept her going. She fainted and was tiresomely ill. Her mother, Georgina, spoke to her plainly and prepared her for what was to come. Georgina would have given her own life if it was possible to save her. Then, one hot summer, she had gone into remission and was never ill again. But the thing she most craved was wrongly timed. It made her race through life to catch the tail of what had escaped her. The idyll with Alec Hooper — what was it, an hour? — was her taste of utter acceptance. At seventeen she had left home to become a dancer and actress, and at twenty had a son, Guy. She tolerated the despair of Georgina, the youthful mother she loved, and the non-involvement of her depressive father, Kelvin, and she bore with the long, philosophical letters she received from Jim D'Inglis, her uncle, who always seemed on the edge of making claims on her love that Kelvin couldn't make.

She had thrust her family from her life by going to live in England, and had put Rupert Hampton — the father of her son — through two postgraduate degrees, and remained his main means of support while he rose to prominence as a biochemist in the UK. Their separation had been amicable, but the day Rupert married Lady Pamela Moore the terms and conditions of Ida's life changed. It turned out that professors, even gangly, vague, dimply-smiling ones like Rupert Hampton, were standard pricks when it came to custody of children. Ida returned to Australia without her son. They had exchanged a whispered promise. It was understood he would come soon. Now it was six years later. He would soon be twenty-one. Unnatural coolness was a charge levelled at Ida D'Inglis. When recently Guy's pale features had appeared in *Tatler*, damp hair shielding flashbulbed eyes, skinny arm around a glazen-eyed young deb, Ida had laughed aloud. There was nothing else she could do. Who was Guy anyway? She could hardly tell. She thrust away thoughts of her son, outside her somewhere, banished them into orbit like space junk. (Only sometimes a molten rush of devastated feeling came thundering down, and she had to hold still until it cooled and became commonplace.)

Mal had no interest in the English part of her life,

never sympathised with her feelings about those lost years, looked bored if she ever talked about Guy, and believed her life only mattered when he was in it. She'd had parts with the Royal Shakespeare Company, starred in fringe revue, and appeared in BBC dramas, but when it came to working with Mal she was just another casting agency contact, she had to prove herself, and she had, by God.

EACH YEAR AROUND EASTER MAL Fitch remounted *The Yabby Stealers*, his first success. It was originally *Root the Boot*, written and acted by three ex-university playwrights, Carmody, Mason, and Todd, who drank with Mal in Push pubs in the 1960s and projected their fame into the future, where it was never to arrive. Mal was King Yabby in a black-lacquered helmet with eyes on stalks. *Yabby Stealers* became a hit. At the end of one production Mal jumped to the next, not acting except in returns of *Stealers*, but directing, putting on stories 'where life boiled up again like yabbies in a drum'.

Among the vivid props and teetering flats there was comical lust, hilarity, conspiracy, malice, grief, and cruelty, always. The various spirited beauties and notable ratbags always came good in the end. For a few seasons lately Ida had played a part. Women who came with their children liked the rough charm of the heroes, the extravagant silken costumes, the mythical satisfaction of love-blessed happy endings. Men who were dragged along fell in love with Ida's understated style and moody gaze, with whatever had bewitched Mal. These days they couldn't take their eyes from Yvette Danielsen, Ida's successor. She had long shapely legs, a dancer's energy, and a smoky, taunting voice. Away from Whale Belly she sang in Real Ale cafes and on resort islands, one slight hardworking woman and a bunch of lazy, hypnotised male musos.

King Yabby's eyes shone like malachite pinheads in the dark. Up close they were huge. His shows were crazy roistering brews, pitched to a crescendo. Mal Fitch knew no greater triumph than to see his actors drained of emotion standing centre stage, while their audience stood on their seats, pelting them with Jaffas, hysterical with feeling. The Whale Belly way was a version of the old schoolyard game, a punch in the guts or an unprovoked knuckle grinder — 'Pass it on'. It was an instruction to Mal Fitch himself. He got it with his life. The atom was there to be split. Isolate the thing. Wear yourself out. Squeeze the cods. Go down to the darkest space where a pinprick of light awaits enlargement. Down through the schoolyard into the back lanes of Logan's Reef with their morbid old dunny men and crazy old bitches. One standard: the decisiveness of childhood. Don't leave it behind, but try. Sex beyond everything, coming through, though not here yet, on the dusty stage. Whale Belly Players thrived on the collision of absolutes, the ringleted child in lace petticoats gutting a trout with a pocket knife, the parson who lived in a tree, the fettlers who never got off the line, with their exploding sandwiches and clattering billycans.

Way before Ida ever remembered knowing Mal Fitch he had done something cruel — allowed her, as a baby, to crawl off the edge of a bed and fall on the floor. She'd forgotten being dropped on her head but something in her remembered the unknowing chain of hurt. With *Prosperity*, Ida had taken Mal's characteristic brew — folk tales in an Australian setting — and got back at him. She had heightened the mythic pull away from slapstick. It was *Yabby Stealers* for grown-ups, as Mal would have done it himself if he could. The passions were above board and recognised, the love was sexual, not buffoonishly mistaken or merely ideal, the problems bared to the bone in a world of action and consequence. Ida said that she'd hardly known what she was doing as she wrote, which was true, but when the drafts were done she saw clearly that what she had delivered to Mal was what he had never been able to get for himself. He was stuck in beautiful or frightening effects. He was a haunter, like his creepy dead father, the water man Gunner Fitch. *Her* characters made clear statements about what they wanted. 'One who loves you sends you this, wishing you the happiness that she will never have, unless you give it to her. I am ashamed, ashamed indeed, to reveal my name, but if you ask what I require of you, I should like to plead my cause. You can have evidence of my wounded heart by looking at my pale cheeks, my thinness, the expression of my face, my eyes, so often wet with tears. My sighs, that have no apparent cause, tell the same tale, my frequent touchings, as perhaps you have noticed, can be felt to be different.' These lines were lifted almost straight from Mal's childhood treasure, *A Boy's Adventures With Gods and Heroes*. He had often used the book himself. He was always restirring any old plot. But Ida had done it tellingly.

Mal resented this, of course. It strayed onto his patch. Hardly an original patch, but it was where Mal found his feeling.

Ida didn't believe much in originality. She believed what you had came down to you, and the trick was finding it in yourself. That was the hard part. That was where claims to originality lay.

Mal doubted this, believing that nothing in his line of work came from either of his parents.

'But Mal, you idiot, your father was always on stage with that old truck of his, and my God, there aren't just the legends he cultivated, there are all the photos he took. You don't think he wasn't after an *effect*, do you? He was a dramatist. And your mother, you know, *loved* the art of pastiche.'

Mal snorted. 'Pull the other one.'

She reminded him that her mother Georgina, William D'Inglis's daughter-in-law, and Mal's mother Rosan, William D'Inglis's lover, used to sit in the kitchen of the old shop concocting anonymous letters to William D'Inglis, trying to puncture his pomposity. It was about the only fun Rosan had at a time when D'Inglis's coldness was upsetting her.

'Is that all you mean?' responded Mal offhandedly.

ON HER BIRTHDAY DURING THIS preparation time with *Prosperity*, Ida went to a restaurant with Mal and they fought once again. It was over his attitude to her as a playwright.

'I can't believe it — you're treating me as if I don't exist.'

'You don't at this time.' (Another of his rules.)

He sawed at his octopus, elbows up. He attacked everything, even the most delicate food, as if he were eating stringy mutton.

'Am I actually here with you now, in any sense at all?' She demanded to know.

It seemed that what interested Mal most was the wine. He read the label, tore it idly in strips, then held his glass to the light and studied its colour. 'Honey or piss?' he wondered. He slurped some back on his tongue, and gulped a refill, outdrinking Ida. This was typical Mal — going for weeks without touching a drop, then bingeing. He snapped his fingers, signalling for more.

Ida folded her napkin, pushed back her chair. 'I think we should stop seeing each other for a while,' she said.

Mal blinked and said nothing, except to fix his attention on the waiter. 'Another of the same?'

AWAKE AT FOUR IN THE morning, heart racing, all Ida D'Inglis could think about was the Cropp River — how it had diminished, forming a dark, weedy, snaky ribbon of water hardly one pace wide in drought-time, making its way through a dim expanse of waterworn stones stretching from bank to bank. The innumerable drought-stranded stones of the Cropp made Ida think of her life as it was now: words arrayed impressively, with her bloodflow disappearing into them — and herself left still standing on the bank, all mystery withdrawn from her, wondering what next.

Ida knew that her family — mother, uncle, father, grandfather and brother — had never been hers to cast off as she chose. Life hadn't done it. Writing hadn't done it. The miserable, exploited gullies of Logan's Reef were the deepest part of her. Hurt plucked at her veins. She would have to go back there. She thought about the twenty Mills and Boon romances written by her mother under the pen name Alexandra Stroud. Georgina had always said that writing was a bad dream made beautiful. After the return of Doc Jim to the property Georgina hadn't written a word. Now, said Georgina, with a faint smile, what was there to write about?

Here it was on stage — what Ida was left with — the family trudging to the forefront of her mind, and standing around disputing in her nerves. It was intolerable. She had only imagined them into action, not lived them through, making them better and worse than they really were, leaving the originals

intact, still bothering her. She was asking for comple-
tion. She had expected a payoff of peace, but writer
and written were not the same. In one of Mal's
playtexts she found an Eliot speech. *There's no vocabulary for love within a family, love that's lived in but not
looked at, love within the light of which all else is seen, the
love within which all other love finds speech. This love is
silent.*

She read it out. Mal angered — he'd had no family
in any proper sense, he claimed — while Ida said it
summed up her and him too if he'd only give it some
thought.

MAL CALLED FOR QUIET. The rainbow arch of skylights
and the shining metal rollers of James's on-stage
flour mill were like the glass and metal of a cathedral
made to outlast time. It was as if everything had been
shaped and polished by dedicated craftsmen over
countless years. In the playscript all Ida had written
was: 'Mill interior — dusty sunlight'. The words were
a miracle of fabric and fibreglass, polystyrene and
paint. In the eyes of audiences it was going to seem as
if nothing but dynamite and bulldozers could make
an impression. This was how it should be, how

theatre was made at Whale Belly Players — illusions of durability. If Ida were to jump from her seat, bound up onto the stage, and take something as tiny and harmless as a sharpened pencil and rip downwards, she would do damage.

She gathered up her coat and umbrella. It was time to go.

Everything had stopped again. Ida looked around the theatre to see if there was anyone who might join her for a drink. It would certainly not be Mal. A young man a few seats along met her glance. He was hardly older than her own son. He kept turning to look at her in the half-dark — he was a reporter Mal was cultivating. Storm Wilde always had an effect on younger men. Not entirely accidental, either. Making eye contact, she conveyed hesitation and sexual nonchalance — those tired, melancholy smiles making any young reporter worth his ballpower want to sit next to her on a barstool, and confess that she was the first older woman he had ever wanted to try it on with. Men came to Storm Wilde wanting to wake her from a sleep of not knowing them. Mal hated that — it was too true for him. He felt he had woken her into her life somehow, but it wasn't going well.

There was an organised movement on stage, and Ida leaned forward in her seat, her chin cupped in her hands. She would wait for this. A bright light was reflected in her secretive grey eyes. James's scene shifts consisted of a succession of snappy images. Midge came sliding down a delivery chute, hair flying, her copious skirts fanning around her waist. That two-hundred-pound bag of flour tipped from a ledge, and came crashing down on old man Finucan's shadow. Offstage, banks of electric fans were set racing, and the rows of rainbow skylights flipped over, becoming clouds that descended in loose arrangements of parachute silk, the mill rollers (cylinders of foil) rippling open to reveal rows of varnished book spines. In the patriarch's study, old man Finucan railed against time and change, and the faces of men were seen looking in through the windows. These men dragged another world in with them when they entered. Even as they walked towards centre stage they were somehow magically walking outwards, so that the room's interior became a grassland, the bookshelves were flattened to an inky pool, and the cloudy sky-ceiling became clear blue. Following the pattern of the play, the staging thrived on opposites. The actor playing old man Finucan also played Lachlan Strong, the youthful drover. It was fantastic to see Finucan doubled up with rage over a mighty mahogany desk, clawing at jacket and waistcoat while suffering the angina attacks that made him mortal, spitting obscenities, howling in hatred, and then in paroxysms that shaded through to gently rhythmic brushing motions (the jacket becoming a gum-branch used to dust ashes from a damper), standing erect, shedding years, and as Lachlan Strong the drover singing a ballad of love and wandering in which a pretty young missus would wash his greasy moleskins on the banks of the Condamine.

THIS WAS FINE. THIS WAS enough. Only at night was it terrifying, when she slept, the way the rider came and took her hand, and led her along the shore of a dark river, and she remembered she was marked for death.

Tin Torch

ON SPIDERY METAL TOWERS ARC lamps blazed against a pale evening sky. They drained electricity from the rural grid and dimmed house interiors to a dusty brown, causing refrigerators to shudder and television screens to diminish to pinpoint stars.

Late winter. Cold. Mal Fitch was back in Logan's Reef for a spell before *Prosperity* opened in the spring. He looked at the bright lights of the paceway and remembered a torch with a long silver handle he'd used as a boy. If he held that torch close against his eye he was blinded, but when his vision adjusted he saw a face in the curved reflector, a man's face with gunpowder-dusted pores and sun-blasted flakes of peeling skin. The man lived in the brightness of the sun, but when the torch went off he became a shadow, a dancing, dissolving shape wearing a black 1930s suit, a wing collar, a gold watch chain. It was the father he'd never met, who was dead before Mal was born.

Drinkers sat on the steps of the old Criterion Hotel, or leaned on verandah poles on the cold footpath. When they were full enough they went over to the trots. Across at the paceway could be heard the creak of harnesses, the rushing wheels of the gigs in the improver events, the pad of hooves on the hosed dirt and the snick of the drivers' whips.

Mal Fitch went up to his room, which had been kept for his visits from Sydney over a stretch of thirty years, and lit a cigarette in the dark. Disappointment rose from the lips of the crowd with a roar. Mal stood looking down into the empty grass-filled yard of the hotel, where the paceway lights threw pale shadows. Dust motes swarmed against the glare. He lit another cigarette from the first one. Dust created an aura around the lights; he tried to see past it, into the deepest dark. After a while he lay back on his bed and stared at the curtains tugged to one side with a piece of unbleached calico tape. He'd kept the torch on a fruit crate near the private entrance to the shop, and one night on his way out William D'Inglis had picked it up and taken it.

Mal remembered the snap of wooden curtain rings. He'd asked himself, panicky, *Where was the torch with its long silver handle?* Mal hated the way Rosan lazily said, *Mal, let him keep it. Let him have it, Mal,* when the man already had everything. He remembered Rosan's warning: *Ssh! He's here,* as if Mal hadn't known. A man who was a century old this year, when Mal himself was past fifty.

Mal remembered a narrow hallway in their shop, a curtain dividing the living area from the front, the mouldy smell of bread, rancid butter and sour milk, dead-smelling newspapers carrying news of hydrogen bombs. There were sticky drinks, lollies stuck together like rocks, and dry, flaky, intensely burning meat pies in the steel trays of a Keepwarm unit. Under the arch leading back was the pressed-tin ceiling patterned with briar roses, the too-many rooms for two — the bedrooms, places where William D'Inglis could be heard talking in a low voice, laughter leaning against a locked door, caution stalking down the narrow hall in expensive socks, creaking a loose floorboard, trailing cigarette ash, making the knock of a drinking glass on the brass tankwater tap on the wall next to the stove. Always the same man despite what people said — he was her only bloke — always William D'Inglis of Croppdale humming, pouring foaming beers into slender glasses. And Rosan calling out while he cursed and said, I love you Rosan, I do.

Despite all his frantic activity at Whale Belly Players, Mal Fitch lived in a mood of waiting. It grew stronger with the years. He could never tell this to anyone — it was too absurd. The Gunner had gone away before Mal was born and was never coming back. He was more than just dead. He'd been blown up and reduced to atoms. His last lettercard was sealed under glass with a photo: *I can't say where I am exactly. I hardly ever know.* Rosan used to scorn that. It was so bloody typical of the Gunner, she said, tossing back her head and laughing bitterly. *He knows now.*

William D'Inglis always brought presents for Mal, shiny toy cars and heavy, muddy-coloured, cardboard-bound books no longer wanted by his growing sons. He courted him until he saw it was pointless. The presents were wrapped in thick, cloudy cellophane. Mal saw that the wrapping, crinkled and greasy, had been on other boys' presents before his. One of the books he still had, *A Boy's Adventures With Gods and Heroes*, in which an English boy named Edwin, who wore a floppy cap and plus fours, travelled in time through mythic ages. Mal loved the places Edwin found along the way, castle walls to scale, tree roots like armchairs, and swords bonded to stone. At the end Edwin knelt at the feet of bearded giants and rode chariots into the sun.

In Mal's company William D'Inglis was uneasy. 'Bring me a cigar, sonny.' There was always a box in the top drawer of the dresser. He scorned Mal for his clumsiness and resistance.

'Don't wanna.'

'It won't bite you.' They challenged each other.

Mal would only obey if his mother came in and frowned. She made her dark eyebrows square on her beautiful, intelligent wide forehead. She frowned at Bill D'Inglis, then, and made him read stories. He'd roll his eyes. But he'd obey, and sit on Mal's bed smoking, reading Hans Andersen's Fairy Tales — The Little Match Girl, The Dog with Eyes as Big as Saucers, The Tinder Box — frightening, unpleasant tales to make a small boy sicken. William D'Inglis smelt of hair dressing, dusty leather coats, sweet tobacco. On winter nights the smell was wet dog. He travelled with a shaggy, useless retriever, and kept her chained under his car when he was visiting. On his drives in from Croppdale she rested her bristly nose in his lap. Late back there, he said, he went to the meathouse and fed her liver and heart.

Then in the frost he'd cross to the far bank of the river and call for a dog named Nell. She was a wild stray, he said, who lived in the mined-out hills. She'd swoop on the leftovers and disappear.

'There isn't any Nell,' Rosan would say tightly.

But William D'Inglis always said, 'Bugger me, yes, there is a Nell, she comes down to the far bank of the river and I feed her liver and heart'.

Nights in the shop as a boy Mal would wait, feeling a tension in the hills where from fifty miles away he imagined he'd always been able to hear the whimper of a dog, then, for sure, the rattle of William D'Inglis's Pontiac suspension coming along the corrugated dirt road.

It was in the shop that Mal first saw Ida. Her mother, Georgina, brought her when she came to visit Rosan, and they exchanged women's confidences. Georgina always had a new joke to pass on in her jaunty, smoky, quasi-Bohemian twang. 'What's the definition of a tomcat?' Things like that convulsed them. 'A ball-bearing rat catcher.'

Georgina didn't like her father-in-law, but she wanted happiness for Rosan with him.

Mal was always inquisitive, trying to make sense of their fractured world, glancing from his glossy black eyes under straight eyelashes while sitting on the floor with tender, year-old Ida, getting her to eat a rusk.

'Mal, take Ida through to the back bedroom and see if she'll take a nap, would you?'

Their voices faded.

Ida had alert grey eyes. The corners of her mouth were turned down in a beautiful frowning smile. She put up a fist and shielded herself from his gaze. He became a person of importance when she paid him attention. She roused a troubled emotion in him. He had a lifetime ahead of him to think about this.

He didn't know why but he wanted to hurt her.

While the mothers smoked and drank gin-laced tea in the kitchen, shrieked, confided, blamed and consoled out of earshot, Mal knelt on the floor beside the bed and watched Ida haul herself up to the edge on her stomach. She raised a fist and smacked the sheet with the flat of her hand. When she reached the edge she slipped, and he watched her tumble to the floor. It was quick. She didn't cry. He lifted her back again. He felt no emotion but love, watching her bewilderment watching him. It was strange.

Later he was asked, How did Ida get this red mark, this *bruise*? Mal?

He couldn't say. He would have to think about it.

NIGHT. FROST. THE UNDERSIDE OF the year. Mal Fitch sat on a cold granite rock above the Railway Hill cemetery, under the glittering canopy of winter. His mother Rosan had been buried now for thirty years. A deep, black, sparkling arena of space confronted him. Glass without reflection. Shooting stars slipping away from a standing start like skaters.

Mal held a pair of binoculars, which he raised to a section of sky in amazement. He found the comet instantly, a hanging wall of smoky stars motionless where there was nothing before, and behind that wall a cone of light suggesting a torchbeam. It was as if someone was crouched in the sky, creeping along a wall.

It was the big heavy torch Mal imagined up there — the one that had been taken, loved by the boy who had claimed it from the toolbox of the old Diamond T '211'. Whenever the batteries went flat Mal hacksawed their soft zinc jackets and shook out the ashes inside them, trying to extract the black pencil-like cores without breaking the graphite. The idea of invisible charged poles made him who he was. They charged him even now. He rolled the smooth fractured cylinders in memory. They were soft and whispery on his chunky palms. He felt himself reverse the way the poles did. Now he would be someone different, leave his home town, prove himself a stranger.

Now he would return. The years were so much irrelevance against these two imperatives.

Moonrise. Bitter chill. Mal Fitch walked back into town along the contours of Railway Hill, a stomping, solid man with strong shoulders, an overlarge head, and a quick, curious manner. His black overcoat-tails slapped behind his knees like beetles' wings. The huge steady moon turned Logan's Reef and the dusty plateau road leading to distant Croppdale into silvery daylight. Mal raised his arms as if to embrace the night. Foxes screamed. Magpies warbled. Drunks smashed bottles in the lanes. Clear eyelines to eternity on such nights. It was a town Mal knew better than he knew himself.

Mal had really loved that torch, that shining cylinder of mercurial grey. He really remembers it now. Fit it into your square palm, Mal, and feel the greasy, big-headed, inappropriately pretentious weight of the thing. The ivory on-button. The crafted, satisfying grip. The letters EVEREADY swimming from the detailed ridging. The recessed omega shape holding the wire hanging-up hook in the base. Just about the right torch for Mal Fitch. Exploitation of loss is Mal's trade. The smallest molecules of loss condense under his direction. It is where his life stems from, where his productions arise — why should the critics ever notice? They don't have a feel for his soul, his moods of waiting and watching patience in the midst of activity. If they turned their eyes from the stage and looked at Mal during the madcap action they would understand things differently: his eyes burned, he was lonely.

Years ago, in the 1950s, just before the torch was taken, Mal had taped it to the barrel of an old single-shot .22 and gone rabbiting. He'd found a hare. Its eyes were cigarette stubs glowing in the dark. It danced on its hind legs. Wherever the torchbeam had gone, parting the dry grasses of Railway Hill, the hare had mocked and led on, twitching its nose and arching its back. When Mal fired a shot, the tip of the barrel had broken off and gone flying back over his head with a deadly hum. It had almost killed him. Spits of hot metal smoked in the grass.

Mal had torn the torch from its mounting, thrown the useless rifle into the dark, and found his way home.

BEHIND RAILWAY HILL THE COMET was cobweb fuzz in the rows of bare frosted canes in Noel Fitch's vineyard. A last look back from the crooked corner under Rosan's grave. Trains went into a famous tunnel here, a tourist attraction now, Logan's Loop, describing a muffled underground circle. They emerged at a ninety-degree angle two hundred feet lower, leaving a hieroglyph in the brain, a cipher for dreams. When Mal was a boy, there were still steam trains and churning smoke instead of rumbling diesels. A plume of bituminous filth would drift into the sky, scattering grits. For minutes the gully would stand silent, wagtails distinctly trilling. Something great went pounding away under the cemetery. Finally the engine burst out into the lower end of town, its headlamp dim in daytime, a choking fury. At the Criterion Hotel drinkers kept ordering schooners in a kind of test. If they missed the train at the top station they had time to sprint down to D'Inglis's mill siding and catch it there, where day and night a beautiful red and blue spluttering neon sign spelt D'Inglis' Self Raising for the benefit of interstate travellers.

Mal clumped down the road towards the Criterion Hotel, past the reservoir lane with its dead and dying Cootamundra wattles, down rocky ridges of dried-off Paterson's Curse, black in the night. A mist of woodsmoke layered the freezing air. The galvanised iron roofs of the town collected cold moonlight. Down by the glinting angles of Logan's Loop were the towering twin wheat silos and the dark brick flour mill, D'Inglis Castle, so-called. The old man's son, Kelvin D'Inglis, had been a kindly but ineffective manager. Now Kelvin's son Stuart, Ida's brother, was buggering the joint. Coils of dead, broken neon tubing spelt the name of the product in dusty pencil-lings on a high concrete wall.

In his sagging bed in Room 17 at the far end of the upstairs corridor, Mal buried himself under heaped bedcovers and drifted off to sleep. It was one in the morning. Water in a glass on the verandah table was skinned with ice. The blinds were drawn in the public bar, where old ladies sang 'Yellow Submarine', his cousin Tutter Fitch and Tutter's wife Betty Fitch, the former Betty Kingling, warbled along, and a distraught woman beat the back and front doors, screaming, 'Bloody old fuckhouse Fitch, I know you're in there. What are you doing with our men, you bitch? Let them out of your fuckhouse, Fitch.' There was a note on Mal's bedside table from Yvette Danielsen, the actress he'd brought down with the designer to experience the atmosphere, to say she couldn't tolerate another minute of this dreadful hole, and she'd moved to the Golden Horseshoe Motel — might they leave in the morning?

Mal Fitch dreamed of the shadow of a rocky escarp-ment falling on the sea, of bushfires on the country's rim reflected in water, glassy, sinuous heat waves writhing, three hang-gliders with rainbow-coloured sails appearing from the smoke with wingtips ablaze, the eyes of the fliers blind as lead weights.

A Stand-Off

STUART D'INGLIS CARRIED A TORCH but didn't use it. A big heavy torch he'd found in one of his grandfather's saddlebags. He navigated by gravity the sharp tussocky paddocks that had been burnt last winter, feeling the bristly cores of the tussocks unbalance his bootsoles. The crunch felt like stepping on an old man's face: William D'Inglis's rough and freckled features. A pity. But there you are.

He shifted the weight of the torch and the shotgun from hand to hand, meaning to rise and move along the bank of the river and come up the eroded gully behind the cottage called Bob's, and when he got a view of them, his mother and Doc Jim, to use both barrels. If Georgina was in the way, God help her. Doc Jim he intended to shatter like glass. The stars were brighter than he ever remembered. He didn't need the torch. Dry grass, dry earth. Stuart D'Inglis could wander here without effort for eternity. The kingdom of the dark. But it would never be that because morning shattered the feeling. A mob of sheep pattered around in a panicky circle, breathing hard, never a bleat. Stuart was like them. Who would ever understand him? Too much rested on his shoulders. He climbed through a barbed-wire fence and snagged his shirt. It took a minute of concentrating to work himself free. He thought, 'What if I just hang here? Feed for the crows.'

In the cool darkness the poplars along the dry river bank gave out their sweet honey odour. They were not drought-stricken like everything else. Their roots stretched under the riverbed, strangling the last drops of moisture from clay. Stuart pissed into the black near the useless pump shed. His nerves were a tangle. He imagined a drill head cutting into the earth between his toes, biting, spitting, shaking its way through various strata and penetrating permeable rocks, releasing water with a rumble and a jerky gush.

His grandfather had shown him a letter from more than fifty years ago, dated 1939. It was a cost estimate from the water driller, Gunner Fitch, who was killed at the siege of Tobruk. Grandfather talked as if everything that happened in the past was still going on. Fitch had a debt to pay. He was a thief. Fifty years ago was sharper than yesterday. Grandfather said that if Gunner Fitch had done the job he'd been contracted for, they wouldn't be having the problems of supply they were having today. 'Think about that, Kel.'

'It's Stuart, Grandfather,' Stuart yelled.

'So it is.'

Stuart thought that if only he could have his grandfather's undivided attention they would be able to work things out. William wasn't the senile old man people thought, despite his always harking back to a period when Kel was the promising heir. There had been a time when the name D'Inglis had meant respect in Logan's Reef. When D'Inglis Self Raising, with its insignia of maroon Christmas bells, was nationally known. Now instead of dignified national brands like D'Inglis the market was awash with no-name blends.

It was after midnight. Stars beginning to fade. Moon gathering itself behind granite boulders at Croppdale. This was it, what he had come for. Stuart left the big-headed old torch in the grass, face-down with its half-metre-long handle sticking up so he would be able to find it again.

There it was, the lit window. When Stuart thought about Doc Jim he almost choked. The bastard stayed up late. Stuart had often seen him peeling open the pages of the *Land* at the kitchen table, reading the classifieds and looking for bargains. This was the supposed healer. And she who used to read everything, and had written twenty books on her own account, now only stared all night at the same old copy of *Tatler*, and smiled agreeably at Doc Jim, going around in bare feet on the cracked linoleum, even talking differently. 'She's lost her plum,' is what they said in the town.

There were no secrets in the small wooden house that Georgina and Doc Jim occupied, with its uncurtained windows and screen doors crawling with dung beetles. It ought to have become a punishment, their living there, but they never seemed to think so — people in their sixties acting like lovesick teenagers. Nor did they show gratitude, just got on with their lives as if they had every right — wrongful Doc Jim and grossly self-deceiving Georgina. His parents, some people called them, and Stuart wanted to job them.

Stuart D'Inglis had a clear picture of the way things were for his father, Kelvin, in his early married

years, long before Doc Jim returned to the property
in disgrace. The wide terrace in front of the house
with its smooth flagstones of river slate had been the
venue for the 1950 wedding. Jasmine and wisteria
flourished, lilac bloomed in the stone cracks. The
photographs, torn from their ashwood frames, were
in Stuart's possession now. You could tell by looking
at them what a secure world Kelvin D'Inglis had
inherited. Strong, young 'fifties faces. Postwar fighter
pilots and bomb aimers running family farms. Determination to validate strongly-held beliefs. Rightful
inheritance of property, and the regular uses thereof.
Georgina maintained that she had never actually
met Jim then — 'the elusive keeper of the family
conscience'. But when Stuart went through the photos he saw Jim in all of them, poisoning her with his
whispers and wimpish lusts. In the past Georgina
had always joined the laughter about Jim, ridiculing
the clothes he wore in newsclippings and UN press
shots — crude native sandals fashioned from truck
tyres, shirts with obscure tribal weaves. In other
photos Doc Jim sat on the bonnets of Land Rovers
and Jeeps with UNESCO, WHO, UNRAA, or USAID
markings, in the company of pretty, ponytailed
nurses with long glossy shins. 'That a do-gooder like
Doc Jim should have a love life is an absurdity,'
Stuart recalled his mother saying one day as she

shoved the family albums back into their murky cupboard. The exact words stuck in Stuart's mind. He was just leaving for boarding school. He sat in the train all day musing about the perfection of his family. They weren't like anyone else's.

A few years later Doc Jim returned from Africa, worked as a surgeon in various hospitals, then gave up doctoring altogether because of a court case in which he was sued for negligence. A woman had died. Shamed, Doc Jim settled at Croppdale with all his belongings in one suitcase the year Stuart turned twenty-three.

Stuart saw it happening. Georgina going silent around Jim, pretending he wasn't there. Kelvin having his fits. Jim refusing to help, on a pretext of ethics. Kelvin's brain on fire. Jim having a go at him at last. A night of panic. Jim treating Kelvin with a slimy bottle from a dusty black bag, with Stuart shouting, *Do something, you withering bastard*, and Jim stating evenly, over and over, *Phone me a doctor, sonny*. Cause of death given by Dr Carmel Battacharya of the Logan's Reef Clinic as a brain infection from the eardrum. Kelvin D'Inglis dead in the dark-panelled living room, head back, jaw open, tongue blue, saliva trickling. Above him framed photos of wheat trucks traffic-jammed at the Logan's Reef railhead. Wedding photos. Jasmine in the air. Honeysuckle vine.

Weathered stone. An unfortunate death. Not the first in Doc Jim's career it must be said.

Kelvin (this was incredible) became a family joke. Except Stuart wasn't laughing. This Kelvin they chuckled about was always sitting on the verandah at Croppdale with a packet of cotton buds, poking around in his ear and claiming there was a beetle in there. 'Oh, Stuart,' Georgina would sigh. 'Can't you see that we loved him? If we hadn't, how could we have gone on?'

Stuart curled a lip.

Soon after Kelvin's funeral Stuart saw Georgina in Jim's arms. They were dancing to scratchy records in moonlight, on the cold flagstones.

Until then Stuart had a serene future planned. His grandfather would soon die. His mother would depart the property and buy a unit in the city. A beautiful young woman would marry him. He would bite the bullet of tradition and close down the flour mill and stop subsidising town employment. He would loosen up. He would breed horses as a side-line, and play polo with Andy MacPriam. He would build a cliff garden overlooking the river. He would harvest the plantations of Monterey pine and edible nuts that Kelvin had planted. He would set dingo traps and bait for wild pigs, and surround Cropp-dale's two thousand hectares with high-voltage electric fencing. In the long term, he would drive a shaft into the cliffs behind the house and create a duplicate living area. It would be a secret. He would not tell his wife, or his children, if he had them. The hideaway would have a hinged door fashioned from stone. There would be a ledge in there, just big enough for a bed. In the darkness Stuart would hear nothing, see nothing, feel nothing except the brush of air molecules against his face.

But none of that would ever happen now. Soon after Georgina and Doc Jim declared their love for each other and moved into Bob's Cottage, swearing to live there till they died, another complication occurred. His sister returned to Australia after many years abroad. Ida. She was a total stranger to him, to be frank. It seemed to Stuart that she had ruined her life over men, and now she had started again. She was in love, she said on her first trip back to Cropp-dale. A man had pursued her who had loved her as a child. She had fallen for him. Georgina blushed with pleasure. Stuart took a stab — 'Andy MacPriam?' — naming his friend and mentor, the handsome, ageing polo enthusiast.

Ida tried not to laugh. 'It's Mal Fitch.'

Stuart felt sick. The Fitches were Logan's Reef originals. They were ordinary working stock. You went to them if you wanted something — that was their point. Mal Fitch had grown up in that back-street store in town, where his mother sold dusty packs of cigarettes and tinned peas, and bottles of soapy soft drink and sulphurous cordials. One story was that she sold herself. All Mal Fitch's relations were in the service trades, baking bread, chopping meat, pulling beers, driving taxis. Mal himself, and his late father, Gunner, were the only exceptions. They got out of the place. Gunner was a prominent asterisked name on the Logan's Reef War Memorial. Everyone knew the Fitches' story because Mal retold it each time he was interviewed, and he was inter-viewed a lot. Ward of Legacy. Never knew his Dad. Left school early, the dunce, and worked in the mill. Was a clerk in the Court House. Went to Sydney. Discovered theatre, another world. But never forgot the Reef. Anyone who wanted to locate Mal Fitch between early December and the end of January any year, had only to look for the acting yardman at the Criterion Hotel (C.J. 'Tutter' Fitch and Betty R. King-ling, Licensees). He was always up early, hosing down the bricks of the old courtyard and rolling empty barrels out of the cellar. He was always boast-ing about his small-town background, talking about isolation, backwardness, stubbornness in the face of change, incest, alcoholism, poverty, meaningless crimes, and dismal economic desperation.

'Head in the gutter, eyes on the stars, that's our definition at the Reef,' Mal Fitch would boast.

COMING UP THE LONG GULLY there was a noise. It could have been anything, a wallaby, a wombat, a water rat nosing through leaves. Or it might have been Doc Jim on his night walk. In still air, bark peeling from ribbon gums could wake the dead. Think on that, Doc Jim, if it is you I hear. The banshee shudders of the departed. The brother you betrayed. The birthright you scorned. Your hundred-year-old father lost to reason, getting down on his hands and knees in the cold fireplace and eating ashes, his freckled old face a grinning yellow moon and his tongue an earth-eating echidna's. Lay your healing hands on his, Doc Jim, if you dare. He will remember your name. He will recall which son you are. And he will laugh at you.

Stuart put to one side the fact that Jim called on his father up at the house at least once a day, supervised a regime of vitamin supplements, smeared Ungvita on his ulcerous sores, and if anything in the way of a medical consultation was required, was punctilious in fetching the tireless Dr Battacharya. That wasn't the Jim Stuart was maddened by.

Crash of a footfall. A shape against the sky.

There he was. The man Stuart wanted. He thumbed the safety of the gun. The man faced him, skinny and tall, holding nothing but a walking stick.

Stuart?

Doc?

Hardly men any more. Just trembling pillars of feeling in the transparency of midnight, where it was possible strangers might love each other at last.

Not this time. (Stuart.)

Not this time? (Doc.)

In the silence Jim D'Inglis cleared his throat. Placing his stick at his feet, he lifted his arms, raised them above his shoulders, empty palms outwards. It was some sort of pretentious tribal gesture. It would never be his part to find words in the struggle of understanding in which he was involved with Stuart.

Stuart stared for a moment, chin trembling. Amazing willpower of the man to bother him like this. Why weren't these people dead?

Turning on his heel, Stuart retreated into the night, creeping away on soft footfalls, becoming a shadow, a ghostly pale nothing, a small boy daring himself to be brave, a mistaken man creeping over the crusty, unbroken face of the earth. The stars were like smoke. The Milky Way was the tongue of a glacier.

Bits broke off — shooting stars. Mount A.A. Hooper ink-blotted the distant sky like a dusty nebula. A fox screamed. This was madness.

Stuart recovered his nerves near the pump shed by thinking about water — how he would bring it up. Here was the place where he had once seen a flood, the Upper Cropp in full spate. He'd been around twelve at the time. Filthy chocolatey chunks of broken bank and whole trees had gone sailing past, the water thundering, pushing, jostling, slamming. The next morning the river was itself again, the banks dripping and glistening, the grass flattened. Since then it had never risen so high. Mostly it was a chain of ponds, and by the time it reached Logan's Reef it was dry.

THERE WAS A CHARACTER IN Ida's play whom Stuart resented. Captain Jacks was a young travelling Salvo. He evaded chores in the camp. People would ask him to do things and he'd say, 'When I've finished m'shave', and go back to concentrating on himself in the mirror that hung on string from a bush pole. Down at the billabong he went crazy. He said he'd found Christ in the water. He went marching between the campfires, rattling a tambourine and singing 'Waltzing Matilda'. He believed that Midge was in love with him. He wanted everyone to follow him — 'Who'll come?' he preached, but they only laughed. Midge mocked him and sang, 'Beware, my friend, of crystal brook or fountain, lest that hideous hook, your nose, you chance to see; Narcissus' fate would then be yours, and self-detested you would pine, as self-enamoured he'. She burst into laughter so wounding that Captain Jacks tried to murder her, wrestling around in the dirt. When the lights came up he was fighting his empty swag.

The Captain was based on Stuart. He knew that. (He'd never liked the size of his nose, for one thing.) But Ida had pointed her accusing finger in the wrong direction. She was the one who never achieved anything, all her runs on the board being phantom victories, vanity her downfall, her love mistakes endlessly repeating themselves, and she couldn't make anything last, could she, not even this play, which would close without an extended season, Stuart noted with satisfaction, and she had returned to Croppdale miserable and dissatisfied, visiting Georgina and Doc Jim for meals and nightly conversation, camping in the old dairy that she was architecturally restoring for her own use, and avoiding Stuart most of the time, which suited him perfectly, because it saved him the trouble of avoiding her.

Stuart intended to sink a bore. Water would erupt, churning from the bore hole. He would doze a pool near the outlet valve, and create an artificial lake. He would watch stars reflected in the liquid. He would grow vegetables and irrigate seedlings. He would drink the water, putting minerals into his system. (He would ask Rennie Logan to pack a picnic basket, and they would sit there at twilight. It would be the place to tell her he planned to marry her. She would like that.) There were plenty of drilling-rig operators around who would do the job, offering special deals and enticements. They stencilled their names and their toll-free numbers on sheets of tin, and nailed them in trees down all the off-roads. But they were all crooks. Andy MacPriam at Thistle Corner had one camped on his property for months. Andy's idea, as an adjunct to his Tablelands Whisky enterprise, had been to offer bottled water under the MacPriam's label, and sell it in the northern hemisphere, where they'd stuffed their supplies. Eventually all he got for his dollar was powdered rock. There was a better way of doing this. Ida knew about it too if only she was brutally honest with herself. In an interview she'd said, 'Down our way we have a saying: "Call in the debt". Sometimes it's not very nice. I've turned this on its head in *Prosperity*. I mean by this that nothing is without endless consequence until it's understood, and the more it's denied — as when people say a thing's over and past, period — the more revealing it is of where the real changes need to happen, what needs attention. So we call in the debt, so to speak. We are owed something if only we can work it out. That's where, or should I say *why*, the transformations occur that have divided the critics so — you know, are these just effects, they're so brilliant, or are they inherent in the action?'

Stuart didn't know what all this meant, if anything, in the theatrical realm where Ida existed. But it was a statement he recognised otherwise. It was in the D'Inglis blood. It was what his grandfather always said. 'Call in the debt.'

There was that beauty of a debt Stuart knew about, that had been biding its time for fifty years. It involved water. His grandfather had shown him the documentation, a yellowing invoice and a receipt for monies paid. Call in the debt, a knockout.

Back at the house, Stuart was amazed by how clear his head was, how at peace he felt. He looked around his room. He couldn't believe he hadn't loaded the gun. The shells he had chosen lay in the ashtray on his bedside table. He must have left them there before he went out. They were waxy blue, the colour of a deep sky. It always happened like this. Stuart goes out. He takes things with him. But they are there waiting for him when he gets back, taking the pressure off him — feeling like the swinging open of a door to allow a fresh breeze in, as good as the touch on his forehead of Rennie Logan's cool hand to prove she loves him.

THE NEXT DAY, MAKING CONTACT with Mal Fitch wasn't the problem Stuart thought it was going to be, bearing in mind the hatred Stuart had expressed over Ida's play, his vow never to speak to the man ever again, blah, blah. Stuart walked straight over to where Ida was camped in the old dairy, and put the question to her. 'Give me Mal's number.' She didn't blink — although her hands trembled, he noticed. She gave him the unlisted number. She and Mal were not seeing each other at present, she explained, but would Stuart do her a favour and give Mal her best wishes?

Stuart swivelled on his heel, let her simmer, walked back to the house, and got straight through to Mal. It was all talk about Ida at first. Mal was anxious about her, and so he should have been. Stuart's thoughts interrupted Mal's questions (something about Ida's health). His sister was a woman without aim or principle in his opinion. He didn't say this, of course. Just made sympathetic grunts and mentioned that the great Andy Mac-Priam had been dropping in since Ida arrived, practically drooling while she mixed concrete topless. Mal was listening hard. 'Uh huh?'

A feeling of finding himself on the same wavelength as Mal changed Stuart to the core. 'How's the show?' he asked.

Mal glided over Stuart's earlier hostility with practised charm. 'Fine.'

And before Stuart could state the business of his call, Mal asked him when he'd next be in town — they should get together for a drink. Stuart said he happened to be coming up the next day, leaving before dawn. He would be there by noon. So Mal named a Woolloomooloo pub he frequented, a veritable bloodhouse — a natural habitat, thought Stuart, for a Fitch.

STUART WAS THERE WAITING TWO minutes before the appointed time. Mal arrived on the dot. Over a schooner Mal told him how it was when he first came to the city from the Reef. Just up the road there, where the expressway cut through, used to be a row of old terraces where he boarded for three quid a week. His cousins Tutter and Noel used to doss on the floor. The old Betty Kingling, too. 'They'd make trips to the city to buy cut-price catering equipment, dough mixers and heavy-duty sausage-making machines. Tutter used to be round as a melon, now he's thin as a match. Noel was always a blimp, cheeks like polished red apples, trouser size matching an elephant's. Betty Kingling the Rubens Venus, a stunner. Once Tutter brought a woman home from Macleay Street. He put his arm around her on the couch, and she turned out to be a bloke. Hairy chest in the frock.'

'Hmm.' Stuart wished Mal wouldn't carry on like this — as if these small-town types with their clown-ish confusions were legends in their own lifetimes.

'You'd know them, wouldn't you?' Mal asked. He was making an effort. Undoubtedly seeing Stuart as a way back into Ida's bed.

'Oh, yeah,' Stuart knew them — the crippled Fitch with the speech defect was licensee of the Criterion Hotel, the lardbucket Fitch was always jammed behind the bar of the golf club, working for seven bucks an hour to subsidise his winery, Railway Hill Estates — only Stuart would never acknowledge knowing them to their faces, not unless he badly wanted their attention on some point, such as, in the case of Noel Fitch, wheedling out of him a dozen or so of his ten-year-old Saffron Thistle Semillon, a gold medal winner, would you believe. The woman, Betty Kingling, was amazing — tits like dozer blades knocking blokes to the side as she surged through the bar, greying hair piled up on the top of her head and always with a flower here, a purple thistle there, her voice like dynamite going off, but would you believe this, at her age, lowering the voice tones flirtatiously, and gotchering blokes behind her husband's back, even looking Stuart up and down with her glad eye on a rare occasion when he dared the Criterion for a carton, and saying, 'Well, look what the cat dragged in, willya?'

Mal eyed the blackboard menu and chose the grilled garfish with green salad. Stuart went for the steak and kidney. Stuart said it surprised him that Mal had never been to Croppdale. No, said Mal, never. Ida had wanted him to come plenty of times, and Georgina and Doc Jim had pressed the invitation, of course, but Stuart should know, said Mal, what an inhibition he had about the property. Croppdale had been a mythical location to him as a boy, like Mount Olympus, home of the gods. Nobody ever did any work there, it seemed. ('Bullshit,' interpolated Stuart.) They lived and slept and feasted on ambrosia and nectar and listened to Apollo's lyre. ('Crap.') Work was reserved for when they came to town, and old William D'Inglis roared down from the plateau with a fistful of thunderbolts like Zeus. ('Good on him.')

'Come out at Christmas. Don't worry about Ida — be *my* guest,' urged Stuart.

Mal said he would be spending the Christmas season as usual at the Criterion Hotel. It was his home away from home. He spoke of it in his deep, plummy voice as if it were the Ritz. The Cri was to Mal like a monastery to a holy man, he said. The sacraments there were Railway Hill Shiraz and Betty Boob-whacker's house special, lamb-burgers. He'd given an undertaking to help Tutter at the hotel until Australia Day. He would come out to Croppdale after that, though, he promised at last, if things were okay with Ida.

'*Forget* about Ida. You're welcome any time,' Stuart insisted, leaning forward over the table. 'You don't have to wait for Ida to give you the nod. You don't have to camp in that dairy, either. Come and stay in the house. My grandfather often mentions you.'

'Does he?' This surprised Mal.

'Relax,' chortled Stuart. 'He doesn't know about the play. And I'd prefer it stayed that way.'

'Nothing to do with the play, Stu — your grandfather doesn't want to know I exist.'

Stuart knew that Mal had been a clerk at the mill in his time. He drew a conclusion. 'He was always like that with workers.'

Stuart wasn't getting Mal's point. 'Do you know about my mother?'

'Sure. She ran a shop. You're always mentioning it when you're written up.' He had to get that dig in.

'That's all?'

'I know she was a Logan,' added Stuart reluctantly. 'Like my girlfriend, Rennie. Except, you know, Rennie isn't a true Logan. Her natural mother was an impoverished university student. That's a confidence, by the way.'

'Did you know that your grandfather had a woman in town?'

'He was a rogue,' chuckled Stuart. 'I know that.'

'Do you know who she was?'

'Some old type,' said Stuart uneasily, 'I suppose.'

'She was my mother,' said Mal.

Stuart looked him in the eye. 'Well, I did hear that one, but honestly, I didn't believe it.' One thing he remembered was that his grandfather had said, without naming names, that once he'd known a woman made for love.

They continued eating in silence. Time was wasting away.

After a minute Stuart took a yellowed slip of paper

from his pocket and passed it over the table. 'Have you ever seen one of these?'

Mal took out his half-moon glasses and studied the paper. What he saw excited him. 'It's a work order, with receipt of deposit paid, for a well-drilling contract at Croppdale.'

'In my opinion,' said Stuart intently, 'and I'm no lawyer, it's still valid.'

Mal wasn't listening. 'I had a blank of these forms as a kid. I'd give a million dollars for them now. Look at this stamp here: "Gunner Fitch, Water Man". And this blurred outline, it's a midget water diviner. The same figure was on the radiator cap of my old man's Diamond T truck.'

' "Was"?' Stuart echoed, grabbing the docket back again. 'Grandfather says the Diamond T's still around. In a shed somewhere. He says it was your inheritance, but you never did anything about it.'

'That's not true.'

'Grandfather says that Gunner Fitch walked over the hills above the Cropp, and found an underground river he said would flow for a thousand years.'

Mal smiled into the distance. 'I like the sound of that.'

'The thing is,' said Stuart, 'I thought I would try and do the job myself, times being what they are.'

'You mean buy the rig somehow?'

'I thought maybe call in the debt.'

'Get it done for nothing?' Mal interpreted.

Stuart nodded decisively. 'This thirty quid your father was paid in 1939 would be worth heaps by now. It's our money and we haven't had the use of it.'

'Your thinking is out of date,' said Mal curtly. He couldn't believe this bloke. 'I sold the rig twenty-five years ago.'

'To a local?' persisted Stuart. He wasn't going to let this slip by, now that the idea had hold of him. With any sale of a tradesman's goods went goodwill. Stuart knew that.

'No.'

Mal told Stuart what had happened. The deal had been arranged by his cousin Tutter. Mal had allowed it for reasons he didn't understand. On the day, he'd felt totally blank, right outside himself — he'd traded away almost the last remnants of another life for the sake of a whim. *Root the Boot.* In a shed at the back of the Criterion Hotel the truck had been raised on blocks and packed in grease since the departure of the Second AIF. The purchaser was a man named Erwin Schmidt, of Gideon Hills, South Australia, who had answered Tutter's ad in the *Land.* This was in 1967. Schmidt had paid Mal a thousand dollars. It was good money at the time, enabling Mal to produce *Root the*

Boot, renamed *Yabby Stealers* when it became clear that children went for its raucous slapstick and nobody else did. *Yabby Stealers* had become a money spinner and put Whale Belly Players on their feet. Each year since, Mal had remounted the production and received a card from Erwin Schmidt.

'I put an act on for Schmidt. I said anything that came into my head about Gunner. Christ knows why — I didn't want to face anything, I wanted out. I said he could make stones give off steam, and that he'd once eaten a live chook. I said he'd found gold by reading his fingernail clippings. When it came to water he was the master. The town supply of Logan's Reef ran through a system of underground fissures charted by Gunner from vibrations on cigarette papers. He'd find water to cure cancer, fight TB, make you shit, stopper the runs, make you potent. He knew where there was water that shone in the dark — he'd bottled some and left it for me, hidden somewhere. I said that Gunner's power had preserved that shining water, and when Schmidt asked me what that power was, had I ever heard, I said it was love. Schmidt said he'd always honour Gunner — it was his rig. But the one thing I really cared for in all that stuff was a torch. This was a kid's thing. I'd fallen in love with rusty nails and a ball of spider's web and then this big long silver torch I found, distinctive, the kind cops carried in gangster movies. Your grandfather took it, Stu. He never brought it back.'

'He kept it,' said Stuart abruptly. 'So he did. But he never throws anything away. *I* lost it.' He looked at his watch. There were phone calls to make. 'It's out in a paddock somewhere. It'd be the same one, for sure — like a stick of old silver? I can tell you where to look, if you like. Down near the pump shed. You'll find it. If it means that much to you.'

Mal had no words.

'You okay?' Stuart glared at him.

No words, no words. A feeling of fear. Alarm at the thought of losing everything he had. Fear of the death tied up in that torch — of feeling it at last, then losing it absolutely.

'Mal?'

'Just thinking about stupid bloody old times,' shrugged Mal.

'Those were the best days,' swore Stuart D'Inglis, who was never in them.

Erwin Schmidt's company was called Rocky Springs Drilling. They were still in business. After draining a long glass of beer and wiping his lips with a paper napkin, Mal gave Stuart the number.

Stuart galloped through the rest of the lunch, and was on the bar phone trying to get through to Rocky

Springs Drilling on their toll-free number before Mal left. No answer. But he kept trying until he got one. He was back at Croppdale and it was three in the morning by then. This never worried Stuart. He saw what needed to be done in every situation. *Cut the crap. Get through to the essence. Save yourself. Be.*

The Criterion

AT ROSAN FITCH'S FUNERAL, THIRTY years ago, there had been nobody to mourn her except portly, pretentious Mal, aged nineteen at the time, and a bunch of relatives with eyes like his, offended, proud, and remembering.

The Fitches spat dirt from their mouths, shielded their eyes from the glare, and muttered curses at the weather, which had failed them since spring, as it always did, leaving the Logan's Reef lucerne flats in a stunted, useless condition. What was bad for the land was bad for the bakery, the butcher and the pub, where Fitches waited on people's pleasure in eternal half-dark.

The mourners gazed across the railway cutting and up the road to Croppdale, fifty miles away, wondering if a faded gold Pontiac would appear, bringing William D'Inglis down to pay last tribute. He was the one who had paid the debts on the mixed business, had come visiting when Mal was a boy, and who had sent a cheque for the funeral expenses. His cumbersome old car, it was said, had been parked outside the shop as far back as the night when the priest had come round with the news that Gunner Fitch had been blown up at Tobruk.

A different car appeared, a black Morris Minor driven by pale-faced Georgina D'Inglis, then in her early thirties. She wore a jaunty blue beret, and a bright, peasant-cut maternity skirt. Mal Fitch's heart always beat faster when he saw Georgina. Nobody in Logan's Reef was like her. She sailed through the town like a mysterious stranger. She was carrying a wreath of russet whispering gum tips, gathered by herself, which she pushed into Mal's arms. 'I am so sorry. I am going to miss her awfully,' she said, joining the other mourners at the graveside.

Mal stepped forward, knelt, and with measured restraint placed the wreath on the heavy varnished coffin. Then he looked up and met Georgina

D'Inglis's eyes as if to say, 'We know who'll be next —
it's the saddest thing'. This was because over in the
car, parked in the shade of a yellow box tree, sat
Georgina's daughter, Ida. She was eleven years old
and had leukaemia.

Impassive on the outside, Mal was in turmoil. His
mother's death had been a release. But those slanted
grey eyes in the Morris despaired him. Ida had him
aligned in her sight. Sadness flooded him. Nothing
about this day was fair — it was the wrong end of
meanings. Things led nowhere except into dry
ground. Mal placed a forearm across his eyes to
shade the sun and catch a tear. The priest was
reciting the funeral service but would soon lick his
dry old Irish lips and here at a woman's funeral get
down to what always brought the fervour of love
into his voice, anecdotes about a real man, the
Gunner.

PEOPLE RECITED STORIES OF HIS father to Mal at every
opportunity. When the shell went off at Tobruk,
Gunner had reverted to atoms. There was that one.
Ex-diggers said there wasn't a shred of him left for
the burial party. When Mal asked what he was like,

he was told that the Gunner was good at showing people what they already had — 'what they didn't know about, but needed'. Trying to imagine him, Mal went around in a circle, and was never close. Coming backwards through irrevocable obliteration, the closest he reached was an image of magnified, sooty pores in silvered reflector glass. No one would tell him where Gunner had died, at what instant, what he was doing at his last connected moment in time. Was he crouching, running, leaping, huddled in fear, close to his mates, or isolated, off on his own somewhere, silhouetted on a sandridge under the starburst of a shell? 'None of them things,' they shrugged.

Wherever Gunner went he had made a photographic record of his jobs. His snaps were kept in shoeboxes, prints mixed with negatives. Gunner was sometimes in them himself, a tall, square-jawed man wearing a tieless white shirt buttoned at the neck, and a tight-fitting black suit. A felt hat was pulled down over his eyes, leaving a bar of shade across his nose. It seemed he wore the suit everywhere, even in the bush. Mostly his photos were just for the record — inky clefts in hills, overbright claypans, blurry rock pillars straddling dim bush tracks. Certain shots, his best, blown up and framed, were hung on the dining room walls of the Criterion Hotel. The mark of Gunner's departure from a location was a steel pipe in the ground, bedded in a square of cement, with a knobbly gate valve bolted to the top.

The drilling rig was still in Logan's Reef then, 1960, parked in a tin shed at the rear of the Criterion Hotel (James Patrick Fitch and Donna Maree Logan, Licensees). Mal and Tutter lifted the stale-smelling tarp. Mice were nesting in the low-slung headlight wells. Slaters lived under toolboxes. The wheels were wide apart, the chassis high off the ground, the black, chipped tyres hard as Bakelite. It had twin flat windscreen panels divided down the middle, and rear-vision mirrors jutting from the tops of the doors. The drilling unit, folded down on the back, consisted of a motor, a stumpy shaft, a box of worn bits, and ten or a dozen lengths of rusty piping stacked on either side of the carrying tray. It didn't look big enough to penetrate the earth to any depth. On leaving for the war, Gunner had cased the moveable joints in grease. He must have stood back and hurled grease in places because dollops lay on the flatboard like cowshit. When Mal scratched the ancient dust-grey surface crust of the grease with a fingernail it was translucent as green aspic. It was Mal's rickety inheritance — this and a dry gum stick wrapped in calico and kept by his mother. On the radiator cap of the Diamond T was the potbellied figure Gunner had elected as his trademark. He'd had a rubber stamp of it reproduced on his invoices. It was a zinc, chrome-plated ex-PMG-style Hermes with its snake and pole pliered off, and a V-shaped divining rod made out of rusty fencing wire soldered in its place. A sandalled foot rested on an orb threaded at the base. The figure lurched forward like a baby learning to walk. Mal ran his fingers over it, feeling the pits made by flying stones and weathering, and stared into the blank, tiny eyes. 'I don't want you,' was what the figure seemed to say, 'I'm after better game.'

'I don't want *you*,' Mal riposted. Chemical stain from boiled radiators coated the statuette like frost. It called attention to a feeling: getting on with what really counted, finding water and bringing it up. Mal knew that using the rig would involve lifting pipes, swinging chains, and turning the crank handle of an auxiliary compressor motor mounted behind the cab. It would be manual labour. Not Mal's style at all. The sun would always be burning overhead. The metal would be hot. It would mean making appointments, keeping commitments, sticking to a timetable. And Mal wouldn't know what he was doing.

IN HIS TEENS MAL FITCH had a black curl flopping over his spotty forehead, and he sulked. People called him lazy. All his energy went into dealing with himself. He hated who he was, and couldn't choose who he might become — only rattled the fences. He sat around all day eating meat pies, reading comics and library books. Inexpressible lust made him leering, facetious. Flakes of pastry worked their way into the wool of his navy jumper, which he would sulkily tweak in class. The only girl with any time for him had left school. But anyway, he didn't like her. Betty Kingling worked in the telephone exchange and was always charging over seats to be next to him at the pictures, where they sat without touching (Mal and the next town bike, Tutter derided). Mal was stuck on the out-of-town girls who arrived at nine at Logan's Reef Intermediate High and left at three-thirty on rural buses. They kept their mystery wrapped, mirroring his own, he despaired, its perfect opposite. The ones who lived on the Croppdale run were specially enticing. He could never approach them. If they called to him he would snarl. In class he met their idea-making with scorn. They came from hard-working small-farming families, but they seemed connected by a fine thread to mysterious Croppdale. Their self-containment magnetised him. Their meagre snobberies made him burn. They wore white ankle socks, pleated navy tunics, had rosy cheeks from the morning chill, and their eyes were shiny with factual ambition. Years later they would write to Mal Fitch, trying to place him in school plays, and he'd write back, rudely, telling them that although there had always been an annual play, and although he had always tried out, he had never been chosen. *They* had been chosen. Whatever it was he found in himself later had been unwanted then. He was only ever the class fat boy, the clown. Remember? He was only ever in the lower ranks of a miserable country school where even the top students were dunces, and where one day a teacher had caught him cheating in maths. So Mal slammed his desktop and stomped out. It was the end of school for him — a convenient act, a stroke of luck. He refused to go back. For a while he helped an uncle on a pie run. Then he became dispatch boy at D'Inglis Mill. It was there, one day, that he roared at Ida — she was riding down a delivery chute on an empty flour bag, her plaits flying in the air, her tartan skirt fanning around her ears. Mal caught her at the bottom, saving her from a six-foot drop into an empty concrete loading bay. He ranted about dangers while she palpitated with fear. Splinters and rat bites. Accidents happened here all the time. A two-hundred-pound bag of flour had smacked a worker between the shoulders and broken his spine. Things like that.

The thanks Mal got at the end of his rave was a frank stare from her clear grey eyes, and a kick in the shins.

'Fatty Fitch,' she braved him. 'Sitting in a ditch.'

'Ho hum,' responded Mal, folding his arms and standing his ground. Years later, when they were lovers, she accused him of twisting her ear that day. 'You didn't like me calling you Fatso.' But Mal had luminous memories of that day. He hadn't twisted anyone's ear. He'd wanted to protect her, not hurt her. 'No. You couldn't help yourself,' said Ida, with absolute conviction.

All surviving Fitches were fat. It was a Fitch tradition to feed up. They were deliberate movers, always short of breath, purse-lipped and with blankly thoughtful put-upon expressions. They died at early ages from heart attacks, kidney failure, alcohol-related diseases, or accidents, falling asleep at the wheel, or drowning in their own vomit, as Mal's own mother had. At nineteen Mal weighed sixteen stone and was on the way to meeting his fate — just as Ida D'Inglis was on the way to meeting hers, being consumed by an aberration of blood cells.

IF MAL PESTERED HIS MOTHER she would agree to show him how Gunner found water. But only after she'd had a few drinks, when she was in a good mood, because she often turned angry, remembering Gunner. 'He'd fight for his mates and his team — they were his everything,' she always said. She'd grab Mal's hand, wrap it around the old forked stick, and say she had never been able to feel anything, but because he was his son he might get a tickle. In Gunner's hands, apparently, the stick had leapt about, torn flesh from his fingers, and smacked him on the breastbone so hard it left him bruised. Something had pained inside him, too, at the level of his kidneys. Mal felt nothing. Rosan would rewrap the stick in its bag and sigh. She'd examine the small expensive diamond wristwatch she wore, trying to make the action look casual. The watch had been given to her by the man who was there as long ago as the night the news came from Tobruk. He had come with a demand — when was he getting his water? He had stayed for love. That was her story.

'TIME'S GETTING ON.' ROSAN FITCH would pour herself a brimming glass of sherry. 'Aren't you going to the pictures, tiger?'

It was typical of her when she wanted to be rid of him, the way she coaxed and cajoled, shook loose her hair and crossed her slim legs, smoothed the floral material of a summer dress across her knees, and reached into her purse to give her son money.

'You'd better hurry along or you won't get in.' They could already see a car's headlights coming down the long lonely road from Croppdale. 'It's your cup of tea, darling, Tutter's been round already, looking for you.' It was 1950. What would it have been then — Danny Kaye, Randolph Scott?

It was the night William D'Inglis had slept under their roof until breakfast, complaining that his homestead had been taken over by a wedding party.

WITH HIS MOTHER LAID TO REST under the grassy hillside where the interstate expresses droned through Logan's Loop (diesels had just come in), Mal Fitch pictured her as he had often seen her when he came in from school or work — as he had seen her last in this life — flat on her back on the floor behind the counter. The shop had a bell-rope made of clothesline cord, at the end of which hung a cowbell, but from mid-afternoon onwards it rarely roused her.

People used to take what they needed and leave money. Mal didn't know why William D'Inglis had stopped visiting. All he knew was a prevailing atmosphere of hurt and injury. It never went away. It was oily, intrusive, transparent and as poisonous as gin. Barely into her fifties, Rosan Fitch had a cherubic, pink-cheeked face, and gingery corkscrew chin whiskers. She could still have been an old man's plaything. She would have been in that, Mal believed. To characterise her life that day Mal was tempted to get a flagon of Gilbey's, settle it into the crook of her arm like an outsized baby's bottle, and ring the cowbell loud enough to tickle her hearing.

It was a day of high, thin cloud, with a dazzling white heat-haze covering the rocky hills and thistle-dry paddocks of the district. The priest cleared his throat. Mal stared at his shoes the way he stared at the roadside while waiting to thumb a ride away from Logan's Reef at weekends. He thought about words he might say when it came his turn to speak. But the priest didn't invite him. 'I remember it was a frosty night,' Father Vincent remarked, brushing away flies, 'when I came bearing the grievous news to Rosan and the babe. It is a picture engraved on my memory. I entered through the back door, and they were waiting before the fire. The flames glowed rosy-red on their cheeks. She was a lovely woman. I couldn't tell her, you know, I stood there wringing my hands, with tears running down my face, a perfect coward, and she was the one who did the comforting, placing her hand on my arm, and looking at me with great concern, asking, "What is it, Father? How can I help you?" Now for those of us who were lucky enough to know Gunner Fitch, wasn't that a wonderful thing? Because it was the Gunner to the letter.'

It always got round to Gunner, climaxing with tales of his skill as a Group Nine League player, getting right away from Rosan and himself as Virgin and Child and never coming back again. Gunner played fullback, nothing got past him. 'He was great in the wet, and everything.'

Across on the Protestant side of the cemetery was the D'Inglis family plot, where a front-end loader was parked. It wouldn't have to dig a very big hole next time, thought Mal. He glanced at Georgina D'Inglis and read her thoughts. Ida was a skipping, jumping firecracker, full of life and cheek. She was out of the car now, hop-scotching between tombstones. Soon she would be tipped into the dirt, wasted. Mal didn't want to be around when it happened. The knowledge twisted his guts. It darkened the sky.

IN THE WEEKS FOLLOWING, AT lunchtimes, when the mail was cleared, Mal sat on the steps of the Court House eating his customary two meat pies and three sausage rolls. He'd won a cadetship in the public service, and was a trainee clerk in the Court of Petty Sessions. Hating to go home to the shop any more, he lived in his uncle's pub, the Criterion. He had a frightening dream. In a state of terror he met a strong-jawed man on the downward slope of a rough road. He had metal rods in a rough A-shape, heated at the ends. His eyes were blank. His skin was streaked with gunpowder. He pressed the rods into Mal's arm, creating five large blood blisters. Mal broke away and threw stones at the man, who threw some back. Mal went around a corner of thick black-berry bushes into the Cropp Gorge Picnic Grounds. He found a deserted railway tunnel no one knew about, a secret Logan's Loop. He sheltered in it, clinging to a side wall, plucking hooklike blackberry canes off his arms. He thought he was safe, but the man was suddenly there again and Mal decided he had to kill him straightaway, throw him under a train or break his neck. He was in the act of doing this when he woke, drenched in a feeling of hurting himself.

Ida D'Inglis played with her rope on the footpath outside the Post Office. She had been taken out of school in Sydney and brought back to Logan's Reef because her days were numbered — hers to spend as she wished. Her rope spun and slapped the cement as she toppled and recovered. She didn't show that she knew or cared about her illness. But she gazed at Mal with new interest — maybe it was fear. She knew who he was now. He'd yelled for her attention in the mill, terrified her with his concern. He was ashamed of that. He wondered if she'd heard the story about him — that he was her grandfather's bastard. People had only to look at his moon-face and curly black hair to know it was a lie, that he was a true Fitch. However, Mal was snobby and savoured any connection to the D'Inglises. Ida sat with her head between her knees for a moment before tossing it back as if to denote nothing could defeat her. She had pale, freckled skin, and her grey almond-shaped eyes sometimes shone violet. Her straight nose and kid-sisterly frankness of manner broke Mal's heart each time he saw her in the streets. 'Fatty Fitch, sitting in a ditch,' she taunted him as usual. He couldn't banish the smell of the dry grass plot awaiting her, the withered flowers, the advancing spectre. He saw the ashen, dried-out clumps of Paterson's Curse and the heaps of roly-poly grass piling against the fences on Railway Hill. He saw the temporary wooden cross that would be hammered home, and dust blowing across the valley. Over everything came the desperation cry of crows. Her death would be his death.

It was always a drought year at Logan's Reef. Anxiety about the seasons made people feel unfinished. Until they reached their ideal — the sky darkening, the barley grass sprouting green, the rails and bridge timbers glistening wet, the dry creekbed thundering with white water as only ever happened in imagination — they led a suspended life. Mal Fitch was about to leave, to change his life, to enter a profession nobody from Logan's Reef had ever practised before (and the function of which they would never be able to understand, except it was to make Mal famous). But he too led a suspended life. He would always be one of them.

Georgina emerged from the Post Office and waved to Mal. He raised a finger in acknowledgement. 'Howdy.' She came over, leading Ida by the hand. He loved being greeted by this clever woman. To have a writer in Logan's Reef made Mal feel that something in himself might be dared. Her stories always featured doctors. Her latest, set in Nyasaland, was being serialised in *New Idea*. Everyone guessed that she gathered authentic details from Doc Jim, her husband's brother, whose aerogrammes arrived regularly from abroad. It was agreed around town that she had married the wrong brother.

Georgina D'Inglis talked about Rosan, saying how much she missed her. Mal missed her too, tears welling up when he thought of the airless weatherboard shop. When he went there, the cowbell clanged, he said, with nobody there to snore through it. Georgina smiled (she loved a detail), touched his arm considerately — 'There now' — and asked Mal to come out to Croppdale some time. Mal felt himself blush. It was typical the way people like the D'Inglises showed their hand by making these offers too late. When he was ready, she said, she would fetch him in her car. No, he replied, he would like to come, but was leaving for Sydney on the Tuesday Mail. He was going from Petty Sessions to the Electoral Office. It was a phase of his cadetship. 'Regrettably, I shall have to decline.' Ida waggled her hips and poked out her tongue, mocking the way Mal talked. (He'd been doing a correspondence elocution course lately.) Georgina shook his hand and wished him well. 'Some other time, then, Malcolm.' When Mal looked round at Ida again, he caught her studying him. It made his scalp prickle. Previously he had absorbed her. This time it was her soaking him up. He went back to his pie, blinking away tears, and watched until mother and daughter climbed into their car and drove away, the child's pale face looking back at him through the rear window, the vehicle disappearing into the hollow at the bottom of the town past the dark brick of the flour mill, and then reappearing on the dusty plateau road leading up to Croppdale.

SUDDENLY THERE SEEMED SOMETHING MAL could do about all this. He threw away his pie, and squeezed through the Court House railings into the adjoining park. Away on the hill, the small car swayed like black jelly in his eye. He strained after it, reaching for Ida D'Inglis to keep her attention alive. It was as if he was trying to say, *Listen. Wait. Do this differently. Come back to life.* In desperation he tore a green stick from a gum in War Memorial Park — this being what he was born to do, no mistake — then, clenching his jaw, bending a knee and tilting forward as if learning to walk, he gave himself over to a feeling. He sensed the dying child wondering what everyone was going to become, what the world would be, fixing her steady, speculative eye on people.

Tutter Fitch and big friendly Betty Kingling watched from the upstairs verandah of the Criterion Hotel. This was good. Mal the clown. What an act in the empty, cicada-ringing day.

There was a heaviness at the centre of Mal's chest.

His kidneys felt as if they were going to burst. His shoulders quaked. His wrists ached. A sound came against his ears like the humming of tin sheet in a steady gale. *You.* If he'd had an arrow, he would have drawn back a bow and loosed it. The stick fought him; Mal was drenched in sweat as if there were someone on the other side breathing fire and wrestling him hard. His eyes were streaming. *I'm thirsty. Bring water.* The car shrank as it climbed onto the plateau, with Ida's pale face still framed in the back windscreen.

The only road east from Logan's Reef climbed a thousand metres and ran for eighty kilometres through rough grazing until it reached Croppdale, a refuge in the sky. There summer nights were cool and tree ferns grew in abandoned mineshafts. On the eastern horizon was a glimmering mica-tipped peak — Mount A.A. Hooper. From there, on a clear day, it was possible to see the Tasman Sea. So Mal had heard.

The thought of Ida filled the sky. A current of cooler air writhed from the east, ran through the town and stroked Mal's cheeks. Betty Kingling cupped her hands around her mouth and yelled, 'You're nuts, Fitchy!'

There was absolute stillness. Not another sound. And then the cicadas started up again, shrill and tinny in the ear, and Mal crossed over to the Cri,

climbed upstairs and joined Tutter and Betty Kingling on the verandah where they were drinking
schooners of flat beer drained from a warm keg left
over from a teachers' poker game the night before.

BETTY KINGLING STRETCHED HER BARE legs in the sun,
hitching up her cotton dress. 'Garrd, this is good,' she
sighed, fingering open her cleavage and tipping a
splash of beer into it. A soiled bra was visible with a
tiny, pink embroidered rose at the centre. She was a
big eater, like Mal, and now she had discovered
drink. Mal looked at her as if for the first time, seeing
something delicate, the angle of a wrist as she tipped
the glass, the fine blue veins revealed.

'What are you looking at me like that for?' frowned
Betty Kingling. Mal looked away.

Tutter kept asking her to tell him things she'd
heard over the phone at the exchange. 'I couldn't be
bothered,' she said. She bunched her seersucker skirt
into her lap and stared back at Mal. 'Well?' Her eyes
were a shiny beer-bottle brown.

She leaned over and placed her hand on his leg.
'You shouldn't waste your time always wanting to
leave,' she said intensely, 'because what you want,

Mal Fitch, can be right where you live. Even them precious D'Inglises know that.'

'They don't have much to be happy about,' said Mal.

'All I ner-know is,' observed Tutter, 'they never know who I am, no matter how many times they come for a dozen beer. Which is about every three months, or m-m-more. That's that der-dimwit, Kel.'

The other two weren't listening.

'Mal?'

'What?'

'Did anyone ever tell you,' she said, grabbing his curly neck-hairs in her fingers while Tutter rolled his eyes and looked away, 'that you have the most beautiful straight eyelashes? A girl would kill for them.'

MAL FITCH REMEMBERED THAT DAY. A mood of eternity hung over it. Inland parchment sky, doom-laden, replete with the inequalities of love. Old spring blinds drawn down with a rip. Room 17 with a chair-back jammed against the french doors leading out to the verandah so Tutter couldn't walk in. The single metal bed. Light flaking on the walls like shavings of zinc. Too much happening too fast. Betty Kingling saying that she loved love, and did he too, it was the only thing. His trousers around his ankles. His fingers cramming him into her. One foot on the floor, his own, the leverage of a skater. Sweeping through him, what seemed to be his future, his life mounting a curve, rising, clamouring, perfectly attainable, and spent in a shudder.

'That was great.' She held him too tight.

A minute later Mal stood at the window in his singlet, scratching a chubby leg. The afternoon light lengthened into evening. Her arm reached out to grab him back again. She wanted a sincere kiss. Through a chink in the blind the white, winding road to Croppdale was visible in golden light. A column of dust hung there, a motionless plume dangling above the first ridge. It seemed to have been there all his life. Why did his heart feel like melted tin, squeezed out, hot and exhausted?

The girl who was dying wouldn't die. He seemed to know that. He seemed to know things through dissecting the chain of events leading to his standing at this window. In some future year he would find that he couldn't live without Ida D'Inglis, though for years on end he wouldn't give her a thought. Then he would make his return to Logan's Reef and begin a search for all things lost.

Under the floorboards the roar of drinkers swelled as the day-shift finished at the mill. Betty Kingling said she had always loved him. Mal replied that he hadn't known.

'Mal?'

'What?'

'Don't you even like me?'

''Course I do.'

He didn't say, but he wanted to be out on his own somewhere, with his .22 cradled over his arm, ranging over the rocky hills above the golf course, potting at rabbits in the low-shining afternoon light, and when it grew dark, sitting on a rock somewhere, checking the stars. After that he would like to come in again, and find her here.

Betty was propped on her side with a sheet pulled up, her breasts spilling out. He was going to have another go at her in a minute, he could feel excitement stirring again, but she wasn't so welcoming, didn't seem to like him as much any more — what was this about?

THERE IS A SPACE AROUND MAL FITCH that is the silence of someone waiting. He's come to know this after years of professional activity. When he was tiny, he used to wait for his father to come back. 'I'll sit here and wait for him,' he would stubbornly insist. It made Rosan cry. 'Mal, darling, he was only ever half here, the poor bastard.' People hadn't told him the truth about Gunner — that he was dead — until they thought he was old enough to understand. By then he had worked something out for himself. A need. A hurt. A space that was never filled. Mal played dumb, acted the fool, stuffed his mouth, sulked — it was who he was, and all he would ever be. At Rosan's wartime parties Mal would sit under the kitchen table watching pairs of legs, trying to work out what their movements meant. Their voices were detached from their bodies, and his game would be to fit them together. When Rosan fiddled with the radio and music started, the legs began moving in time, dancing would begin, and the game didn't seem important any more. Mal always fell asleep then. Dreamed. *A dark space, a curtain parting to a square male hand, the snap of wooden curtain rings.* If he felt afraid he would shine the torch with the long tin handle across the briar roses on the ceiling. Rosehips dangling from thorns threw slim shadows like the streamlined headgear of spacemen.

Mal was twenty when he stumbled on what would become his primary ritual of expression. It was when he first came to Sydney, and walked into the old Capitol where a play was in rehearsal. The forest of Arden seemed shaped from coloured chalks, the girls' busts were tighter than melons, their voices were shrill poetry. Absurd males gallivanted around, wearing Errol Flynn moustaches and green leather jerkins. Mal followed them outside between acts, sitting in the Haymarket smoking Craven As. He sucked style from their contrivances like a lizard sucks eggs. He'd do anything to belong — sell tickets, swab toilets of spew, carry loads, take abuse, learn friendship, and give himself electric shocks with zinc hoops lowered into antiquated lighting buckets. It would take thirty more years before he recognised in everything he did the reiteration of that single image. The dark space. The heavy velvet parting to a callused hand. The knowledge of a man in the house gained through the imperative snap of wooden curtain rings. The line of life along which he grew older, became absorbed in activity, became brilliant, but never changed, never could.

IT IS NOVEMBER. *PROSPERITY* IS in its last weeks. Mal has made the final alterations, there is nothing more he can possibly do, and now he feels detached, fearful, alone. Success is a negative experience for him because he's been concentrating everything on arousing emotion in others that he doesn't have in himself. So achievement is a reproach to his emptiness. The end phase of production has always been Mal's most difficult time, when he's moved with the intensity of a sleepwalker back into life.

Before Ida, he would inevitably pursue an affair at this time. It would be with someone unexpected — the least likely candidate is how the woman would characterise herself as she woke to him. For Mal too — it would be the same for him, he would claim. She would be someone who hadn't seemed fully attentive to him previously. He would seek a quality of indifference to disturb. It wouldn't go smoothly, ever. At the start she would ask him to stop calling her for a while, to give her time to think about his rush of attention on her otherwise calm (and, had he noticed, married) life. She would have conflicting motives contributing to her confusion: she would always be an actress, for one thing, and never a lead, for another, and she would ask herself why Mal Fitch, with his influence over actors' lives, had barely acknowledged her as a living person in his previous dealings with her, in whichever of his productions she had happened to appear. He would say that she had come at him from the side. She would say (sharply) that she hadn't come at him at all. Mal would say, I mean you surprised me. Your unhappiness. Admit it. He would watch her with lizard-like concentration as if each particle of air was charged with meaning. And she would be, she was, unhappy. That would be true. Oh, and she might be open to persuasion, she would say. All the intensity of Mal's work, his troublemaking demands, his confrontations with Whale Belly Players' board of management about extending a season, and his tongue-lashings of the moronic press, would find a focus in persuasion then. She would eventually concede, thinking all the time that she was not sure if she even liked him. But that would go. That would change as Mal knew it would. It wouldn't matter. There would be nothing else then except secret meetings, charged silences, the compulsions of touch. Then in December Mal would go to Logan's Reef without much explanation. In February he would return to the city. By then he would have a stack of playscripts to read, the rhythm of a year would be beginning again, nothing would be changed. Mal would be back with himself again, disruptions banished, the only penalty being a trail of hurt and destruction not touching him, nothing to do with him, invisible, gone.

IDA IS LEAVING HIM. HE KNOWS that. She appears naked in a dream, blue-skinned, a living corpse. The setting is the foyer of a theatre with smashed glass all around, a serene Ida advancing towards him, terrifying him. So he pulls out the chef's knife he uses in the kitchen at the Criterion Hotel and plunges it into her heart. Five, six times it goes in without effect. The purpose of the knife is to make her feel something for him, a passion. It's getting to be a problem. He cannot speak to anyone about this. Mal never confides — and it is strange, the only person he feels attuned to his bewilderment is the brother, Stuart, whom he finds not very bright, probably unstable mentally in some fashion, and in every way — age, background, social assumptions and professional sympathy — as different from Mal as anyone could possibly be. Yet Mal feels, since their manic, disjunctive lunch together, that they are mates. He likes him.

THESE PAST SIX YEARS MAL'S waited for a revelation from Ida, and what she has delivered is a play, as if all she can tell him is this: her life isn't hers. This is no surprise to Mal, whose career in theatre is based on collective assumptions. But, personally, it is impossible for him to accept. Her life isn't hers, it isn't his. Yet he has always felt that her death would be his death. The scorching November day she packs her car for the six-hour drive down to Croppdale she tells him about the feeling she has of her life-flow disappearing into the rainbow stones of the Cropp River. She is going to recover herself there in whatever way she can. It's her only choice.

'I know that feeling,' says Mal beratingly. 'I get it every time. It's the workaholic syndrome, or something.' He tries to make light of it, implying an everyday affliction. 'It's artistic depression,' he adds cunningly, 'that you're suffering from.'

'Thank you.' She's always flattered by the word artistic. After all, she's only a minor anglophile cabaret artist (as a critic labelled her). 'But I wish you wouldn't always try to take over what's mine.'

'Spare me the cliches,' Mal rolls his eyes.

The pain Mal feels about Ida leaving simply will not come out. It's as if he's in some kind of brittle, outdated time warp — a wartime English drama. Going down with the sub. Clinging to the conning tower while the waves pound.

Ida's small, neat jaw is tight, her sad and secretive eyes avoid his. She is still beautiful at forty, but not ethereally so, he would like to tell her, maliciously, as she was some years ago. She isn't going to age very well. She'll be overwhelmed by a look of exhaustion, which even her mother doesn't have. This will be irrelevant to her power to break Mal's heart, but malice makes him store things. The hurt goes back before him, twined with thorns like the stems of briar on the pressed-tin ceiling of the old shop.

'It's not hopeless. I can help.' He tries to get warmth back. It doesn't feel good.

'No thanks.'

Mal can certainly help, he thinks bitterly. Reverse the charge. Get down to the level of connection. He's done it before. Always. Not just way back with Ida when she was a girl and he waved a stick at her, and her leukaemia frighteningly, marvellously, went into remission. Not just years later, either, when they first became lovers, and she lived in delight at their newness. But plenty of times in between in the murk of cheap rehearsal halls with the disposable talents of his players. And now, too. He rolls a news magazine into a tight scroll, and peers at her through it. Makes her concentrate on her innards.

'Oh, the problem is me. I know it,' says Ida. 'The play keeps circling around a point inside me. It never gets out. The transformations only postpone the moment of helplessness. My moment of helplessness.'

Then there's nothing to say for a minute. She has

said this better than Mal has said it for himself. She's made it clearer, truer.

'Shall we have a whisky?' asks Ida.

'Too right.'

Ida passes him his drink. 'I am only ever going to do this once. It's all too much.' She looks intently at him. 'You haven't told me what you think of the rewrite at the end of Act Two. The hysterical horn-pipe and the blowflies. Midge catching blowflies. The reveller bullockies stacking up on each other at the back of the inn.'

'It doesn't seem so new. I mean, it's exactly what I was getting at. My mother was a great blowie catcher, I've told you that.' They're at it again. 'I see it every year in the pub yard. As a matter of fact I took Yvette and James down to the Reef to get the feeling.'

'When?' Ida is startled.

'There was a late frost. When the comet came.'

'Ah.'

He knows that hooded look. She thinks they spent the night in the pub, Mal and Yvette Danielsen in the same room, the middle-aged man and the manic, bristly-headed singer who plays Midge. He once described Yvette as an amorous leech. She didn't think he meant it negatively.

'What did they find?' asks Ida in her neutral tone.

'Tutter drowning himself in grog. Betty Kingling

the earth mother. I should say earth grandmother, almost — Fiona's expecting. Hangover and drought, freezing frost, remorse, desolation. All the waiting that goes on. They got the feeling, all right. Your brother's mill-hands eyed her off in the public bar. Alec Hooper was there. He was the only one with any decency. He stretched out a hand and stroked her scalp disinterestedly, as if she were a live animal.'

'She is.'

'James came up with that completely new idea involving the swing doors, to suggest an alternative existence rather than the idea of life after death or whatever it was, which we could never get right in the text, could we?'

Ida says, 'I thought it was all there in the styrofoam river stones when she walks through them in bare feet, when she comes backwards to where she was, so it's not the least bit New Age, as you kept going around saying it was, as if I had to be rescued from my own stupidity. No, I can't see the reason for the changes — they're just there to aggrandise the production. Like a cattle prod to extend the season. The feeling has *nothing* to do with your old hotel. You don't know the river at Croppdale, how it shines when it's dry. I thought James had it beautifully right — the moonlight a road into the sky.'

'It was when people snored. We had to activate the interest.'

'Someone will always snore.'

Mal stares into his glass and adopts the hammy Scottish accent he uses in commercials. 'MacPriam's Tablelands Malt, famous for poisoning the emotions.'

'I'm just stating a few facts.'

Mal lifts his large head and glares at her.

'You look as if you want to hit me,' she says.

'What I feel like now,' he mutters, 'is twisting your ear. *Don't go.*' But he doesn't believe he's actually said the last bit, because there's no sign it registers with Ida at all, and he's never pleaded with anyone. She goes.

CHILDREN COME AWAY FROM MAL Fitch's productions with a feeling for the excitement of life. To kids, there never seem to be any cheap tricks, although the critics say otherwise. Now *Prosperity* has seriously impressed the critics. It is as if audiences, grown adult in a rush, have fallen in love with the desperation of experience, its hurts and consolations. They go outside into the streets again, and things they saw on the stage seem to happen right through them, becoming part of their lives. 'I saw young Lachlan with his silver spurs, his bullocky's whip gallantly furled, rise from the ground like feathered Mercury, and vault with such ease into the saddle, as if he were an angel dropped down from the clouds, to turn and chase a big red kangaroo, and twitch the scrub with noble horsemanship.'

Prosperity is 'deep'. But the theatre parties that bus themselves weekly from Logan's Reef return soothed to their town. The rhythm of the bus whomping wallabies and wombats in the dark is satisfying. They don't know why. More important than any gossip or betrayal as emphasised by the likes of Stuart D'Inglis in his rantings is the townsfolks' feeling of mystery. This is them. How very strange, this way of being moved. When they greet Mal on his home turf, or smile shyly at Ida D'Inglis buying her groceries at the Co-Op, there is little sense of separation from the material. There is confidence of possession on the part of the Reefers that astounds Mal and honours Ida. It's as if this is where the play is really happening, and has been all along, and Ida and Mal will have to get into it now, not stand outside it the way they have, possessed by their individualism.

MAL DRIVES DOWN TO LOGAN'S Reef in December. He stays in the Criterion Hotel, where Tutter keeps his room, and Betty Kingling cleans it and airs it in readiness. Absurd of Ida to think he might have had it off with Yvette Danielsen here (or anywhere). She preferred philosophising contentedly with James in the Golden Horseshoe Motel. The only people Mal's ever been to bed with between these walls are Betty Kingling, all those years ago, and Ida herself.

Mal pulls beers, waits on tables, washes dishes, and joins the life of the town. He adopts a distanced manner. But he does his Santa for the Lions Club, recalling the Torchbearers for Legacy Christmas parties when, because of a dead father, he was always given better presents than anyone else — beautiful electric train sets, cowboy suits made from real cowhide, and roller skates before anyone else in Logan's Reef ever had them. He gets drunk every third night. The hot insect-filled nights find him walking out on the cemetery road, where he sits on his favourite rock catching subtle changes in air temperature and watching the stars. The crammed, dense sky tells Mal that he's lost somewhere in his life. A shooting star slips its moorings in the Milky Way and plunges away to phosphorescence.

Last winter, out here in the frost, comet-watching. A memorable night. The vision of the torch. The long-lost torch of Gunner Fitch shaped like a wellhead in the old photos, the octagonal ring clamping the reflector glass like a gate valve fitting. Mal turns it over in his mind. The dented tin. Stuart called it silver. It has never changed, only gone ahead of Mal, telling him where to go. It lies in the grass at Croppdale, a rusting jewel. When Mal goes to Cropp-dale at last he will find it there. He cries clumsily in the dark, wiping his eyes with flapping shirtsleeves.

For the whole two months Mal's been at the Reef over the Christmas season he's been sinking down. He doesn't shave, sometimes, for a week at a time. He ties his trousers with binding twine. He's started chain-smoking again, for the first time in years, and manages a creditable early morning coughing fit that rattles the window-glass above the beer garden. It's as if personal decay, letting go, becoming a nobody, is the only proper state of readiness for what happens next.

FROM THE PUB VERANDAH MAL watches the flour mill manager, Harry Frawtell, a black-browed, square-headed hang-gliding enthusiast who boards in the pub, launch his glider from the rocky bluffs above the

Cropp River Gorge picnic grounds, and float down across the tin roofs of the town. He carries a fox whistle on his tongue and makes the squeal of a wounded rabbit. He angles his head and stares at people from low over the streets, then flips a rainbow-coloured wing and whistles up high on an updraft, reducing himself to a small wailing shape in the sky, attracting mystified hawks and curious wedge-tails.

Wind-filled sails return to haunt Mal's dreams. Blind beggars roll up their lids, revealing eyeballs of cold white quartz.

WHENEVER MAL HEARS THE SOUND of a truck engine groaning on the far side of Railway Hill, and sees the blue arc of headlights propped in the dust-moted night sky before the vehicle comes into sight, he feels a choking, trembling excitement. Stuart D'Inglis had told him — the truck, his father's old truck, is due any day now. The men from Rocky Springs Drilling are on their way back. Stuart roars into town from Croppdale in a panic of looking for them. He sees Mal sitting smoking and reading on the upstairs veran-dah of the Criterion, overlooking War Memorial Park, and yells from the window of his table-top ute, 'Seen anyone?'

Mal gives the thumbs down. He knows that when the truck does appear, and if the radiator cap symbol is intact, he will follow along.

IDA CAME IN AND HAD drinks with him on Christmas Eve, and then again at the New Year's Jockey Club dance. Between them was the tension of unhappy lovers. Ida had asked for normalised rapport, but the concept was a fiction. Every worthwhile nuance had to be remorselessly dulled in case it ignited bad feeling. And then it did anyway. He couldn't get rid of the idea of Andy MacPriam that Stuart had put in his head. It was childish. Ida referred to him too often, was too casually dismissive. 'Andrew asked me to name his new foal. I suggested "Boofhead's Pride" — isn't he a log?' Georgina and Doc Jim came too, the four of them making a party, eating ham and chicken salad with bulk mayonnaise under the race-course grandstand, dancing jazz waltzes, and drinking old Railway Hill whites, dusty as spun gold, the four of them easily agreeing they were the best kept wine secret in the world, a soothing, ambrosial liquor vintaged by a portly alchemist, Noel Fitch (whose latest plan was to start a Kangaroo Kitchen at his vineyard, serving wallaby kebabs).

When it came time to drive home, Ida slipped into the back seat and gave her hand to Mal through the window. No kiss.

Around town, people didn't make the fuss of Mal they used to, say, when he did his TV ads for Mac-Priam's or appeared on Celebrity Squares. For whole stretches of time it was as if he wasn't there at all, except for being greeted by people his own age, blokes mainly, a handful of burnt-out, work-ruined leftovers from schooldays. Once he would have had little to say to them, except for snarls and challenges and the accentuation of differences. They were former diesel mechanics, train drivers, millworkers, shearers and harvesting contractors. They'd grown up learning alcoholism with Tutter. Now what they'd ended up with in common with Mal seemed like the basis of a real connection, though some would say it was a desolate thing — 'normalised rapport'. An ache in the limbs, a memory of weather, a distinct shared mental picture of where certain buildings were that didn't exist any more, likewise the people that filled them; untroubled silences over a glass of beer; a smiling, no longer dangerous interest in gossip — because it was the fabric of their own story, they'd recognised it at last, their grab for meaning through individuality surrendering to other continuations of life. Each understood something obvious, which they couldn't have done when they were younger — it wasn't the time for it then: there was a rhythm in the cycle of the years they'd found. They partnered it with grog and cancer, heart attacks, breakdowns, gout.

In his room at the Cri, under a dim light, Mal read novels rescued from the ruins of the Railwaymen's and Millworkers' Literary Institute. He turned a page of *Vandover and the Brute* and listened to night sounds. From the bar came the loud, cutting voice of Harry Frawtell trying to persuade Tutter Fitch that there wasn't a God. That afternoon he'd looped the loop over Logan's Reef Central School — 'I had my finger up God's arse and he never even squeaked,' guffawed Harry. Tutter had promised him free drinks if he lived. He was into them. In the glassed-in downstairs office Betty Kingling was doing the accounts. Mal listened to the clatter of dishes as Fiona cleaned up in the kitchen. She was the daughter of Tutter and Betty, thirty years old, pregnant, and could have been Mal's daughter, but wasn't. He heard the thin sound of CDs being played loudly on headphones in the room across the corridor, which was occupied by a tense, isolated young man named Keith Wiencke, who managed the wheat dump out by the railway yards, a job that entailed killing mice with poison, tying down tarps in windstorms, staring at people with a dead eye, and not much else, it seemed.

In the hotel dining room, as he served tables, or, tonight, as he sat in the management corner, reading the small print of the airmail *Guardian Weekly* while eating his roast, and steadily knocking back a bottle of 1982 Fitch's Saffron Thistle Semillon, Mal savoured the atmospherics. The desultory dining room life always gave action a kick when it seemed too late. Someone always entered at the denouement who wasn't in the dramatis personae. He gave that one to Ida. Here was an example — into the dining room slid the shifty-eyed Keith Wiencke. He had showered and changed and come downstairs to a corner table. The only other diners apart from Mal were an elderly couple consulting road maps as they ate. Travellers did not stay in hotels like the Criterion any more, they went to the Golden Horse-shoe, but recently there had been an advertising campaign in city papers and a list of Traditional Country Pubs had appeared. The Criterion's name was on it, thanks to a contact of Mal's having his arm twisted.

After a minute, the other permanent boarder, Harry Frawtell, banged through the swing doors carrying a schooner of beer and a glass of tomato juice, clutching his day's mail under his armpit.

'Jesus.' He put down his glass after taking a long pull at it. 'That's cold.' He was so angry he complained about what he liked. He rearranged his cutlery, putting the spoon across the top of the setting. His knuckles were scabbed from too many narrow escapes hang-gliding.

'Fiona round?' Harry frowned at the grey-haired couple because they were eating and he was not. Then at Mal.

'Somewhere,' answered Mal.

Harry raised a fist and banged the table-top. The cutlery jangled, the empty teacups, turned bottoms up on their saucers, gave a clack. The elderly couple looked up.

'A-bominable service,' he winked, the way other people might nod a greeting.

The elderly couple smiled and sipped their Saffron Thistle, which they told Mal was very good indeed.

'Bandicoot's piss,' said Harry Frawtell under his breath.

Fiona emerged from the kitchen.

'What do yous want tonight?' she said to Keith and Harry. 'There's no choice.'

Harry grabbed her by the back of the skirt. 'How about this?'

She broke free. 'Tekky'd kill ya.'

'Tekky'll never come back,' said Harry.

Fiona rearranged herself. She was six months pregnant. Her boyfriend, Texas Dyball, had disappeared after promising a wedding.

'There's a three bean salad and all,' said Fiona.

'They got a choice,' accused Harry, resentfully indicating the elderly couple.

'They ain't permanents.'

'I ain't so permanent either,' said Harry Frawtell, blinking. Along with the anger went an impression of tears. While Fiona was in the kitchen fetching the salads Harry finished his beer and burped. He showed Mal his latest letter from D'Inglis Mills Croppdale Incorporated, regretting that no position could be found for him in the company after the first of July.

'That's too tough,' said Mal.

'I'll tell you what I intend to do,' said Harry, leaning forward over the table. 'Every night from now until the first of fucking July I'll go over to the mill and I'll find myself the nicest looking bag of D'Inglis flour in the place, and I'll do a big black shit inside it, and I'll sew it up.'

Mal could see the elderly couple toying with their glasses and staring at the old photos on the walls while Harry spoke. The photos showed harvesting scenes in the days of horse-drawn combines, each one signed in white lettering with the name of their long-dead photographer, R.C. Fitch. Beside each signature was a neat white stamp of recent origin, the trademark of Railway Hill Wines. When the elderly diner savoured his wine again he spoke of its 'sweaty saddle' character.

Harry jerked his head back: 'Bullshit!'

Fiona returned from the kitchen carrying the salads. The plates were heaped high with slimy discoloured beans, strips of ham, limp lettuce, tomatoes, asparagus, and bruise-blue chicken legs.

'I want beetroot,' Harry demanded as he started eating.

'There ain't none,' said Fiona.

With his mouth full Harry made the action of a tin opener. He then raised his eyebrows to Keith Wiencke and made a drinking action while he sucked in a string of coleslaw. They routinely shared fetching and carrying. The younger man pushed back his chair and went to the bar for a beer and a tomato juice.

The elderly couple peered at a newspaper as they finished the last of their wine. There had been a football riot in Europe: English fans had caused the death of forty Italians. The couple deplored the incident quietly, using the word 'uncivilised'. Harry

Frawtell reddened. He looked grimly at Mal as if to say, You'll appreciate this one.

'If you don't mind me saying so, what you just said is the greatest heap of crap I've ever heard.'

'I beg your pardon?' queried the man. He looked like a retired man of some importance. The ex-headmaster of a big school. The woman twisted herself around with dignity.

'I'll tell you what's uncivilised,' said Harry Frawtell in a loud voice, 'and that's keeping those poor hungry English bastards on the bottom of the heap. They got nothing. They're outa work and they're told it's their own fault. No wonder they kill.' Harry thumped the table. 'I'd kill too.'

Fiona came from the kitchen with the swing doors thumping behind her. 'What's goin' on here?' she called to Mal as she threaded her way between the empty tables. She set a plate of fruit salad and ice cream in front of Harry. He gave it a sullen, tearful leer, then grasped his spoon in his fist and started shovelling it in.

'Spare a thought for the victims?' suggested the man with a brave tremor as he took his wife's elbow and helped her up from the table.

'Has he been stirrin' again?' Fiona went over to the couple and placed her hands on her hips.

'Bloody "victims",' muttered Harry Frawtell, rolling his eyes.

'I hope yous enjoyed it,' said Fiona. The man put a five-dollar note in her hand, but she blushed and pushed it back at him. 'What did I do? I never done nothin'. Come through to the saloon for a Railway Hill Liqueur Muscat.'

'She never does nothin',' echoed Harry sourly. 'But she ends up in the puddin' club just the same.' He turned to Mal. 'Fuckin' Railway Hill Wines. When I first come here it was just a paddock of noxious weeds and sheepshit.' He burped and pushed his chair back, his chin tucked into his chest. 'A bloke could've bought it for a song.'

MAL AND IDA HAD RARELY spent more than one night at a time under the same roof. With Ida, Mal thought he had got it right where he had failed before. Ida never complained about his Christmas absences. She had her own. In past years, on her visits to Cropp-dale, they met in Logan's Reef for drinks and a meal, as they did now, and sometimes a look would pass between them, as it never did now, and they would head up to Mal's room mid-afternoon, or out to the deserted, blackberry-choked picnic grounds at the gorge, where the Cropp River trickled from the hills and nobody ever disturbed them. Ida loved to hear the gossip when he came back from the Reef; she had her own from Croppdale, and it was the making of *Prosperity*, Mal believed — that sense of town life he gave her that she could never have gained from her family, mixed with the tension of class division she had in her blood.

This year Mal hadn't told management how long he was going to be away, or what he was thinking of next — if he did, he'd have to admit that he was not actually between productions, in this mood, but finished with them. Croppdale was at the end of a road that was still the same as it ever was, a ribbon of dust in the upper corner of his room window. There was nothing after the property in that direction, people said, save crumbling limestone cliffs, blue forests, a distant peak, and hazily far, the sea.

And under the hills was an underground river that would flow for a thousand years.

Mal dreamt of that river. A horse stamped out the water for a well. Cascades sheeted over rockfaces and ferns uncurled hairy clefs. A man clicked a torch, making signals. An old truck sailed across water with its wheels dismantled and loaded on the back.

From the bar under Mal's feet came the thump of country music turned up full volume. A rush of thirst went clear through his sinuses and he wanted to be dancing, pulling someone more alive than he was into his arms — Ida, that is who you are? And then, whenever someone knocked at his door, he had the hopeless wish it was her. But it was always just Tutter wanting him to take over in the bar, or Betty Kingling bringing a pot of tea and two china cups, and they'd get their feet up on the verandah rail, and blow steam from the surface of their hot, rust-red Darjeeling, and she'd refrain from asking the question she was always asking with her eyes, why was he so bloody miserable?

Hatless, Mal went walking in the hot afternoon sun on the plateau ridge leading to distant Croppdale. He knew Ida had come to town without seeing him a few days before. Betty reported seeing her at the clinic, where she'd had a lot of tests with Dr Battacharya, and had looked shagged, Betty said. Then Keith Wiencke, the foxy-faced wheat dump manager, had mended her tyre at the roadside just out of town. Wiencke looked narrow-eyed and heated over the encounter, telling Harry Frawtell about it while Mal waited on tables in the dining room. He hissed to Harry, Why didn't they pack an esky and go driving the back roads until they found her?

'Cause you're a shit, Harry had told him.

GRIT FLEW INTO MAL'S TEETH and every distempered dog from the wrong side of town came at his heels. He could feel heat bouncing from surfaces that rattled all around. Logan's Reef was made of tin, which was loosening, flapping, ready to fly. The sky was a squashed mulberry colour and by three-thirty was black with dust boiling from the west. Harry Frawtell's Commodore slid up behind him with a crunch of gravel.

'Get in.'

It was freezing in the car. Climate Control was jammed on high. The mill manager banged the ventilation grille with the heel of his hand. He was a fastidious driver. They descended the single-lane tar track beside the railway line, went through the underpass, and came up alongside the steel mesh fence of the shire equipment yard. The wind hit again. Grit peppered the windscreen. Balls of roly-poly grass mounted each other and wobbled under the security barbs. Front-end loaders, twin-cab diesels, rollers, packers, excavators, bulldozers and graders were lined up inside there.

'About two million dollars worth of plant, and that's at used prices,' said Harry Frawtell in disgust. 'It's all standing idle while the bastards get pissed for the day. Do me a favour, Mal. If you ever see me on the fuckin' shire I want you to beat me to death with a shovel. Understand?'

Mal said he would do it.

Up ahead loomed the double gates of the flour mill. Harry Frawtell pulled a key from the ashtray and tossed it into Mal's lap.

'Open up, willya?'

Outside, the heat was refreshing. Mal shouldered aside a section of gate that ran on a small rusted wheel. He walked ahead of the car. Yellowed wheat sprouted from the cracks in the crazed roadway where the workers, he remembered, always came out to piss.

Harry Frawtell led Mal along the narrow, weedy path beside the manager's sinister residence. Once Mal had thought old William D'Inglis lived in it, a diamond-cornered house of cards. 'Look at this dump — they expected a bloke to live in it!' Mal remembered when the manager's residence had flowers spilling from window boxes. It had been photographed for the D'Inglis Mills Christmas Calendar. 'Give it to the Hysterical Society,' spat Harry Frawtell. He thumped the dark glazed brick of the residence.

He unlocked another door and they walked down a dark corridor stacked with boxes of yellowing stationery. A dozen cats scattered ahead, then sat back watching while Harry hissed, ran forward at a crouch, hissed again. He laughed asthmatically, enjoying himself. The two men entered the floor of the mill where everything was covered with a film of white flour. Harry made finger-tracks on the pipes and dusty bricks. He stamped his wide soles on the concrete and then angled his head to see animated, larger versions of his feet appear behind him. The steel rollers of the milling machinery shone like mirrors in a telescope. This was a different Harry from the one Mal had seen before, when the shifts were operating and Harry shouted unreasonably at the workers. The workers had worn white caps, long-sleeved jackets, and disposable face masks. In Mal's day they breathed dust and died of emphysema. It became TB in Ida's *Prosperity*.

'What sort of mind would put this under the hammer?' Harry spat in a corner. 'The old bloke's one hundred fucking years old. He needs a nurse and a chartered accountant to hold him up while he signs his name. Only he doesn't, he doesn't sign his name, does he? It's that little shit Stuart D'Inglis who signs his name. He's got his hooks into that Rennie Logan I've done my balls over.'

'Don't blame Stu — he's just the agent of change.'

'What in the name of fuck am I expected to make of that?' raged Harry Frawtell.

They went into the tiny, glassed-in office where thirty years ago, after catching up on paperwork, Mal had swivelled on a captain's chair, fighting boredom. There was the gouged red cedar table where Mal had sat reading the grey, silken-bound American library books donated to Logan's Reef Shire by the Andrew Carnegie Foundation. The volumes of Eugene O'Neill had never been opened. When Mal slit their pages, along with a sensation of entombed riches for the taking, he recognised the grandiose talk of a boozer. The deserted loading bay where Mal had saved Ida from a two-hundred-pound bag of flour was a haunt of spiders.

Harry Frawtell showed Mal his latest letter from D'Inglis Mills Croppdale Incorporated, regretting that no position could be found for him in the company after the first of next month.

'That's too tough,' said Mal, as though he hadn't heard it before.

'I'll tell you what I intend to do,' said Harry, getting into his refrain. 'Every night from now on I'll find myself the nicest looking bag of D'Inglis flour in the place, and I'll do a big black shit inside it, and I'll sew it up.'

Mal shook his head. 'You wouldn't.'

'Let's get pissed,' said Harry.

Back at the hotel he shepherded Mal ahead of him into the bar. Mal watched as Tutter shuttled empty glasses from the chiller to the gun, and rows of frosted schooners filled with creaming ale. Mal felt a prickly sensation at the back of his sinuses as every promise he ever made for himself seemed about to be fulfilled. The piss. The clamour. Torrent of feeling. River of life. Everyone was an alcoholic, himself included. He looked around, his eyes searching through chunks of sun-reddened faces for one to love. Where had Ida gone? What was she doing tonight? He always felt she was wasting her time when she wasn't with him, using up her life. He lit a cigarette and drew on it sharply.

Harry poured a beer straight down his throat and pushed his glass out for another one. 'Your shout,' he said. He looked around the bar. The place was packed. 'How many women,' said Harry, 'would you say are sittin' at home waiting to be goosed by these pissants? The poor bitches. A bloke oughter do the rounds.'

'Hiya, boys.' A handsome, ashen-faced man in his forties squeezed past.

'Alec,' nodded Mal.

'Jesus, they're a mean mob of poor sorry bastards,' said Harry under his breath. He meant the sacked mill and wheat dump workers, who, despite his angry stares, kept touching him on the shoulder as they shoved their way to and from the urinal. It showed something about him. He was no good with them but he believed in them, and he was one of their number, come what may. And they saw that in him. And Mal liked him for it. He was a good man.

After a long deep draught Mal notched up to another plane of feeling. Endless renewal of excitement. Friday night in a bloodhouse. The old home away from home. The fumes of the slops. The roar of the roistering mugs. Lost souls in the valleys of the blood. The heart-churning country music which he had always thought, if he was ever to get anything up of his own that wasn't going to be categorised as kids' stuff, would work for him, evoking this town of heroic losers. Bikies' girls in jeans and black singlets leaned against him while placing their orders. ''Scuse me, Dad.' Tutter put another beer in front of him and winked. 'On the h-house.' So it bloody well ought to be: Mal had just covered Tutter and Betty for the liquor licence renewal — twenty-three thousand dollars down.

Mal was conscious of Alec Hooper staring at him from the other side of the servery. When Mal caught his eye Alec pursed his lips and dropped his head. 'Alec's off the strength at the wheat dump as of tomorrer,' whispered Harry Frawtell. Alec came over. Harry shifted away. Mal and Alec stood drinking side by side without exchanging a word until Mal cracked.

'What'll you do?'

'Go shootin',' said Alec. 'Out there on the Upper Cropp. It ain't legal, but then nor's that Kangaroo Kitchen the cousin of yours wants the roos for.'

'You know that country, don't you?'

'I sure do.'

'You worked for old William D'Inglis, once, didn't you?'

'I sure did.'

It was a false line of questioning for Mal. He knew all about Alec Hooper, who would have heard by now of the scene in *Prosperity* where Lachlan Strong dropped a flour bag on old man Finucan. The real thing had happened at D'Inglis's Mill in 1964. Alec, at seventeen, had been in love with Ida. The old man wouldn't have it. He sent Ida away. A bag had been tipped from the landing and broke William D'Inglis's neck. God knew it was Alec who sent it down.

LATE NOW. TOO LATE FOR anything else except this. Mal Fitch sits on the side of his bed with his head in his hands, and feels the proximity of what he is seeking. There is an ache across his shoulder blades, a pain in his kidneys somewhere. His arms feel heavy, his hands press into his temples, his wrists ache. Excitement eats him. He sits this way in rehearsal halls, awaiting understanding from a cast, feeling devastated till it comes. He knows his part is finished when the production comes alive. Then when he looks back on his work it is nothing. It always belonged to someone else and was never his to express. Same with his life.

BOOK TWO

RETURN

Snake Rising

THE FIRST NIGHT COLIN BYRON camped with Erwin Schmidt and Kurt Wolpers he slept beside the old truck, knowing they were fools and needed him. Towards dawn it was chill, so he hauled his swag under the chassis that still retained heat from the burning day, and slept with his nose almost touching the greasy, dust-caked hump of the gearbox.

Then it was creeping light. The other two weren't stirring in the camp, so why should he? He looked down the length of the truck towards the back. It was all shiny claypan and silvery dawn light out there.

Water where they'd secured the wellhead at dusk spread across the ground in a stain, corellas and budgerigars lining up for a drink.

Colin Byron reached up. Thick wads of grease on the metal crossbeams were hard as scabs. Peeling some back, he found it was green, pure, shiny like bottle glass. It was a beautiful substance, with a smell that never staled. He worked his fingers into it. He'd known there was something about this truck from the first he'd heard of it. They always had work, the two Krauts, yet they drove a truck so old it was laughed at. A 1933 Diamond T '211'. It had a dividing bar down the middle of the windscreen, and flat plates of glass on either side, with wing mirrors like ping-pong bats attached by metal rods to the door frames of a cab on which the words R.C. Fitch, Water Man, were faintly visible in old paint.

Colin Byron could find things that were lost, if people needed him to badly enough. Also for himself. Gold was always at the back of his mind — the metal of kings. He only had to think of something without forcing himself and it happened. Gold lay in the depths of the grease lump, keeping him working cleaning the muck away. It caught the light. Dull yellow. It was attached to an I-beam by a twist of tie wire. It was a ring.

Colin Byron's skinny, freckled fingers found the

greasy metal and he was half-afraid, knowing rings were trouble. People went for rings to tie themselves in situations they imagined would never break. Someone had hidden it there under the floor of the truck. They would have had their reasons. They would have meant to come back for it. It wasn't intended for Colin Byron, anyway, though he would keep it if he could. That man they spoke such bullshit around, Gunner Fitch, for sure, he would have been the one who had taken such care. They said he could make water shine, eat live chooks, you name it. He was the first owner of this truck and he'd been dead fifty years plus.

The ring was in the shape of two snakes joined together, head to tail, their heads facing opposite directions, the tail of one in the mouth of the other. Colin Byron picked at the holding wire with his fingertips, untwisting the sharp ends until his flesh was torn and bleeding and he gained his prize. He could see the golden scales of the skins. He slid the ring onto the fourth finger of his left hand. It was easy getting it on, harder coming off, bulging a roll of blue flesh. With this resistance he felt a tightening in his chest, an ache in his balls — it was strange: he felt a heartache down to his knobbly wrists where love was trapped and couldn't escape but was trying.

Then he needed to do one. He crawled out from

under the truck looking for a place. High on the wall of the dune was a fallen tree with a V-fork of the kind he liked sitting on, staring into the distance, letting it drop. *If you are nobody, nothing, you still haven't gone,* he said to himself. *You are ashes whirling in space. The world is two snakes eating each other's tails. Nothing stops living in light.*

Over his shoulder, the sky was black. Lightning forked and came at him. He was in it.

ERWIN SCHMIDT AND KURT WOLPERS woke hearing booming behind the sandhills. The storm came from nowhere in the empty sky. Morning darkened and clouds raced up — it hadn't rained since Christ was a boy in shorts out here, they panicked, grunted at each other through their hangovers and waded through the empties from the previous night, kicking and yelling. Erwin, a fatty, reached up and hauled the driver's door open, farted his way up while whiplash Kurt fitted the crank handle, bracing himself, fighting the kickback. Lightning hissed across the plain, illuminating the low mulga and groves of Mitchell grass, seeking iron in the earth, ignorant of flesh. Bolts flared, cracked, and reflected blue on the tiny figure of a winged man screwed to the radiator cap whose eyes were blind and whose zinc feathers were edged with rainbows of crusty salt.

There was the rig backing over the claypan trying to get to the made road before it was too late. There was Kurt Wolpers leaping into the cab and slamming the door. There was brain-damaged Colin Byron, getting up with his trousers round his ankles, having made a shithouse from the highest point of elevation around, the top of the sandhill. Leave him there, he was already dead, forget him. Electricity made his red hair stand on end, his lips go dry and blue, his pale muddy eyes roll in alarm. The strike of fire lifted him off his feet and blasted him down the dune, a rag of nothing, spinning and landing on his head. 'Keep driving!' spat Kurt as the first fat raindrops hit and he opened the door on his side and jumped down on the running board, despising the idea of himself ready to save a stranger he hadn't met until yesterday but who'd found them their water.

Colin Byron picked himself up and started running, clutching his trousers and sprinting barefoot across mats of bindi-eye.

'Open her out!' Kurt told Erwin, and flopped back in his seat, slammed the door, stared ahead sardonically. 'He's alive.'

A hand reached down from a cloud with a stockwhip

and flayed a swarm of locusts. The sun's face became the moon, with a nose and an eye looking down on Colin Byron, surveying the nakedness of his life, the circle of the planet, the gold of an ancient ring, the cartwheels of human pain.

Colin Byron jumped onto the running board and stood there shivering with his white knuckles gripping the door, his face grazed, sweating blood, his jaw hanging slack. The drilling rig rocked and lumbered out to the made road stretching forever. A grass fire flared. Kurt Wolpers opened the door and Colin Byron wedged in beside him. 'You shits!' he sobbed.

The Three

NOW THEY WERE BACK. The old truck appeared over the crest of Railway Hill above Logan's Reef. It had travelled three days from the west in answer to a phone call. The agitated caller had made a plea and a promise. He was desperate for water, he said. In order to get water he would pay double the standard rate. He wanted water now.

'Okay, Mr Dingles. We shall be there Wednesday.'

'Morning or afternoon?'

'What is today?' (It was the middle of the night when the call came.)

'I cannot believe my ears,' mocked the caller. 'You got the letter — dated last year — and the deposit?'

'Yah.' (The cheque had bounced. They'd had to ask for another one. Last year was barely a month ago.)

'*D'Inglis*,' the caller barked, 'is how the name is pronounced in this country. And you don't know what day it is? I will keep an eye out for you.' The receiver went dead.

The truck only just held together. It was high-cabbed in shape with a battered bonnet and a dull silver grille. On the old-fashioned radiator cap stood the flaking chrome winged god, the pot-bellied boy wearing what appeared to be a trailing nappy, with a quiver of arrows at the waist and a piece of rusty eight-gauge fencing wire in his fists. Behind the cab, low steel sides and bogie wheels supported a folded, cranelike drilling rig, with bundles of rusted metal pipes along its base. The whole thing was high slung, top heavy. Paintwork on the sides said Rocky Springs Drilling Coy., Gideon Hills, S.A. Under that was the ghostly name of its first owner. Attached to the truck was a long, four-wheeled trailer packed with a refrigerator and a gas stove, cardboard boxes tied with twine, a battered off-road motorbike, fuel drums, wire-framed beds and mattresses wedged into crevices, and an aluminium boat.

The contraption clattered along slowly for a few hundred metres, descending towards the town. Then it swung off the road with a grind of brakes, and subsided to a halt on a potholed bitumen apron. Scattered around was a litter of styrofoam hamburger cartons and empty beer cans. A nearby cairn marked a forgotten event (the dedication of an unusable picnic spot by a one-time shire president, William D'Inglis). It was, as ever, a day of high, thin cloud, with a dazzling white heat-haze.

Three men were squeezed together in the metallic green cab. Such heat did not bother them. They had known worse. They studied a hand-drawn map and argued between themselves while the town's tin roofs rippled in oily light about two kilometres below. The interior of the cab stank of sweat and travel, diesel fumes, the odour of last night's booze-up, the stench of stubbed-out cigarettes. Lying on the passenger-side floor on rumpled potato sacks were a skinny grey whippet and a barrel-shaped, red-eyed Jack Russell terrier. The dogs knew better than to leap up whenever the truck stopped. All they saw all day were the threatening toes of boots. They peered from narrowed eyes, muzzles resting on their paws, awaiting a sign.

'So. We go through the town of Logan's Reef and turn west,' declared Erwin, the driver. He was a fat, ruddy-faced man in his fifties who spoke English with a strong accent. He angled the hand-drawn map across the steering wheel. 'Then we travel eighty-three kilometres and we are there. *Khroppdahl.*'

Erwin's soft grey hair was cut in the shape of a pudding bowl. He had a pink, razor-scratched double chin. His shiny brown eyes were squeezed by fat. He wore a white, coarsely woven cotton tennis shirt, and a pair of khaki cotton trousers undone at the waist, where his gut expanded. He wore rubber thongs because his feet were swollen from circulation problems, and his beefy arms were covered in dry, scaly skin cancers. He wasn't young, hadn't even been young back on the day he bought this truck in Logan's Reef and cleaned the grease away from the metal holding plates in big dirty handfuls.

'Look,' corrected Kurt, the man sitting beside Erwin. 'You've got the paper arse-up, mate. We go east. We come back this side of town and turn left. See?'

Kurt, a wiry mistrustful man, also spoke in a German accent. He traced a route on the paper with a cracked, yellowed fingernail, stating his corrections patiently. 'See here, mate, that-a-way, out that road there.' Kurt had a high balding forehead, short pale hair, sandy eyelids, and hard, unblinking blue eyes.

Lines of tension ran down his cheeks like scars. He
was aged around forty. He had the look of someone
constantly overcoming the physical strain of maintaining cheerfulness, staying within a concept of
himself, whatever the odds. He wore a denim jacket
over a rearing stallion-printed T-shirt and faded blue
jeans. On his feet were a pair of elaborately tooled,
burgundy-red, Cuban-heeled riding boots. They
were disfigured by dust, scuff marks, and ripped
stitching.

'Yah. You're right, Kurty-boy,' acknowledged
Erwin with a sigh. 'You're always right.'

The third man, Colin, was in his mid-twenties.
'Jesus,' he grunted, looking sideways while Kurt
snatched the paper back from him. 'That there's a
shithouse kind of a map. Who wrote it?' He
drummed his fingers on the duco of the side door
and observed, 'You don't want me to see it, do you?
You don't want me to see nothing, you bastards.'

Erwin folded the map away in his shirt pocket. 'A
beer now, I think,' he said.

'You're singing my song,' said Kurt.

Colin rolled his eyes. 'Arseholes.'

Wherever the three of them travelled it was
always the same. Colin Byron didn't count to the
others except for water. They would pay for this now.
His skinny shoulders and spindly legs were just

something to be squashed and pushed to the side of the cab to make room until there was water to be found.

As the truck started moving again, Colin hung from the side window like a spider, his ribcage crushed against the door handle. With fiercely focused eyeballs he watched a team of bull ants dragging a greasy potato chip along the blue metal. This was the way the blokes hauled their gear when he'd first seen them chasing water. Arse-up. They knew about rocks, depressions, signs, but they had no feel. If they found a mug they'd take a punt and sink a shaft. In the end they'd argue, toss a coin. The truck made most of the decisions for them. If it wouldn't start, they'd drill where it stood. By then it would be high noon, they'd be out in the sun with their shirts off, two Krauts, no hats, cooking.

He'd found them on that claypan west of buggery. Kurt wore a gold neck chain, Erwin's jeans kept dropping round his white arse. They yelled and shook their fists in the emptiness. They hauled up the five-metre derrick and attached the drill bit with heavy tongs, wrestled and swore, and then looked over their shoulders to where Colin was sitting under the thin shade of a wilga.

'Where'd you spring from?'

'A bloke dropped me.'

'We didn't hear notting.'

'It was back over the rise there.'

Colin scratched a mark on the ground with the heel of his boot. 'You ain't got a hope where you are. There's a flow under here.' Colin put a hand between his legs, rose on his heels. 'Not much, but a flow. I'd say thirty, thirty-five metres down.'

They had no reason to believe him. But they had heard of someone, and of course this was him, a boy from the Hill who chucked fits and was nuts, who had worked for their rival who'd gone bust when the drought broke: but who found water.

Colin read their thirsty minds. 'There's a carton in it if I'm wrong.'

He wasn't wrong.

If you asked Colin Byron how he knew what he knew, how he found water and things that were lost, he asked you back how you knew it was morning when it was — same way you knew you were hungry or thirsty, dying for a drink. Same way you knew when it was pitch dark and you were going to have to strike a match. Same as when you were scared. You'd have to be stupid not to feel it. Same way you knew anything — because you needed to. Then you felt it. Same as when he knew there was love around, bound elsewhere, always bypassing him.

Colin's curly red hair was a mess from where he'd slept all night jammed on pillows in the boat on the trailer. He wore a checked flannel shirt with a torn pocket, threadbare green King Gees, and a pair of oversized Blundstones without socks. The clothes were clean because St Vincent de Paul's washed everything before piling it into his arms, and Colin was clean because Kurt had forced him into a shower after the truck collected him from a street corner in Broken Hill, where he'd been sleeping in the men's home. The dogs had been round at his married woman-friend's place: she wanted to adopt Colin, but her husband wouldn't have him in the house.

Colin had a lumpy, bumpy scalp, protruding ears, hollow eye sockets, eyes the colour of muddy water, and pale, taut, freckled cheekbones. Froggy blue skin stretched over the bridge of his nose. He had a swollen upper lip from a recent fight, and a scab on his forehead from the fight before that. When he moved his head it jerked slightly, he didn't know why, and when he walked he dragged a toecap.

On the horny third finger of his left hand he wore this gold ring. When he had thinking to do he tapped the metal of the ring against his teeth, making a definite ticking like the running out of time of a wind-up clock when it is about to stop. Say he was in a pub and Kurt was putting the work in on a woman.

If Colin stopped clicking even for a moment she'd give him a sideways glance and then one in Kurt's direction, sum up something inside her head, and get up and say to Kurt, 'Fine. Yeah. Let's go.'

KURT ROLLED A CIGARETTE AND swiftly placed it between dry lips. After lighting it he pinched out the live match with his fingertips. Kurt always did this, riding the pain, fighting it. When he inhaled, his face went blank with concentration and the rearing stallion stencilled on his T-shirt looked savage.

'You are sick in the head,' accused Colin Byron. 'Cracked.'

Getting no response, Colin reached across and jabbed Erwin on the upper arm. 'And you are as bad as he is, fatty. You pretend you ain't, but you are.'

Erwin went up through the gears and the load of steel rattled and shook as the truck gathered speed. Down they rolled towards this old town. The truck sang a low refrain of harmonising metal, the vibrations folding into each other and building to a single powerful hum. Erwin blew the klaxon to echo the feeling, bouncing it off the tin-coloured hills. *I'm back, dicks!* Erwin forgot the rusty bolts of the engine mountings, the knots of eight-gauge wire holding parts of the undercarriage together. The whole contraption threw sparks when it bounced at speed, threatening to disintegrate, scattering wreckage for miles. When this happened at night it lit up the bush at the sides of the road.

Colin spat sideways. He looked ahead through the windscreen as the town shifted closer. 'Okay,' he asked, 'what's the dump called?' He tried to make out the name on a white signboard. Just as the jumble of letters was coming into his brain Kurt put him in a headlock, forcing his skull under the dash. Kurt did this easily, he was strong, keeping his cigarette nipped between his teeth, laughing, snorting, with dry nicotine-smelling fingers plugged in Colin's nostrils. 'Do your thing, you little shit.'

So this was the town, then. Colin didn't need any clues. It was where R.C. Fitch had come from, where Erwin had bought the truck and drilling equipment all-inclusive the day Colin Byron was born — 28.2.67. Erwin had shown him the fat-guy stamp and repeated things that Gunner Fitch's son had told him about his father when they bought the unit. It was like hearing about himself, understanding that people had thought Gunner Fitch cracked because he knew something they didn't, just as anyone knows things — you know, it's raining; you know, the sun shines; you know, you smell like shit, your fingers smell like shit, that ring you wear is the colour of shit — where'd you get it? They'd have to chop off his fingers if they wanted that.

Gripped by Kurt, Colin Byron narrowed his eyes and the light darkened. He saw his boots through smoke. He entered a descending spiral and felt himself flung against an inside wall as he went around a curve. All the time he was sinking, going down fast, twenty, fifty, a hundred metres, two hundred. He felt sick from longing. It gave him a hard-on; he wanted someone who would love him — it wasn't the woman who wanted to adopt him, she couldn't love him, though she always touched him, kissed him, ruffled his hair and picked sand from his scalp, then shampooed him at the kitchen sink. He was a freak.

His head went right down into the floor and greased away on the bitumen. Booms went off like battle guns. Flames belched from a hillside where men stood holding crucifixes and machine guns against the fire of a dragon. *I can't say where I am exactly. I hardly ever know.* Colin said that to the woman once. His mind spun like the time lightning had blasted him from the sandhill, and he'd reached up to the face of the sun that had a special eye. Erwin shuffled through the gears, the truck shuddered, slowed, dipped under a railway viaduct at the entrance to the town, and Kurt let Colin go.

'You filthy, filthy shits.'

The first thing Colin saw was a hotel with an old verandah awning. The Criterion. He looked at the name gummy-eyed, spelling it out under his breath. Whatever a Criterion was, there were a lot of them spread around, north, south, east, west, rotten stinking bloodhouses every one. A square-chested man with curly black hair stood on the verandah rail, fists clenched and knuckles showing white as he stared.

Erwin said, 'That's him. The son.'

Colin thought he said, 'The sun'.

Colin caught his eye. They knew each other.

Behind the hotel were the twin cylinders of a wheat silo, the light-towers of a trotting paceway, and the dark brick of a flour mill. A sign on the mill said D'Inglis Self Raising.

The three climbed from the truck. Colin carried the dogs under his arms. He looked back over his shoulder at the flour mill, spelling the high words Self Raising out to himself. They were written in glass tubes emerging from chipped white sheet enamel. The curves of the S looked pleased with themselves, and the line of the R gave the other letters a kick along.

'So. Let's get a beer inside of us,' said Erwin,

slapping his big belly. 'Say gidday to the son. Then we will go out and look at the site, unload the gear, and so on. What do you say?'

Erwin had a way of announcing things that made these trips all over the bloody country seem like the greatest pleasure a man could get from life. 'You guys do everything arse-up,' complained Colin.

'We have certain habits,' agreed Erwin.

'You're always pissed,' accused Colin. 'Both of yez.'

He trotted after them, head twitching, foot dragging. All he knew was that they needed him and they treated him like dirt. Automatically he spat at the radiator cap. Spittle ran down the belly of the little fat guy.

Erwin eyed the blackboard outside the bar and the words: 'Counter lunches 11.30–2.00: Lamb Burger, Steak, Special Saus, Chips.'

'I'm for the saus.'

The three stood aside while two men carrying golf bags came down the hotel steps. One had black hair, black eyebrows, dark stubble. The other was red and slender like a fox.

'Gidday, mates,' said Erwin. 'Hot enough for your game?'

'Yeah, ain't we nuts,' said the first, sticking his jaw out.

'Don't I know you?' said Colin to the second, grabbing his shirt. It exhausted him the number of people he knew.

'Who, me?' The foxy-faced man shook himself free. 'No way. Wouldn't know you from a bar of soap, pal.'

Later, though, people remembered.

The two golfers hitched their clubs and headed for their car. Erwin Schmidt tilted his head and saw a dark eye staring at him from a split in the verandah boards. The son. Mal. He'd always been a little aloof. Then the water drillers entered the pub, their footsteps slapping on the shiny brown linoleum of the foyer, the dogs skidding as they were put down.

MAL FITCH STRAIGHTENED HIMSELF, STOOD on the verandah and scratched his neck. Noonday haze lay thick over the town. Hot air scraped the inner lining of his lungs, as he lit another cigarette. A vicious westerly whipped up, butting the galvanised iron roofs and pelting grit on windows. Mal went inside, closed the french doors and lay down on his bed, reaching out to rotate the ash of his cigarette on the thick glass lip of a bedside ashtray. He was trembling. It was no joke. He remembered Erwin Schmidt. He travelled rough and dirty. The youngest had spat on the radiator cap. The third looked paranoid. These were the ones he had sold his inheritance to, and for what? To be the age he was and still no further along in life than a boy frozen in time. When his smoke was finished Mal got up again. Someone was coming up the stairs. It was the one who had spat. He appeared at the door holding a meat pie away from two small dogs wheezingly leaping. Mal raised himself on an elbow.

Colin Byron stared through him and said, 'That was bullshit about the cigarette papers and eating a live chook'.

'Who are you?' laughed Mal.

Instead of answering plainly the other said reproachfully, 'I just know this. A bloke who found water wouldn't do tricks.'

Colin Byron dissolved Mal in his gaze and tapped his teeth against the ring he wore. Mal had a feeling for someone he'd never known, a man wading through reedbeds collecting water lilies. A man playing cricket while an electric storm approached the day he left for war, with Rosan in the grandstand shade accepting a letter from William D'Inglis. *Meet me tomorrow. Love me. I'm yours.*

The tapping stopped. Mal wanted to jump in his car and drive up the road to Croppdale.

'Girrouta there, yer mongrels!'

The spell broke. The dogs ran away downstairs and the skinny red-headed man followed them. Mal went outside onto the verandah again. The green truck was like a permanent fixture, parked parallel to the kerb in the wide empty road where the dogs reappeared chasing white cockatoos from the centreline of bitumen. The truck's load of metal creaked in the sun.

Mal went inside again. He looked at his hands. They were shaking. From a hook behind the door he took a pair of old binoculars. Sitting on the end of his bed, he focused them through the flawed glass of the verandah door. His eyeline led through a gap in the ironwork straight down to the potbellied figure on the radiator. He whispered:

I've waited for you.

I don't give a stuff.

What if I follow you now?

That might be all right.

Where have you been all this time?

Sunk.

ACROSS THE TOWN DOORS WERE closed, windowshades drawn. Combating the heat, people stayed inside watching midday movies, eating withered sandwiches from their refrigerators, drinking tea. Sometimes they parted the blinds and looked out into the hurtful daylight. Then they let the shades drop again. To remember when water came at the twist of a tap, hissing under shrubbery from sprinkler rosettes, was to recall a time when the old had been young — before the young had memories. Across house yards locusts moved like cloud-shadows, stripping the leaves from fig trees, grape-vines and fruit trees. Any growth that was left was nurtured with tea leaves and saved slops from washing-up. The locusts devoured washing from clotheslines, ate grassblades down to the nub. They stripped flowers sitting in jam jars in the Railway Hill cemetery. Pushing and pulsing, they lurched the back lanes, clustered on garbage, and slithered along fences where small boys crushed the juice out of their abdomens with twigs. Then came countless more — crouching back on their tails in the dust, extruding their guts with a sickening white dexterity.

Up in the hills above the town, roly-poly grass clogged the sand greens of the Logan's Reef Railways Union and Flour Millers' Golf Club. There, the two golfers from the Criterion Hotel teed up and began playing. Harry Frawtell and Keith Wiencke were the only ones out there. Swathes of blackened Paterson's Curse gave the land a burnt-out, exhausted look, like heaped-up ash. Blood throbbed at the back of their eyeballs. They shaded their foreheads. Their eyes were drawn to a high plateau shimmering in the eastern sky, a mound of darkening ranges to the east. Clouds were sometimes seen there, promising rain, bulging and darkening before dissipating utterly. They wiped their sunglasses on the flaps of their shirts. The distant plateau was the reason they came to play golf on such forsaken links at this wilderness time of day. Up there against the sky a ribbon of dusty road led to Croppdale. The two men were magnetised by the name. They had never been there. They did not speak to each other about it. They were helpless when they thought about it. They could only stare that way.

'Git on with the game, you moron.'

'Your shot, prick features.'

They belted their golf balls hard, taking separate routes to find them in dry gullies and between rocks. They reunited on the sand greens where they used a scraper to smooth oily putting-paths to the holes. They shaped up on the next tee and whopped their Dunlops square on their dimpled, shy little faces while attempting to send them into outer fucking space. They played on the borderline of rage, in cages of feeling. Harry Frawtell was thinking about a young woman named Rennie Logan, a teacher at the Logan's Reef primary school. He had never met her or spoken to her. He'd only clung to his glider, launched himself from a bluff above the Cropp River Gorge picnic grounds, and flown dangerously over the town on school sports day, his jaw hanging slack in the g-curves, using her as a reference point for his fox whistle as he suddenly ascended a screaming updraft.

The foxy-faced man was thinking about a woman named Ida. Two days ago he had changed a tyre for her at the roadside, and she had shaken his hand in gratitude, a cool smooth touch, and then had driven off.

At the fourth tee they faced the distant plateau squarely. A vehicle windscreen glinted far away, a thin haze of dust dulling the glare. Someone was coming to town. Vehicles hardly ever used the Croppdale road these days. The two men made separate unspoken guesses about who it might be. Harry Frawtell believed it was Stuart D'Inglis. He spat. D'Inglis would get his when Harry dropped in on him from the sky. Keith Wiencke fixed on the idea of Stuart's sister — whose grey-flecked eyes seemed to unfold layers of thought when she looked at him. He felt his balls tighten. Ida. Say that name again.

ERWIN SCHMIDT AND KURT WOLPERS drank schooners of dark beer in the interior bar of the Criterion Hotel. Erwin had his plate of leathery pork sausages, stringy mashed potatoes, grey peas and black gravy in front of him. Kurt Wolpers declined food. He got his nourishment from beer and tobacco tar, and from inside himself, from self-control. Colin Byron with his limp and spiderlike fingers drank Coke from a beer glass and ate a meat pie out of a cellophane bag. The dogs were back at his feet. They had pies too, nosing them across the floor. Quick chomps against the skirting board and they were gone. Tutter Fitch watched the men and remembered the slow one, Erwin. He'd swallowed Mal's bullshit and paid the price of an old truck without bargaining. At the time it shat Tutter off that Mal had walked away with the money, a cut of which would have allowed Tutter to buy the liquor licence from his dying father, or maybe get the car he wanted to please Betty Kingling: a soft-top two seater Triumph Herald, colour fire-engine red. Now it all meant nothing. They loved Mal Fitch and would kill for him, the miserable old bastard.

'How about I take the wheel on the way out to this place, Cropper whatsit?' Colin Byron proposed to his companions.

'Maybe,' said Erwin, chewing. He turned to the

barman and genially said, 'I was here twenty-five years ago, the day of the big match, I recall'.

'Don't I know it. It was a good day for what we done, Erwin,' nodded Tutter Fitch, surprising the bloke by fishing up a name. But if you ran a pub and people walked back into your life over intervals of years it was hostly to name them even if you couldn't piss straight any more, and needed a tumbler of White Horse to get up in the morning. Tutter pressed the button of an electric bell that buzzed in the back of the hotel somewhere. '*Mal*?' he barked. Then back to the newcomer, 'R-R-R-Remember Malcolm Fitch?'

'I do, I do,' Erwin reddened with pleasure. 'Now he's famous, yah?'

'He's here on hols.'

'Yah, yah. He was up on the verandah,' said Erwin, winking. 'Watching us park. That ole truck is a fucking bewdy,' he added. 'We say it's looked after by that fat little bastard. He leads us to water.'

'I don't go for that. I spit on him,' intruded Colin Byron vehemently. 'Anyway, mate,' fixing Tutter's yellow eyes with his muddy brown ones, 'what code is it up here? Down here, around here, wherever the fuck we are. AFL or League?'

Tutter stared at him. 'You're kidding.'

'Where *is* this fucking place?'

'He's g-got to be kidding,' Tutter turned to the others.

Colin screwed his pie wrapper tight in his fist. 'Yeah, I was kidding,' he said.

'We'll have the same again,' nodded Erwin.

Kurt took Colin's elbow and steered him towards the pool table. The dogs followed his bootheels. They always played for a dollar a point — Colin already owed him three months' wages.

'This t-town,' reflected Tutter Fitch to Erwin, 'is known for one code, and one code only, and that is League. Where's h-he from, anyway,' he angled his head towards Colin, 'the planet M-Mars?' He set Erwin's next streaming beer in front of him.

'He's kind of simple,' said Erwin agreeably.

'He would have to be.'

'We come from a long way from here. From back over the S.A. border, and then some.'

'I remember that,' said Tutter, resenting implications of forgetfulness. He drew himself a small beer and sipped it sourly, as if he had just discovered the taste instead of living on it. 'S-someone's been ringin' about yers. He said he was comin' right in. He said, don't move an inch.' Tutter leaned backwards, hearing the scrape of a car exhaust in the side lane. 'A D'Inglis,' he added.

Mal Fitch's white BMW made a left turn onto the main road and accelerated out of town. Tutter watched through the bar window. The connecting door to the kitchen banged open, and Betty Kingling bustled in, red-faced and bothered. 'I don't believe this. He's taken his bags too.'

Tutter executed a clean sentence. 'We know where to.'

'No we don't,' snapped Betty Kingling. 'Not after all these years, we don't.'

'Don't we just?'

'Oh,' a hot tear ran, 'you shut up.'

Over near the pool table Colin Byron examined a framed photo on the wall. It showed a tall, fair-headed man at a racecourse turning on a tap. 'President of Jockey Club, 12.2.39,' was nibbed in white ink on the photo. The man had a moody expression and wore a lightweight linen suit. 'Your fucking shot,' demanded Kurt. Colin studied the tap. It would be brass. He stared so intensely at the photo that its parts broke up into swirling soot. He tapped his teeth and the clickety rhythm was like the tread of horses coming down a spongy green straight watered by jets of spray.

'Your *shot*,' Kurt struck him behind the ear with the thick end of his cue, making him convulse sideways.

'Jeez,' he complained.

His ear ringing, Colin lined up the balls on the scuffed green baize and drove his cue forward, seeing stars. The chalked tip exploded on the smooth curve of the ball, and Colin lifted from his toes, following through, feeling as if he were being propelled into space through blasts of explosive.

AT THE LOGAN'S REEF CENTRAL school a hooter blared and movement began. A crowd of children edged along hot footpaths to the War Memorial Baths. They crossed the main road in a careful file and then they broke and ran, racing over burr-brown grass and whirling their coloured towels as they rushed in through the wire gates. They leapt and waved as they dashed for the water and though they were watched by four teachers they had eyes only for one.

'Hey, Mrs,' they yelled, 'it's great. Come on in!'

Their favourite teacher, Rennie Logan, stood near the gate, preoccupied. She watched as a familiar white Toyota ute came down from the high end of town, its engine grinding. Through the heat it dipped, past the Court House and Police Station and past the War Memorial Baths. It was so hot now that the vehicle's tyres sloshed on half-melted puddles of bitumen. The driver, a pale, handsome, dark-haired man of thirty, stared at Rennie Logan standing there, and flicked a finger in recognition as he rumbled past.

'What is it now?' she said to her fellow-teacher Cindy Walker, who glanced that way too. 'He says one thing and does another.'

'It's always the same. I warned you about him but you wouldn't listen,' said Cindy Walker. 'I've seen it too many times.'

'With him?' asked Rennie Logan.

'What does it matter who with?' replied Cindy Walker. She liked playing on lucky and beautiful young nerves. 'With men,' she conciliated, after a pause.

This added to the hurt Rennie Logan felt from seeing Stuart D'Inglis. Almost everything hurt her now. Sometimes she felt that her skin was turned inside out, and she was reacting to things no one else was meant to react to, or ever could. On sports afternoon the kids had started screaming when a hang-glider had whooshed overhead doing stunts, the pilot dangling from a cocoon-like body bag, a silver thread of spittle dragging across the sky. Everyone thought he was great, a mystery man. But Rennie didn't appreciate it.

STUART D'INGLIS SMILED WHEN HE saw the high-sided green Diamond T parked outside the Criterion Hotel.

It was a museum piece, all right. The work would be cheap. In fact he was blowed if he would pay at all. He'd driven to town with one idea, which was to find this truck. And over on the right now there was a bonus: Rennie Logan arched on her toes acknowledging him shyly, he thought, as she saw him and looked away. She wore a white cotton shirt, a slim blue skirt, and flat leather sandals. Very underspoken, very conservative, very nice. The absolute Stuart D'Inglis requirement personified.

His fingers flexed on the steering wheel, and a day that had seemed entirely wasted was not. He would try and have a word with Rennie later if he could, and arrange another weekend away. It would have to be a cheaper effort than last time, though, because the bill at the Top of the Town had made him wince — not because of the room, which had been well-priced as the weekend special, but because of the extras. Rennie had surprised him the way she had cantered through the room service menu, and in other ways made free at his expense. He had thought someone with Rennie Logan's background would prefer doing it hard. Her stepfather, after all, had done it hard on the railways. Her step-grandfather had done it hard in the mines. Her step-great-grandfather had done it hard at the diggings, making a fortune and losing it in less than a generation, leaving behind his name for a shantytown that had grown into this, a town whose name was synonymous with D'Inglis Self Raising.

He walked around the old rig making an inspection. He read the gravel-pitted signwriting on the high metal sides and across the battered old bonnet. The name Fitch was fainted out. There was a free-of-charge, all-hours telephone number painted on (a little trick that would be costed in to the price). Stuart hoisted himself up on the running board and looked inside the cab. The windows were wide open. The interior smelt of baked sweat and hot leather, dog-rug and stale tobacco. The overflowing ashtrays, *Rugby League Week* and the porno magazines stuffed behind the driver's seat, the key in the ignition with its imitation Heineken bottle key-ring — they said it all. Stuart glanced along the sleepy main street with its peppercorn trees and shimmering heat-haze, making certain he wasn't seen. He kicked a tyre, hard. It hurt, but he felt better, forgetting that no action ever went unobserved in Logan's Reef, nor was any gesture, even the most random, senseless, meaningless byplay on the part of a D'Inglis, ever left without meaning ascribed to it. Behind Stuart's back, Rennie Logan watched from the pool. 'Getting his act together,' she thought. Then, for some reason, the day seemed lighter. She thought, What does it matter? Her class clamoured around her, wondering what the joke was — why she stood wiping her eyes with her towel, her shoulders convulsing with laughter. He wasn't even real.

Stuart D'Inglis reasoned through his annoyance. With the drilling rig sitting there, heat turning the ground to lava, anyone might push in and get ahead of him, any water-desperate rival. Dollar was the only loyalty of working men. The drill bits were blunt. The sleeves of the well casing were flaking. 'This is not the A team,' he raged internally. 'I should have known that. I have landed myself with the dregs and scrapings.'

With a bang of hinged doors, Stuart D'Inglis entered the bar of the Criterion Hotel. His eyes blinked adjusting to the gloom. Plucking a sweat-soaked shirt away from his shoulder blades, he went through contortions, blind to his watchers.

Tutter Fitch gave Erwin Schmidt a wink. 'There's your man — as awkward a p-piece of shit as ever the cat der-dragged in.'

In the gloom, two men swam into Stuart D'Inglis's vision. They were playing pool at the half-sized table, one in a T-shirt, sinewy, with dirty blond hair, the other a red-headed, scuttling, monkeylike youth wearing a checked shirt. Meanwhile the third stranger, fat-gutted, with legs planted apart and dirty ape's feet in rubber thongs, turned from the bar and caught Stuart's eye with a look of friendly recognition.

Don't know you from Adam, Stuart told himself.

The youth at the pool table looked friendly too, but the other one grabbed him by the ear and spun him back to the game. Stuart noted, as he always did when he entered the bar of the Cri, that the framed photo of his grandfather turning on the water at the refurbished Jockey Club in 1939 was badly askew. No respect.

There were other people in the bar: several grizzled, stumpy young men waiting their turn at the pool table, and two baggy-necked booze-aged women, all glancing quizzically at Stuart D'Inglis. They knew his identity, as he knew theirs. Half of them were Fitches, the other half were Logans. They did not speak to Stuart D'Inglis. And never in all their lives had they been spoken to by him except on those occasions when he had wanted something from them.

Stuart advanced on Erwin Schmidt.

'You are the water men?' he demanded.

'We are,' said Erwin, nodding proudly. 'Pull up a stool.'

'Look, I won't,' said Stuart. He cleared his throat and rested a boot on the dull brass foot-rail and stared at Tutter Fitch, knowing his name but not using it. Knowing their secrets. Tutter was the one who didn't know male from female, who'd picked up a bloke at the Cross. 'Give me a squash,' Stuart ordered. He turned back to Erwin Schmidt: 'See here, fellow. You made certain promises. I rang you. You said you'd be here yesterday.' His voice whined in the upper register. The people in the bar lowered their eyes and smiled to themselves. *It's on for young and old.*

'No, no, I said today.'

'At *first* you said yesterday.'

Erwin Schmidt eased back on his stool with a look of understanding. So. Of course. A little argumentative. We shall bring him down to a level we know. Lead him to water.

The barman planted Stuart's drink on the counter. Without saying thanks Stuart gripped the cold glass in his long, shapely fingers and brought it stiffly to his lips.

'We have a way for doing things,' said Erwin Schmidt. 'Certain habits. You must not worry. But if it's a problem for you,' he shrugged, 'no water.'

'Fuck that,' said Stuart, man to man.

Kurt came over chalking his pool cue. He asked the barman for another schooner, and sank it while he stood there.

Stuart thrust out a hand. 'I am Stuart D'Inglis. Here

is twenty dollars.' He put a note down on the bar and turned to the barman. 'Get the guys a carton of cold VB will you, um, Tutter,' he said. He turned back to Kurt. 'This beer goes into the fridge at the Croppdale men's quarters. Understand?'

Kurt only stared at him.

'How many of you?' insisted Stuart.

'Three,' said Erwin.

Kurt blew chalkdust from the tip of his cue.

'Then the one carton should be enough for tonight,' said Stuart, smiling at this Kurt but winning no reaction. What was he bluffing towards, a second carton? That would be about the ceiling of the type.

Colin limped over. 'What's the story, yous blokes?' he said.

Colin peeled a scab from his lower lip while he awaited a response. Stuart looked him up and down. There was a plea in those rusty eyes.

'Follow me out,' said Stuart, more softly than he usually spoke to people. 'It's easy to go wrong on the way, and when we get there, there'll be enough daylight left for me to show you the ropes. Then the beer for later,' he added, hardening his voice for the other two, for he was a person who picked his types, knew his men, held out the stick, dangled the carrot.

The barman put a carton of beer on the bar with a small amount of change on top. 'I am the white

Landcruiser,' said Stuart, pocketing the change and tucking the carton under his arm. 'I'll watch for you outside. How long — ah, ten minutes?'

'We shall be there,' said Erwin briefly.

Kurt Wolpers turned his back on Stuart D'Inglis. 'Line 'em up again,' he said to Tutter Fitch.

RENNIE LOGAN CLIMBED OUT OF the pool, holding the hand of Nicole Hooper, the girl said to be her favourite. Other small girls splashed up the steps behind her, demanding her attention while she turned and knelt on the steaming cement and took Nicole Hooper by the skinny shoulders. 'You will have to learn to do things on your own, Nicky,' she said, seeking the seven-year-old's lowered eyes. 'You aren't like this with Mummy, are you?' The other girls stood by, dripping, and sucked their fingers.

'I don't know.'

'Well, I want you to practise for ten minutes. Float. Kick. Will you do what I ask?'

'I don't know.'

'I'll watch from the teachers' umbrella,' Rennie promised. She gave Nicole Hooper's hand a squeeze, knowing it would make things worse later. Someone's finger traced a pattern on the fabric of her swimming costume, all the way around its scooped back. A circle of little girls stepped back, their pain and satisfaction inexpressible. 'Now leave me alone.'

'Yes, Mrs Logan.'

'It's Miss. I do not have a husband,' Rennie instructed them wearily. 'Now hurry, or Mrs Betts will want you for water safety.' The children entered the water. On the other side of the pool Margaret Betts slopped up and down wearing a coarse flowered dress and Dr Scholl sandals. Rennie crossed to the teachers' umbrella where the deputy waited.

'I've been watching you,' said Viv Edenhope, passing Rennie her towel. 'Full marks — a difficult situation for a young teacher. These clingers,' he sighed with calculated sympathy.

'I did nothing,' said Rennie Logan, making space for herself among a litter of exercise books, sun creams, and morning papers. She hated the way male teachers praised her professionally whenever she caught them out — locking an image of her away as they met her eyes. This one never swam, but went around as if he was always about to, in a light blue tracksuit the colour of small boys' pyjamas. Now he was smoking, cupping a cigarette in his hand to minimise the bad example. If she stayed teaching she would become like these others, sealing over their hurts and disappointments with unverifiable maturity.

'None the less,' he persisted, 'you are a natural.'

Rennie Logan shifted her gaze to the world beyond the pool's high mesh, and stared across the dry grass of the War Memorial park to where Stuart D'Inglis's white Landcruiser tabletop was parked in the shade of a pepper tree. The world wasn't much better out there, but it was better.

'Ah, yes,' said Viv Edenhope, following her gaze, 'while you were in the water your boyfriend came out of the pub and reversed uphill like a demon. You'd think he'd been bitten by a snake. There he waits. Till three? You know, I can't understand why the Head tolerates this sort of thing,' he added, taking another quick pull at his Kent. 'Aeronautical gymnasts breaking DCA regs. Blokes hanging around the younger staffers like blowflies. These squattocracy lotharios are the worst of all. When was the last time one married a teacher, I wonder? Hello, here's some action.'

Three men emerged from the Criterion Hotel and climbed into the large green truck that was parked there. Stuart D'Inglis started his Landcruiser. Rennie Logan took a couple of paces into the sunlight, her dark furious eyes following the movement of vehicles. Stuart's went into the lead. The truck followed.

It was as if they were melting into each other in the heat waves. They passed under the railway bridge, disappeared near D'Inglis Mills, reappeared again near the Shell fuel depot, and roared past the Golden Nugget Motel.

A longing filled Rennie Logan's thoughts. She wanted to disappear from the face of the earth. She peeled off her shirt, took a few long strides, then plunged into the water. She floated face-down with her eyes open, staring at the blurry tiled bottom. Children jostled her but she ignored them. Cindy Walker frowned, and began surging towards her. She always feared something like this. Rennie wasn't balanced. Rennie Logan opened her mouth, letting water in. Was this the way to do it? All the other ways she could think of weren't final or even nice. So pick a hot day. Crystalline water. Make it beautiful.

Shades of Croppdale

I N THE HEAT OF THE day Mal Fitch drove through
bare ringbarked country he had never seen before,
though it was over the hill from his birthplace. It was
the crossing of a border after years of exile, and
finding it no paradise, but closer to the worst dreads
anticipated. It matched the going down into hope-
lessness of his life at present. Hundreds of dead trees
were aligned in the same direction like matches
tipped from matchboxes. Sheep with daggy wool
stood in the old timber, others were already dead,
pecked at by crows. An eagle circled above rocks.

Rabbits with eyes pussed from myxo sat on the side of the road. There was no grass, just thistles.

Sunk. Mal was in that mood.

The road never stopped going up. Mal felt pressure in his ears. In shaded cuttings there was coolness. It would be cold at night up here — Ida always shivered when she said that. But now it was hot again, the sun scorching through the windscreen. He entered a zone of burnt-out bushfires, logs puffing smoke, stumps of tussocks smouldering. Both sides of the road were silver, ashen. The road led from one steep gully to the next, oven to oven. This was the same dusty white surface William D'Inglis had followed when Mal was a boy, the large wheels of the Pontiac rumbling and the big, pale-handed man with his limbs spread wide, replete after lovemaking.

Mal emerged into open country at last. It was strange after the lower parts, still droughty but with a light flush of green as if colour could be bought, and a handsome copper-roofed homestead rising ahead, pine windbreaks sheltering it as in a butcher's shop calendar photo. This was Glen Doe, the whisky-and-polo MacPriams' holding. Mal had helped them along by selling their stuff on TV, playing wartime Churchill endorsing 'the fighting spirit'. But he would never be invited to visit. There was a shady English-style garden. Silver sprays watered a chequerboard lawn. A jaunty weathercock in the shape of a galloping pony leapt from the peaked gable of the greenish roof. The MacPriams rarely went to Logan's Reef. The story was that Andy MacPriam took a wrong turn once, and entered the Shire offices seeking directions, wondering whose town it was. If he wanted groceries he jumped in his plane and flew to Sydney, where his leafy sandstone pile was visible across Rushcutter's Bay from Mal's mouldy terrace in cluttered Womerah Lane.

Mal imagined saying to Ida, *By the way, I saw the MacPriams' humpy on the way up. You wouldn't have to worry about the next dollar if you gave Andy the nod. I wish I'd put him in* Yabby Stealers, *say as a dog, say as a great floppy golden retriever.* He'd turn her round, get her to smile, get her to see Andy MacPriam as a retarded mutt, six foot four in a dog suit — he'd done it with plenty of others, reducing their variations to a single shrewd caricature. He'd done it to himself and look where it had got him. *Sunk.*

He travelled on between bleached granite boulders and across concrete causeways on waterless creeks. This was the road where the well-scrubbed schoolgirls who'd struck him dumb with their unattainability had waited each morning on the Croppdale bus run. They must have crept out from under logs. There weren't any decent houses. Mostly there were just shacks and ruined chimneyplaces. His car swung into dips and his stomach rose. He saw no humans. A large corrugated iron shearing shed and a grey, verandah-less timber house of the 1940s appeared on the horizon and slewed down towards him. He drove through the middle of some-one's yard. A tractor was pulled half out of a shed, cogged guts lying on the ground. A red kelpie raced at the wheels. If eyes watched from behind windows, Mal didn't know. The afternoon air was white in the heat, except where willows and glossy-leaved poplars grew in creek hollows, sucking moisture from deep down. In the paddocks only wind-blasted hawthorn trees and rose briars were ignored by sheep. Everything else was eaten. Sandy soil drifted with no vegetation to hold it. Dunes were forming. A few twisted gums survived on rocky knolls. Dead hares lay squashed on the road. Mal gave up longing for change. He was marooned on Mars.

But then he came to a rise like all the rest, and the country changed. A ribbon of road led down to a wooden bridge and a wide sandy bed of river, with poplars lining the banks and a few pools of clear, shallow water in the centre. Mal's square tongue draped over his thick bottom lip as he put the car into low gear, scraping a rock, beginning the descent to the bridge. This was the place. A forest led the eye upwards. It started on the other bank of the river with a few scattered pale-trunked gum trees, and then the trees thickened and spread, rose and became hazy, shimmering blue. On the far skyline, thickly timbered ridges were like black straining shoulders against the sky. The afternoon light caught on a bare mineral slope, Mount A.A. Hooper. Mal had seen this peak from the coastal side, hazy above a beach shack. Logan's Reef lore said Mount A.A. Hooper was unclimbable, tougher than Everest, but it was scaled every weekend by city bushwalkers who approached through a state forest on the other side. That was typical. People in the Reef didn't know what they had. The sky in that direction looked softer, with isolated clouds dangling streaks of rain. There was a smudged rainbow. Mal lifted himself slightly above the seat, and peered forward against the windscreen.

'*Now,*' he breathed to himself, bumping his head on glass and remembering the tightly cellophane-wrapped gifts that had come to him from Croppdale, toy cars, pocket knives, and books. All his life he'd been cursed by grandiloquent longings because of *A Boy's Adventures With Gods and Heroes*. Now he felt he was falling down past the point of his own origins — in through that cellophane.

Wooden bridge-planks rumbled as he crossed

over. The sign said *Upper Cropp River*. Mal thought about Gunner Fitch's thousand-year river, the underground stream. He accelerated with an angry jerk. He would speak to William D'Inglis, enter his house, and if he couldn't get any sense out of a reclusive old man, open his store cupboards, read his files, unearth old letters and get his life exhumed.

On the other side of the river the road forked, and here Stuart D'Inglis had instructed Mal to take a right turn and look for a lichen-stained rock, under which would be a key. The road led along a cutting in the river bank, where wild broom grew impenetrably. Up over a low scrubby ridge he could see a large metal gate framed by a rectangular archway of brown-painted steel pipes. *Croppdale* — the property name plate hung from heavy chains. Inside the fence a sign proclaimed: *Mining Lease. No Through Road. Trespassers Prosecuted. No Shooting. Wild Dog Baits Laid. Man Traps Set.* Mal found the lichen-covered rock, kicked it back and found the key, holding the dull-shining flatness between his fingers and feeling the glory of ordinary time. Here was where the past broke through.

As Mal jiggled the battered brass of the padlock and untangled the chains he remembered a recurring dream. He was invited to appear in a play, and put all his feeling into rehearsal, but went dead in the play itself.

Not this time, he resolved.

TO IDA ON NIGHTS OF FULL moon the roofshine of the many farm buildings at Croppdale appeared like scattered dams. Ducks came winging in, crash-landing on corrugations. Magpies erupted at intervals, wagtails sang in thorn bushes.

It was drought-time. In other years Ida could reliably add to the night-time effects of Croppdale the percussion of stones, a clatter created by powerful, low-level sheeting water.

On most nights Ida came down to those stones. They were like acres of stranded, scrubbed potatoes. Bone dry. Each took in light and shone it back from a pitted surface. This was where Ida was born — within earshot of a river under a brilliant night sky. She would not be taken away from here again, by herself or others. She walked the dusty tracks between ramshackle farm buildings feeling elated and weary. Croppdale. The name was a taunt. The soil was thin and rocky. Things had never grown well here. But ideas about people were transformed in the silvery light. Mal Fitch was humbled. Stuart went quiet, reserved his criticisms, asked himself questions about himself at last. Jim's weaknesses and evasions flipped over, becoming the strengths they so often seemed. The love of Georgina and Jim took flight from time. Ida's memories of Kelvin, her father, were untroubled and kindly. The scratchings of a geology hammer recorded dates in old cement — Feb 1939 had a shaley mollusc cemented in, like a crown or a headshield. Her grandfather William D'Inglis's always-burning attic light was dimmed under this sky. His nightmares were granted peace. That once he'd hit her was a meaning that flew back down his life. May he die, she prayed, delicately awake to himself. Ida, having approached death once, half-remembered a feeling of grace. She clung to the idea. Any moment now she would step from her clothes, and a pair of headlights would sweep around the rocks on the road, and she would dance in the moving light, arms above her head and fingertips joined, eyes closed, her life complete and disappearing into the sparkling mica of the sand.

Ida had been three months without a roof overhead while she made repairs, spending her time with a masonry hammer and chisel, going around barefoot, wearing an old checked cotton workshirt and a pair of torn jeans. She was happier at Croppdale than she could have imagined. It was just that she was terribly tired. Only today she had stretched plastic sheeting across the gap in the dairy roof for Mal's sake. He'd hate it there. It was done in a cold sweat, under the noon sun, with waves of darkness pulsing across her eyes.

MAL ARRIVED AHEAD OF STUART and the water drillers, scraping rocks in his old, two-doored, low-slung BMW. He unpacked a briefcase stuffed with whisky and dusty vintage Railway Hill reds from the pub cellar. He barely looked at Ida at first, just handed her a cheque he'd been holding for weeks, comprising the closing royalties from *Prosperity*. He wasn't humbled, no. Truculence was more the mood. Fishing out whisky this early, he proposed a toast — 'To Croppdale?' — and kept sending surly glances around, taking in the mess of the family compound, aching to get it inside himself after a lifetime of resistance.

In the heat and glare Mal looked his age for once. Curling a lip, panting, almost toppling forward under the pressure of the experience, he objected, 'You expect me to sleep *here*? Your brother said there'd be a room for me in the house if I didn't like roughing it with you.'

'Stuart said that?' Ida was amazed.

'Ah yes. We've become mates. One of life's surprises. He's a poor sorry coot. I offered him a choice of paperbacks and he picked *Siege of Stalingrad*. He's ready to break out.'

Ida watched Mal adjust, the refugee from the corner store and the small-town pub, all defiant sensitivities at the brink of his grossly materialised myth, Croppdale. Maybe this shouldn't happen to anyone. Ida had always known the hurt Mal had felt, but could barely express, from the visits of her grandfather down the plateau road into Logan's Reef. His hands shook. He downed a hefty glug of raw MacPriam's, lowered the bottle, and appraised Ida in her jeans, checked shirt, and braided hair. He'd always liked this hillbilly-heartbreak look of hers. But it was a drowning regard this time. He wouldn't be angling to sleep with her this time. His full lips were wet as he drew the back of his hand across them. 'Are you well?'

'Well?' Ida sat defensively scraping her bare toes in the dust. 'Of course I'm well. Why do you ask?'

'People do ask,' he shrugged. 'And you seem tired.'

'I am tired. Naturally.' Her voice reflected gratitude.

'I had a different picture of this place,' said Mal. 'How you fitted into it, and so on.' He opened the boot of his car and took out an old army hat. It sat too high on his overlarge head, making him look absurd. He rolled down his sleeves and buttoned them at the wrists. 'I'd like to take a look around. Do you mind?'

He was off and away. She didn't exist for him, then. It was always the pattern. He lurched off around Croppdale as if this was his next production and Ida and the rest of them were just routine disposable talents to be kept waiting for their call.

CROPPDALE LAY IN A TAWNY narrow valley of tussocks and splintered snappy gums. Limestone crags formed a cliff behind the homestead, which was built from river stones and rubble, and sat on a terrace alongside the Cropp River. The rocks told a story. The grey ramparts along the river were limestone, yielding whorled shells and shadowy tendrils of carboniferous fern to the patient searcher. It was a gloomy place, pierced by the shrieks of peacocks and the troubled honking of geese. But Mal loved the ambience. Part of him had always been here awaiting his arrival — jammed up there on the heights with the vantage point of a god or lodged in a crevice like a lizard. The cliff-face was sheltered, ferny, attracting sunlight and shade, while the homestead underneath was mostly in shadow. It was a wide, deep, sombre building in a heavy bungalow style, with a roof of rusting galvanised iron. Mal went in without knocking while Ida watched and wondered about him from the shade of the old dairy.

Passing under a stout, crudely adzed doorframe, Mal's feelings boiled up suddenly. He was wild at never having come to Croppdale before. It was all so simple and direct. He felt bruised and bruising, rough, invasive, unleashed and troublemaking. In the silent hall he grabbed a hook on a rickety hat stand and twisted it off in a scatter of rust. Otherwise he would have smashed the glass on the family portraits hanging in a line — Mal summed them up — Sir Magnus (responsible), William (sociable), Kelvin (unfocused, woozy), Stuart (alarmed, afraid). The line-up lacked only a woman made for love, and a proud intelligent kid from the wrong end of town, and a home-wrecking prodigal brother.

Mal leaned out of a window. At the back of the house, against the cliff, was an old, neglected garden — empty bird cages and bush-carpentered flower tubs in a jumble of pathways marked by white-painted rocks. A dead gum tree had a flood marker in its upper branches, where hawks nested. The legend was that every forty or fifty years the house went under water. The last time was in the 1930s. The Gunner had been called when the last excess of water had disappeared. It was a D'Inglis tradition, the boast ran, to shovel out the mud, lower the furniture from the roofbeams where it was trussed, and move back in again to breed another generation. Ida had never witnessed such a flood, but in her childhood, she had told Mal, it threatened from the eastern valleys, where storm clouds brewed black on Mount A.A. Hooper, thunder rattled and shook and died away.

In this house, Mal counted, were at least eight bedrooms, a library, a billiards room, and a low-ceilinged echoing kitchen with zinc-topped benches. Cavernous doorways were connected by cold, damp corridors. In a pantry Mal found green frogs covered by crystals of sand in wall spaces where the mortar had worked loose. He found a sharpening steel and poked it in to the hilt, remembering doing this as a boy, in a room like this one. Had Rosan ever brought him out here, before he was old enough to remember? Had William D'Inglis courted him and he'd refused? In a rage of waste Mal slapped the walls, and impotently jabbed the lumpy, imperfect old window-glass. Every minute of his prowl he expected to come face to face with the old man.

He stood at the foot of the attic stairs. Someone was thinly snoring up there. *Leave him, Mal. Leave him alone.*

In the long, gloomy living room were innumerable framed photographs, a number signed R.C. Fitch. Sweat poured from Mal as he scanned them. The photos were of agricultural shows, beribboned wheatsheaves in harvest displays, children, dogs, horses, cats, horse-drawn wagons and motor trucks queueing at the Logan's Reef railhead.

At one of these pictures Mal leaned on the side-board fighting tears. It should have been famous, this shot. Its vitality astounded him. It showed Rosan as a young woman Irish dancing against a painted stage-cloth in a flashbulbed wooden hall. The bones of her clear intelligent forehead were strong with the spirit of living. Her eyes were clear and lovely. The lower half of her body was in shadow while her hands reached up into brighter and brighter light, which seemed to shine more intensely as Mal peered closer.

Mal staggered out to the verandah and sank into a squatter's chair in the shade. He sat heaving with exhaustion. He was changed. He heard a sound, a roaring, grinding back in the hills. It was the old truck coming towards him again. Its engine noise rose to a racing pitch, then stopped abruptly. Distant voices shouted in the heat. A bee buzzed against a waterbag hanging from the roof rafters. Mal closed his eyes.

Sleep was where he would find what he needed. Only in sleep.

Mal blinked, raised an arm and passed it around the silent hills, bunching a fist and then uncurling a stubby, trembling finger. He wanted something for himself as badly as he had ever wanted anything. The action wouldn't take anyone from themselves, this time, but return them to who they were. His nerves went into spasms like jumping pianola keys.

'Ida!' a shout escaped him.

What did he want to tell her? Something about the river. How it roared, jumbled, foamed in the mountain. Something about Rosan and the man who slept upstairs making tinny snores. Something about Mal's whole life — how it seemed to have come from a dream at Croppdale.

Hopeless.

Ida left her shade and crossed the bare dirt yard from the dairy. Mal rubbed his stinging eyes. She was so slight, so determined in the heat. He would always love her. But he would grant her something he'd never attempted before — separation from his need. It was the hardest thing. *Let her have it, Mal, let her have her life.* Everything that had been bunched in Mal Fitch, making him who he was, he felt separating out. The thousand-year river cleaved through the messy details of his life. He rode along into the darkness of the mountain, abandoning hurt.

'God, Ida,' Mal heard himself saying as she joined him, 'when you were a kid, and you were sick — remember that day?'

'What day?'

For her there'd been so many days. He hadn't known any of them then, really. He'd never told her about waving the stick at her and divining a different fate. He couldn't tell her now. He sat with his fists bunched, head down, agonised, accepting humiliation. She couldn't be expected to make any sense of this. Her life had an importance that was destined to escape him.

'Are *you* okay?' She stared at him.

'Ida, I'm sorry,' he said with a catch in his voice.

'Don't worry.' She turned aside. 'It's cooler here.' She seemed to think he was apologising for making her walk through the sun. She filled a mug from the waterbag, cupping a hand and splashing water on her neck, slicking her hair back from her ears.

Stuart's truck came racing around the corner below the huts, the horn blaring. It drew up parallel to the verandah in a lather of dust.

'Jump in! Make it snappy, for Christ's sake!'

Mal looked enquiringly at Ida who folded her arms and shook her head. Mal climbed in, and they roared away.

THE WATER DRILLERS' TRUCK HAD hit a boulder on a corner of the track and was jammed there. 'No offence, Mal, but it's a heap of shit,' Stuart confided. He drove in spurts around the farm compound, getting Mal to fetch tools for him while he sat in rage in the air-conditioned cab. 'Crowbar, jack, wooden blocks — there, over *there* — are you blind?' He rolled the window up and his nostrils flared while Mal dug his arms into boxes of junk, glancing up into roof-spaces stacked with saddlery, a cradle, cupboards, ladders, a rocking horse, cedar chairs — a treasure hoard. As they drove along Mal made offers. He was into a Whale Belly mode. It beat depression. *You sell*? He bartered through the wreckage of Stuart's enthusiasms until Stuart realised he was being used by an expert, and grinned. 'You ever shut up?'

'You always angry?'

'Touché.'

Ida should hear us, thought Mal. Mates.

Trailing out from the house were the dairy, shearing shed, machinery shed, defunct generator shed, stables, abandoned potting sheds and a decrepit tree nursery. There were rusting pine planters. A broken weighbridge. A history of Croppdale was written in ruin. Round yards for horsebreaking. Innumerable plastic tree pots. A grading shed for nuts that never ripened — genetic failures. Drums of arsenic for impregnating pine logs in a treatment plant that was never built. Further along the track were the men's quarters, a rectangular twelve-doored hut made from galvanised iron. It was where the water drillers would stay.

They came to a hilltop on the rough track out. Stuart stamped on the brakes. Up the valley from the homestead could be seen the old weatherboard cottage, Bob's, where Doc Jim and Georgina lived. It stood in a bare, tussocky paddock. Georgina had started a garden — wasting water, said Stuart — and Jim was encouraging her, and her roses now were as high as the guttering, with surges of startling purple sarsaparilla hiding the septic tank. 'You can't get into that house without getting your face ripped off,' he grunted.

The water drillers' truck looked like a skinny arthritic skeleton with a hip in the air. It was sixty years old. The loaded trailer had been unhooked, and wheeled under a tree. Colin Byron lay against it in the shade while the other two stood in the sun and scratched their heads. Mal watched as they disagreed about what to do, arguing with Stuart who shouted: 'I'm telling you in plain English, my friends, that I will not be financially responsible if someone gets hurt here. Everyone hear that? I can see you've been drinking. Erwin, isn't it? Mal, you're my witness. Not a cent. Not a bean.'

'We get it, yah.' Erwin lay under the chassis with just his boots poking out, a stubby within reach. When he emerged he saw Mal. His moon-face creased with smiles. 'Matey!' he boomed. He shook Mal's hand with a thrashing motion. 'Find the boy a beer,' he instructed Kurt. 'Remember dem things you told me about your Dad?' He tapped the side of his head and whispered. 'We've got a fella on the strength who's as good. You met him. Col.'

'Is this going to be a party?' interrupted Stuart, clumsily manhandling the jack into position. 'Come on, you men.'

They raised the truck until it teetered, swayed, and hung precariously.

'That's the best we can do,' said Stuart.

'I don't like the look of it,' said Erwin.

Stuart stood back with his hands on his hips. 'Who's getting under?' It wasn't going to be him. 'All it needs is two men and a chain fed around the rock and we'll whip it out in no time.'

He was met by silence. Kurt spat in the dirt.

Mal went to the front. The truck looked as if it was about to flip onto its back and struggle like an insect. He stared at the angled, battered, potbellied figure on the radiator cap. It had shaken loose and was wired back on. *Dare yourself*. It was barely holding. *Dare yourself and know me*. Mal felt a tap on his shoulder. Colin Byron breathed hot spittle on him. 'Come with me,' he tugged Mal's shirtsleeve and dragged him over to the others. 'We'll do it,' he announced. 'Me and the son.'

'You're off your head, Mal,' brayed Stuart warningly.

'It's okay,' said Mal, but it didn't feel okay. Just compulsive. He expected he would die. He found himself wriggling on his back on the rocky, dusty ground, with tons of metal in the sky above him and a twitchy maniacal youth at his side. 'You'll appreciate this,' hissed Colin Byron. '*See*?' He pushed his knuckles in front of Mal's face. On the fourth finger of his left hand was a shiny gold ring.

'So bloody what? What do we have to do? Let's do it!'

'That's where I found it. Up there.' Colin Byron reached up, grabbed a crossbeam and held it in his fist. 'It was wired on.' The truck swayed back and forth. The whole weight of it seemed suspended in the sky, supported by one hand. 'I brung it back for you.'

Mal peered at the snakes for a moment in the dim dangerous oily shade. 'It's not mine. I don't know anything about it.'

'Someone here does. It was his last job. That Stuart wants us to finish what your old man started.' Colin

Byron twisted his head and called out, 'We need the chain! Stu, git yer ute up!' Then more quietly to Mal: 'You know there's a river. That's the word. We should go look for it together.'

UP AT THE COTTAGE, THAT night, Doc Jim D'Inglis took a piss and looked around, scratching his bristly grey-haired neck and swivelling his eyes towards the extreme corners of his vision. He saw a movement through the rocks. Stuart was out there, engaging in a silent reconnoitre in the nightscape.

This was where they came face to face. This was where Jim had dropped his stick and shown his palms. Where Stuart hissed, 'Bullshit,' and turned away. Anger rose to the surface of each twenty-four hours like a symptom demanding examination, an assignment of meaning, the contact between them contradicting what Stuart said, that he would have nothing to do with his uncle any more, that he had cut Doc Jim from his life and thoughts, that Jim meant nothing to him, was a nobody, a no one — just a marriage wrecker and a culpable physician — and he would deny him every facility that Croppdale had ever supplied to that workman's cottage called Bob's in honour of a long-dead, forgotten shepherd who had once had a slab hut on the site. Kelvin had left the place, and ten surrounding acres, to Jim, otherwise Stuart would have had him out. Stuart was unable to deny power or telephone to the cottage — that would be risking the law — but he controlled water and road access. Now the water had been cut off. There was no message about this, no word. Just the gargle and dry shudder of the kitchen tap when it was turned on tonight.

Stuart, thought Jim, knew nothing. He was like a child awakening every day to the newness of action. There was no previousness in his experience; he behaved as if he had answers. Stuart had been like this since childhood, only ever swinging into a different mode when change was inescapable. As when Kel had died. As when the last water dried up. Then he panicked and seemed to be in pain so acute that he'd need to grow new limbs to cope. He summoned these water drillers from interstate. The reason why things were the way they were in his life, he always said, was because of what other people had done. He was never able to get through to the one person who could set matters right, because he didn't know who that person could possibly be.

There he was around the back of a rock again. Jim believed that Stuart was trying to scare him up like game. And he knew what Stuart hid from himself — that he wanted to talk, reveal himself, but could only approach self-knowledge dumbly. That it was himself he was trying to trap.

'Stuart? Come over here — there's something I want to say.'

'What would that be?'

'Let's talk.'

'What good is talk?'

But at least they were talking.

'What about our water?'

'We're all in the same boat.'

On these nights of prowling Jim knew that he and Stuart were thinking the same thoughts, dancing the same dance, manoeuvring, in their different ways, together. If only this need to talk could rise to the surface, declare itself for what it was, then Jim would be able to see Stuart through his trouble, get him born to himself, have him understand himself better. Jim had a vocation for this kind of thing — healing wasn't just in his hands. He wasn't just a culpable surgeon with no way back through the miasma of error. He'd faced the rot.

For now, Jim could only imagine them blowing each other's head off at the same instant. Past that point he could see them doing something matey together, like fly-fishing on the Upper Cropp.

'Stu, come one night for dinner?'

'Listen.'

'What?'

'*Listen.*'

Up at the homestead end of the valley, headlight beams moved around the men's quarters. Stuart sprinted away under the hill, and then the throaty roar of his ute could be heard. Then came the groaning of a heavily laden truck. It was a sound that had been coming since late afternoon and early evening, grinding over the rocky Cropp hills. From this distance, in blazing moonlight, vehicle lights were pastel. The spotlight on Stuart's Toyota cab roof danced, hitting buildings, fences, tracks, hillsides. The beam hovered on the crags above the homestead, creating a mist, illuminating the blackwoods and peppermints that grew there, lingering on the glossy kurrajongs. Down two kilometres of paddock Jim could hear Ida's actressy laughter in the night. 'Welcome!'

Jim went to the top of the rocky knoll above the cottage and breathed the night air. The atmosphere was faintly smoky from distant fires. Every shape in the night including the grey cottage with its rust-patched iron roof seemed encased in a molten, barely cooled, mist-smoking silver. Music flowed from the cottage, a Chopin nocturne on a scratchy record. Music was everything to Georgina. The notes searched out and found Jim, starting a flow of memory. He remembered talk of the old well that flowed here at Bob's somewhere. It was said to have tapped an underground river where a blue phosphorescent light made the use of lanterns unnecessary. It came back to Jim then that he and Kelvin had known the well as children. They must have been very young. It seemed like an implanted memory, a story told in firelight by their lost, romantic mother. Jim felt that if he could only peer into the place where he was before ever he was, where his mother had been with them, before she left them, he would know it.

Jim went inside to ask Georgina about the well, whether Kelvin had ever described it, finding her mending pillowcases by the light of a reading lamp, sitting at the dining table with her work spread in front of her, her dark braided hair only just beginning to silver in her sixties, and her wide freckled face and look of surprised acceptance catching Jim by the heart as usual. Georgina said she had never known any well. Kelvin had never mentioned one.

HE WENT DOWN TO THE old swamp where he had played as a boy. The approach was through a colonnade of flaking, frost-shattered, blue-grey granite boulders that were perfectly made for games of Cowboys and Indians. It was easy to imagine Tom Mix making his camp nearby, building a fire of old fence posts, opening a tin of beans to blacken on the embers. There Jim D'Inglis had played, aged eight or nine, a cap gun in each hand, blazing away at imagined enemies, his leather chaps flapping on his skinny calves, the green fringes of his waistcoat tickling his ribs. Now Jim was well past sixty. The brother he had played with and protected was long dead: poor Kelvin in an Indian headdress of white cockatoo feathers.

Wallabies favoured the swamp in the evenings and left their droppings on the close-cropped grass. Generations of sheep drifted through. Cattle bogged here in droughts, leaving their skeletons in mud.

In a cleft of rocks was a high, gritty ledge. There Jim had crouched as the US cavalry rode in, calling to his brother with an owl-hoot under the full moon. Kelvin had come to his call. In later years they had made bombs from gunpowder, nails, and galvanised pipe, and tested them ready for the Jap invasion, once killing a cow.

Jim studied the flaking rockface, trying to locate the footholds and handholds from half a century ago. He remembered how Kelvin had scrabbled and how he had held him away from the blast. He would not be able to scramble up that rock again if his life depended on it — not unless his old suppleness of spine was restored by hot packs and sessions at the physio, and then, tapping that blind surface, where would he place his boots, where would he ever begin?

The sun moved across a bare sky. As it sank in the west it turned a pulsating beetroot-red in the smoke of bushfires. Curtains of purple cirrus were revealed in the high atmosphere. While it was still light the moon rose under the hill behind the cottage. When others in the country complained about the dry, Jim D'Inglis felt a special elation. He had never fitted in to local thought. He was like his father who always resisted that idea, yet had buckled down, becoming a dealer of fates. When the land was dead it came alive for Jim: the smell of waterless earth, wagtails moving into night-shift, shallow birdbaths and algae-thick water troughs reflecting slithery moonlight. In Ethiopia when Jim straightened his back from a night of suturing wounds in the hospital tent west of Dombidolo, and walked out into such a nightscape, the smell of dry earth had been the promise of himself. The eucalyptus plantations had rustled. His life had become useless, and it only wanted one more devastating proof, the death of a woman under his care when he returned to Australia.

At the high edge of the swamp the boulders opened onto a smooth, shiny expanse of grass. Somewhere around here was the old dump. As boys, Jim and Kelvin had smashed bottles and watched them break in flashes. Jim remembered dippering mud, watching trickles of undrinkable water emerge from the ground and run into microbe-laden, debris-slickered puddles where dead greenflies floated among mosquito larvae. They had found a rusted jewellery box here, with paste diamonds clagged with soil crumbs and a collection of old rings like eaten-through bottle tops, which they took back and stored in the kitchen of the men's quarters, their wet weather play place. One had a snake's head peering through dirty crust, but when they went back later to clean their find, this particular ring was gone. Kel said he saw their father wearing it once. Then never again.

There was a slight drop in the level of the ground here, a change from coarse curry-coloured sand to black, peaty bog. There had always been a neat circle of rocks jutting from the grass around here. There had been no tree as there was now, a weeping willow.

It had never occurred to Jim that the old well was so intimately close, always known, under the haphazard circle of stones. Yet it was so obvious now when he thought about it. Whenever old-timers spoke of an abandoned well Jim had failed to make a connection to the swamp. He thought it was just a soak. He thought the well would be up in the cottage yard somewhere, because the swamp was too far away from the cottage to pump from. The ground was hollow near the cottage. It was where old caves had collapsed. There was a sink hole in the limestone which had been a garbage dump for years. The cottage had been tied to the water supply at the main homestead for almost a century. The rusting, skeletal galvanised iron pipe arched from the riverside pump-shed and ran across bare ground for almost three kilometres, loping hauntingly over gullies and rocky hillsides to its destination. Jim's grandfather, Sir Magnus, had installed the pipe so that the low-ceilinged slab and daub cottage on the site, Bob's, would have water available at the turn of a hinged brass tap-handle which jutted out from the kitchen wall beside the stove.

In the past month the river had retreated to a chain of miserable soaks scooped from the sand by a tractor-mounted front-end loader. Now even the soaks were finished. That was what Stuart told Jim a day ago, shouting the news from the cab of his Toyota without bothering to switch off the motor and step down for a proper talk. 'You're in deep shit,

Jim, like the rest of us. You'll have to dig your hole in the bloody sand too, and pray for bloody rain.' Then Stuart sped off, staring back for a moment at his mother, who leaned out of the window of the cottage and watched him go. Stuart greeted her neutrally. 'Mother, speak to Jim.' He thought he could aim things at Jim without damaging her one way or the other.

That day Jim went down to the swamp with a chainsaw, an axe, a crowbar and a spade.

Across the moonscape of sandy paddocks the few trees left — tortured snappy gum, viminalis, hawthorn and false acacia — were shedding their leaves from water stress. Desiccated cattle carcases dotted the gullies. Jim stomped around the willow tree's massive twin trunks. Its leaves were still glossy. The ground was still damp. The circle of rocks was still there, responding hollowly to the thump of Jim's boots. The rocks were covered in thick tree roots and a matted, fibrous wad of red capillary tubers.

Of course he remembered the well now. He had seen it alive. He had walked with his mother across the bare steep slope of the mountain above the cottage, and they had seen the sun glint across the surface of its clean water, as certain as love. It was a dream Jim uncovered as he worked on the well. It explained all the lives around him: the chain of hurt reaching down from a courageous, cruel action taken by a barely remembered woman in the name of love. She had gone to England at the outbreak of war, had joined her lover there, and had died in the Blitz. She had sat by the well dangling her toes in the water — Jim and Kel must have gone on forgetting the well even as they played around it — just as they went on forgetting their mother. But nothing was forgotten in time. It was just difficult to conjure up, identify and name.

Jim moved in and began clearing the tree away. He lost himself in work. When he was surrounded by fallen branches he dragged them back, and began axing the roots into sections, slowly revealing a circle of stones resembling a sliced open human skull. They were what he remembered best. Roots. He hauled a nest of stinking pulpy mass upwards. The brains of the earth. The well-top was full of sloppy mud. Jim was at the top, at the beginning, ready to go way down. He thought he would deal with Stuart this way, by clearing out the well. Also with himself, Ida, and Mal. He felt down with a long stick, and at two metres struck a hard and even obstacle. It would be laborious getting it out. The point of his stick traced a maze of curving grooves, each coming to a dead end. It seemed like a chunk of metal with a pitted surface. It seemed like a fossilised egg. It seemed like the top of a head.

Slugs and leeches slid from the blade of Jim's axe. A green frog hopped free of his spade, peppered with soil crumbs. A cold peaty smell came from damp earth. Here the ground had been dark, sheltered, damp and cool for years, while the rest of Croppdale hurtled close to the sun. Here life had developed in secret, awaiting its time of change. Putting the stick in was like taking a biopsy. The smell was like green body gas.

PRE-DAWN WAS AN EXPLOSION of galahs wheeling overhead in hysterical metallic frenzy, white cockatoos outriders in the flock. It was dark at ground level, but flushed with pink in the upper sky from where the galahs dropped in flashes of grey, rose, and white.

The birds settled on a bare electricity wire strung between two poles across the Croppdale compound — more than a hundred of them, some spinning upside down, hanging from their ancient claws before righting themselves. The air was cool this early. The galahs' breasts were smouldering fires, their wing feathers ash. They had hot red faces, and thatches of white head feathers. It would be a scorcher later. Nothing would move under the noon sky. At evening the country would lay waste all around, grey, pink, and ashy white spread wide and useless, hopes leached through into darkness again, stars coming out, moon rising in a drought sky.

Ida D'Inglis was in the shower under the tank-stand near the men's quarters. Two of the water drillers, Erwin Schmidt and Kurt Wolpers, were asleep on their camp beds, surrounded by empty beer cans and torn VB cartons. They'd had a piss-up the night before. The third driller, Colin Byron, was out in the paddocks looking for water. Nothing would happen until he returned with a message about where it was. Stuart D'Inglis was out there with him. So was Mal Fitch, being jerked around in the hard-sprung vehicle and loving it.

WILLIAM D'INGLIS SAT AT an attic window of the Croppdale homestead smoking a black cigar. He munched phlegm and worked his toothless gums against each other as he stared into another day and tried to remember what a cigar should taste like. Not like this. Not like pulp. It should burn with bitterness and rich odours. Galahs perched on the roof iron and strung themselves out along the shortwave antenna that had been strung up by Jim and Kelvin when they were boys, so they could listen to battle reports from North Africa.

Once William D'Inglis had been keen, acquisitive, competitive, strong. People looked at his hands and thought he was soft but soon learned differently. He could pack a punch. People resented millers because they made their money with grain, the earth's free ripening priced by the bushel, and William D'Inglis, building on his legacy from Sir Magnus, inflaming the envious more, had started growing his own, squeezing the whingers out, winning awards at the Royal Easter Show, his golden sheaves perfectly bound by his wife Peg before she left him. He'd done the fifty twisting jolting miles from Logan's Reef to Croppdale in ninety minutes as early as 1921, when the road was just a two-wheeled track. He had blasted out of constriction like a stallion at the gate, outstripping his rivals, battling the government, the railways, the Wheat Board, the growers — as President running the shire, mounting re-election campaigns, drinking younger men under the bar at the pre-war Criterion Hotel and maintaining the lowest golf handicap in the district until he was sixty, when he still loved the woman in Railway Parade, Rosan Fitch.

Now all that was gone. His hands shook. His joints ached. He pissed in pain. He was skinny as a strung hare. His kidneys and bowels were packing it in. His son the disgraced Doc Jim deferred to an Indian, Dr Battacharya, who supplied him with Lanoxin, Slow-K, Gerovit and Chlotride by the fistful. Active angers had distilled to an acid bitterness in William D'Inglis now. He liked to stay clean, but woke with his galah-grey flannelette pyjamas fouled with shit spray. His black stub of cigar pulsed and glowed pink in the early light while he puffed it down breathlessly. The barking of a dog in the hills made his heart beat faster. He had avoided the mineshaft-riddled hills above the river for almost thirty years, never going around via the track past the pump shed and up the steep ridge over the Chinese water races, because he wasn't ready to die yet. Life hadn't offered its last up to him.

He sorted through objects on his dressing table, hairbrushes and shoehorns, razor strops, tobacco tins, tortoiseshell cufflink boxes and broken fob watches, and ran his freckled hands through drawers crammed with old papers, receipts and letters. He put his hand on a tin and gave it a shake. Where was that gold tooth ever? A million tiny threads of satin whispered. Seed! He scattered a fistful of millet out the window. Galahs came crashing from everywhere. It made the old man's heart pound to loosen phlegm from his lung spaces, detach it from his throat, bring it along his tongue and whoosh it free with cannonball accuracy. He got a galah.

William D'Inglis had started life with a grain of wheat, as a boy splitting wheat under a kitchen knife, growing grain on damp cardboard, feeding wheat to chooks, scratching it in, when he was twelve, on stony acres with a horse-drawn combine. Wheat was his token and he always felt as a kind of promise for the future that he would split and ripen himself, and give off his harvest incessantly through the years, but things hadn't gone that way for him. Not quite. His father Sir Magnus had sat in the first national parliament. They called young Bill the miller's calf.

In the First War, as a junior lieutenant in France, he'd organised supplies for the front, driving pack trains under gunfire on black nights, setting up Soyer stoves and soup cauldrons in the mud. He was always in peril. He took food as far forward as he could. Patrols from one side were as frightening as the other, attacking friend and foe in the dark. The habit of burning a night-light started then, a stub of candle in the dugout or a tuft of the flannel they called fourby soaked in gun oil and flickering. Later he inherited the mill at Logan's Reef and expanded the acreage of Croppdale, giving it over to sheep, cattle, and to the forest trees that Kelvin had loved but neglected, and that Stuart, now, another lifetime later, was unable to harvest because no sawmill wanted them. D'Inglis's flour wasn't what it used to be. Breadmakers always said they preferred D'Inglis Bakers' Plain to any other. Sconemakers liked D'Inglis's Self Raising with its insignia of Christmas bells. The Australian army marched on D'Inglis Forces' Blend at Tobruk, El Alamein, and Kokoda. In the 1950s under Kelvin, the mill had started its long decline. Now the old man didn't know what was going on. With respect to D'Inglis Flour, advantage was no longer pursued. Human shit infested flour bags. Unhealthy, cakey black shit, the product of someone who lived on mutton and potatoes — a man named Harry Frawtell according to Stu. There were merchants who condescended to pack D'Inglis's plain as No Names and market it at a loss. His grandson Stuart, whom he loved, was in charge, and Stu was grin-making crazy, emu-crazy, racing around and crashing through fencelines.

Now what was that noise?

William D'Inglis was breaking into pieces, rotting away, blurring, farting and dribbling back to where he'd budded from the earth in 1892. His losses made him howl with resistance. But he still had good hearing. This morning it was Stuart's utility he heard, upriver from the homestead, circling Bob's Cottage and bothering Jim. And he could hear shots from a 30-30 back over the clifftop somewhere: shooters from Logan's Reef daring a foray into the rough paddocks high above the house that had once raised fine bullocks but whose fences were broken, giving feed to flourishing numbers of roos, pigs, and goats. Sometimes they came tumbling over the cliff and landed on the rooftop. A quarter of a century ago William D'Inglis had sent a boy to patrol those tracks, a handsome, razor-eyed kid who sank spikes into shooters' tyres and pumped saltpetre into trespassers' arseholes on behalf of the property rights of D'Inglis Self Raising. That lean stockrider was an Abo. He'd tried to have Ida, William always believed, grabbing her warm from the saddle on a sandbank of the Cropp. He'd read it all over her when they came in, her eyes glazed in the fashion of a cheat while the kid carried a dying dog in his arms. How old was she then? He had an impression of her in her twenties. He'd slapped her on the face. Pretty darned terrible it was. When he told Kelvin, suggesting he do something about it, Kelvin sent the kid into the mill, and employed him in the rail loading section.

But Ida couldn't have been in her twenties, century-old William D'Inglis worked out with a stub of pencil and a crumpled piece of paper. She was only fourteen then. Ages that seemed at the bottom of a well, small points of light from the years he had reached: irrelevancies that still haunted, though, and that he needed a hold on. He knew what it was that had made him hit Ida, rant and rave, and send Alec Hooper to town, denying him the work he loved. It was because Hooper and the girl had found the dog he'd been feeding in the hills since it leapt on him in the dark of a crumbling Chinese mine adit.

TWO SHOOTERS WERE ACTIVE ON the tops. Keith Wiencke, who stood with his back to the pre-dawn light, and Alec Hooper, still razor-eyed in his mid-forties.

Just as the day strengthened, unveiling shapes and perspectives in the chill air, Keith Wiencke loosed a shot. The roo didn't fall over. It only sank despondently, as if suffering a mood change. Blood ran from its chest and it turned its head and gazed at the shooter from sad eyes. He would have to kill it properly now. Second by second the light changed. The sun would soon burst up over the horizon. The wallaby would be realising this too — it was a living thing, not separate from Keith Wiencke, as he tightened his finger, the excitement of death-dealing flushing through him, the rifle kicking, his ears ringing, the roo flung back among the rocks.

Alec Hooper went over and started skinning it.

Keith Wiencke sat on a rock and watched him.

'You should be doing this,' said Alec. 'Deal with what you kill.'

'I'd only botch it, mate.'

'Uh huh.'

In the dark, all the way up from town, Keith Wiencke had been thinking of what he was putting behind him by coming up here. The wife and the boys. In the back of the Hi-Lux was a bag of clothes, a loaf of bread, a few tins of food and some smokes. It was Alec Hooper's Hi-Lux. Keith Wiencke had decided to walk upstream along the Upper Cropp, and then double back. Under his plan he was thinking of the woman he'd met. He asked Alec if he knew anything about her.

'A little.'

'Like what?'

'I dunno — she's on TV, pisses her family off, done a play, *Prosperity* it's called.'

'She's a looker.'

Alec threw the carcase into the back of the truck and wrapped it in sacking. He rubbed his hands in the dirt and wiped them clean on a tussock.

'Yeah. She's okay. A bit old for you, though, fella.'

They left the vehicle and walked down a winding, overgrown track Alec knew about, emerging onto a platform of rock overlooking the property of Cropp-dale. They sat there smoking, looking down on the dull unlit roofs of the house and the sheds, on the men's quarters and the dairy. In a purple shadow they could see the drilling rig and the drillers on their camp beds in the open. They could see dogs in the dust attached to their chains. Past there, up the high valley of the Upper Cropp, was a point where the cone of a headlight was visibly fading, going around steep drops. Some kind of magic must be guiding the vehicle because the whole area was riddled with Chinese mineshafts. Alec had lost horses and stock up there without warning. The time he'd rescued an old dog from the hills, with the help of Ida, was the last time he'd been through those paddocks.

A faint green line at the far foot of the sky bulged as the sun swelled under it. A glistening peak caught the first molten edge of light from the sun a few seconds before it nudged over the horizon. 'What are we looking at here?' Keith Wiencke was amazed. The line seemed like a cloud and maybe it meant rain. The peak angled across it like a hatchet blade.

'That's the ocean,' said Alec.

'Pull the other one. It's more like a fucking cloud.'

'That peak up there is the head of a giant eel that got stuck when he was crossing the grass, mate. It's called Mount A.A. Hooper.'

Keith Wiencke tossed him a cigarette. 'After you, I s'pose. You are such an old bullshitter.'

'This here's the home of my ancestors,' said Alec Hooper matter-of-factly. 'They come up here from the coast in summer. They arranged the stones, held the ceremonies, ate the moths, gave names to them peaks. It was women's country. They was an ancient race, mate, but I tell you what, they weren't ancient enough for this place. They got the rough end of the pineapple.'

Any moment now the sun was going to burst into view. Alec Hooper wrapped his arms around his knees and shed every trace of truculence.

'I used to work them paddocks,' he continued, 'from when I was a nipper. I was adopted to people round here — them Hoopers. They had a block in the scrub. They're dead now.' He paused. 'Them D'Inglises, they'd bring me out here to chase stock from the upper gullies. I got the cattle operation running smoothly, and then they sent me back to the Reef. They turned me into a townie. I was made assistant foreman in the mill under Kelvin D'Inglis. He was all right. Soft as they come.'

'Who hasn't worked in that place at some time, eh?' yawned Keith Wiencke.

'Yeah. I was dropped from the workforce after Kelvin died. Stuart D'Inglis found I had holiday entitlements and sick leave credits stretching wayback.'

'So you did know that Ida D'Inglis, you sneaky lying old bastard.'

'Well, when I done the overseeing, and run the horses up at Croppdale, Ida used to come out with me. She was fourteen. I was a bit older. We were mates.' There was a long pause. 'We clicked.'

'Did you root her?'

Keith Wiencke's head exploded as Alec Hooper got him on the ear.

'Hey! What'd you do that for?'

'I could kill you.' Alec stooped over the younger man as if he might skin him the way he'd done the roo.

'You could try.' Keith Wiencke cowered. He looked down at the 30-30 with its German scope. Alec had his foot on it. Then he took it. Keith Wiencke moved away and sat on a rock, rubbing his head. His brain raced in circles. Why the fuck couldn't he concentrate on what was important — getting the firearm back from Alec? Why these thoughts now — his angry young wife furrowing her eyebrows at him while holding tight to the hands of their two sons, the baby and Bennie, Bennie being the one Keith

favoured and wanted with him in a new life, prefer-
ably with an older woman on tap, tolerant and never
bothering him. He'd gone off and got on the piss that
night. It was when he had seen that water driller, the
skinny red-headed one he had passed on the steps of
the hotel in Logan's Reef when he was on his way out
to play golf. He'd seen him outside the Night Train
nightclub. The bloke had been lying on the ground
chucking a fit, but he came to when Keith walked
past. Everyone else had walked past without helping, too, so what made Keith Wiencke so special,
what was the reason the bloke picked him out,
implied he was top-grade shit? The stare from those
epileptic eyes made Keith stroppy.

Alec dusted the rifle and gave it back to him, ammo
and all. 'Here, look after it, you prick.'

Keith Wiencke blinked. He was amazed. It meant
he could kill Alec Hooper if he wanted.

THE SKY WAS CLOUDLESS ACROSS the pale blue where
the morning star faded. Galahs flapped down to an
empty water trough, jostled along the tin lip and
argued about it, then gathered in close-packed
dozens on the bare dirt, scratching for grass seeds

that weren't there. Their cries hurt the ears. More galahs and cockatoos flew down from the hills, shading low along the length of the dry Cropp riverbed in twists and shreds of movement, at one bend invisible against the drought-stricken silver ground, flicking over, then, at the next bend, their changed body angles catching the light these moments before sunrise, each bird of the flock etched at speed, stiffened feathers biting the cool air precisely — then at the men's quarters wheeling as if with an application of brakes over the crowded electricity wires, sinking clumsily, creating downward gusts of air, grabbing the wires unsteadily.

The Croppdale compound of buildings was a ghost town this early. Stuart D'Inglis had left in pitch dark, the purr of the diesel motor hardly louder than the orchestra of frogs in the sludgy pools of the riverbed. Only the vehicle's tracks showed where it crossed the tussocks, and went up into the bare hills.

Hawks roosted on dead branches above the feed sheds ready to take mice. Mangy foxes watched from sandy dens on the opposite riverbank. Eels pulsed in brackish leftovers of river, getting fat on cattle carcases bogged and rotting. Old yabby claws whitened in crevices of rock, crusted with salt. A ram dragged along the lower roadway between buildings: it had a broken foot and matted, dirty two years' wool.

Whenever anyone had a rifle ready it disappeared into the scrub where it lived.

Up at the cottage, Doc Jim studied a glass jug of crystalline water with a faint line of mud in the bottom. Well water, settled overnight. Jim tasted the water: it had smooth freshness and a slight effervescent tingle. He swilled it around in his mouth and swallowed. Then he drank more.

Working on the well each day, Jim had only reached the one-and-a-half-metre mark, laboriously dippering sludge from the steps of a ladder suspended by rope, and climbing out every few minutes to pluck leeches from his shins. The hard object he had struck with the pole was shifting. It was a boulder. It went down as he went down. When he stood on its surface he felt himself descending like a parachutist. Then he scrambled up the ladder again. Parts of the gnarled surface of the rock were exposed, then covered again as the water swilled around, a rusty, muddy, flaking bulge.

Georgina told Jim she didn't want him doing the work. She would scorn him if he told her. She remembered what was put down wells in her girlhood — rusted scythes, split plough discs, messes of barbed wire. In other extremes, animal carcases and human bodies, dead babies and suchlike. Georgina feared that Jim would bleed to death down there or drown.

A man she knew at Thistle Corner had died, expiring in well gas.

But Jim exulted despite the slowness of the work. He felt, in his actions, that he was going back past despair and frustration, down past cycles of waste. Cleaning the well offered redemption of a loss of himself somewhere. He said this to Georgina and she turned aside, thinking about Jim's excitements and enthusiasms and his tragedy of negligence. He was like Stuart in this. No wonder they faced each other, blank to their similarities. Jim kept thinking he was finished, rounded, complete. So did Stu. Jim spoke about it a lot. But then he always turned the next corner. He said a door had banged in the wind, in the hospital corridor, and he had looked up. The theatre sister had looked away at the same time. Into this chance abandoned space had fallen a life — had fallen, unseen, point first, a peritoneum-piercing scalpel. Georgina would never forget how, in their first love, back when she was engaged to Kelvin, Jim had thought that what they discovered with each other was enough. Georgina knew that he had never sacrificed anything for her. He had gone away from her into personal idealism, leaving her confused, angry, and pregnant with Ida, and then had begun coming back, for years just in letters, and then in person. Always in her thoughts, however. She had loved him yet married another, just as Rosan Fitch had loved Bill D'Inglis yet married another — two threads in two lives never again neatly woven back into the smooth pattern of experience. Who would speak for poor Rosan now? Georgina always felt that a moment would come when she would. When she would have to.

'Let's have Mal over for dinner tonight,' she suggested.

'Okay. I'll tell him to bring his own water.'

'That's not funny.'

Jim peered out the window and saw Stuart parked in his Toyota on the barebones hilltop high above the cottage, using binoculars to focus on the well. A second figure was in the truck with him, lumpy Mal Fitch, wearing his dark blue rollneck sweater in the early cool. Mal had taken to Croppdale with a vengeance, doing a job on it like a theme at Whale Belly. Soon he would use it all up, predicted Jim. Georgina wasn't so sure — she'd noted a big change. It was there in the relationship with Ida: they both had something serious in mind for themselves — not the same thing with each other, that had given them so much trouble in recent years, but a preoccupation verging on revelation.

There was a third person out there too, Jim noted, someone wearing a red checked shirt — higher up than Stuart, signalling to him, calling 'Stu! Stu! Stu!' because he seemed to think the name was beautiful, echoing the way it did, yodelling down the bare gullies. Stuart was leaning out of the cab, signalling back — making a stiff-armed pompous gesture.

On the ridgeline overlooking Croppdale this third figure zapped into the sunrise.

FLAME-HEADED, FROGGY-SKINNED Colin Byron springboarded from loose rocks, stepping from boulder to boulder, smelling for water. A displaced heaviness affected his thin, overlong shins, as if his brain were filled with weights and they needed to nod down through him to his toes before he could feel good about himself. High overhead, a line of migrating pelicans beat north, seeking water, forming a long, slow, twisting line. Colin aligned with their passage. His sharp, scaly nose followed the birds. But when he tipped back his head he could feel the weights tugging his brain. He could feel what it was — water under him, flowing, taking him away. He drifted across the rocks and gullies, constantly overbalancing. There was a whole world under this place awaiting uncovering. Colin had the feeling he'd come home — he wanted to live here, settle down. He wanted to die here. This was the place. It was where he'd been coming to all this time.

'Stu! Stu! Stu!'

They said he was simple, but *it* was simple.

Wherever Colin Byron travelled, Erwin and Kurt were on benders the whole time and tried to lose him, never telling him where he was. In their sleep he drove and they cradled cans of KB against their armpits, their contents slopping everywhere. Now and again they shifted their arses, sucked piss, blinked at the place they were in. Then down came the shutters again. They farted without saying sorry. They reached across each other and threw their empties out the window, and felt around in the carton and selected another one. They had this carton to drink now, and the boss's one ahead of them. This one, the next one. It was the way they lived. Colin found his way all the way back from the north of S.A. and western Queensland, where there were no signposts and the tracks divided without clues. They could never lose him properly no matter how hard they tried, though. At Rocky Springs, where the Schmidts and the Wolpers were the only people, Erwin had an old wife, Dora, who grew cactus plants in a garden surrounded by star pickets and sheets of cracked green alsynite. Kurt had a wife too, a skinny woman, Davinia, who bred Arabian horses on a patch of dirt in a wide gully, where they had yards and a windmill, and lived in a tent. Colin remembered each and every turn-off they'd ever made. In his mind, if he had to, he could trace their journey all the way back to Rocky Springs, all through the day, all through the night, into the next day. He always knew where he was but couldn't say it. Sometimes he dreamed of arriving at Rocky Springs with the news that the other two weren't ever coming back. He would put the truck into the shed, drain the oil, roll up the windows, put a tarp over the cab to keep the dust out, pack the joints in grease, reposition the snake ring, and then move back through the doors and shoulder them shut, padlocking the catch and rolling a piece of steel against the doors to stop them banging in the wind. He would suggest to Dora Schmidt that she ought to disconnect the phone because there would be no point in taking calls any more. He would tell Davinia that Kurt had pissed off with another skirt (which he would have done), she had better forget him.

Then he would go and sit in the hills, light a fire and look out over the land, waiting for what happened next. He thought one day a spaceship would come for him. He would rise with his arms outspread like a singer. But why think all this when he was here? He would work for Stu, his new buddy, and get Mal, his new mate, to teach him to read and write.

On yesterday's drive out to Croppdale whenever they came to a fork in the road, Stuart D'Inglis stood beside his ute with the door open, pointing the way with a straight arm. Colin loved him for whipping them along. 'Step on the gas, there, chum.' His face all twisted in the sun. His pain wasn't fake. He was in need, Col saw, and Stu knew it, which was rare. Col could help by bringing it up. He didn't have a name for it. It was love.

The road had grown narrower and less used as they'd gone along. At one turn he saw a hollow log with a kelpie pup chained inside. There was a little wooden house with a tin fence hard against wheel ruts. 'I could live there,' Colin had told himself. Old tree stumps, starving horses, and the carcases of dead sheep were scattered through the paddocks. 'I could clean them up.' There were miles of slow going. 'I could plant a crop here, if there was water.' (His scabby nostrils twitched.) On a gravelly ridge they passed a mine derrick and a heap of rubble, with a truck backed up to a loading ramp. 'I could get it going.' The truck had no wheels, only rocks under the axles. 'Maybe there's gold,' thought Colin. They went through scrub where a fire had been. Black everywhere. Colin could smell the deadness of ashes.

He must have been born in a cold fireplace to like this smell so much.

He knew that here someone had lit a fire to warm himself, but it hadn't worked. Colin held his knuckles up to the light.

'Where'd you pinch that fucking ring?' Kurt had grabbed for it.

I could do anything I wanted, Colin told himself. *Stay anywhere. Be anyone. Catch fire.*

Near the end of the drive, just as they had come to the gates, Colin had felt a fit coming on. He'd learned the signs: the light hurting his eyes, tears pricking, a dry mouth, fear in his guts over whether he'd hurt himself. He had to match himself to a rhythm to control what happened. On the road it was always the truck rattling, the tyres humming and whining. Then the moment would fade — Kurt and Erwin had never seen him have one. But yesterday the road hadn't had a rhythm to offer when the fit came on. Col gripped the stiff wheel with his wrists hurting as they ground around the side of a cliff and approached the gates where Stuart D'Inglis stood with chains at his feet waving them through. On the other side of the gates Colin knew what was what, and jerked to a stop and muttered, 'I need a shit'. He shot into the bushes out of sight. When he came round Stuart D'Inglis was crouched beside him, holding his clammy hand, and staring at him wordlessly.

Now he was where he wanted to be. He loved it better than all the other dumps. Elevated Croppdale close to heaven.

SOON COLIN BYRON WOULD RETURN to the camp and Kurt and Erwin would wake, glaring at him in their special anger, raising their hungover heads and untangling their dirty eyebrows.

'What's the story, Col?'

'See up along that line of rocks above the river there?'

'Yah.'

'That's where it is.'

Only it was going to be different this time.

See up along that line of rocks above the river there?

Yah.

It's dry. Not even a thimbleful of cat's piss for yers.

AT THE POINT WHERE COLIN was about to turn around and head back to catch a ride to the men's quarters with Stuart D'Inglis and the other mate, Mal Fitch, his foot struck something soft. He looked back over his shoulder and saw a shadow settle on the dirt. Only it wasn't a shadow. It was a hole in the ground the size of a fist sucked from under. He'd stepped it into existence with the pressure of a heel. Now it trickled open to the size of a hollow footprint. Cripes. It grew wider. The heavy feeling inside Colin's head slid loose as he investigated the hole on his hands and knees, his bony arse jutting upwards, his face into the earth like a rusty axe blade. Gravel hissed down. A stream of cold air fanned his cheeks, curling its currents behind his ears, up under his shirt front. He cupped his hands around his eye to the hole, and looked down into darkness. Pebbles bounced, pinged, tumbled away far below. He knew what he'd hear if he waited long enough — a splash, a tiny, pinprick-like, concentrated noise of surface break-age. Just a small gulp far away.

There it was, too. A small gulp far away.

Colin Byron felt a thinner, longer shadow come up from the darkness of the hole and wrap itself around him. *You are mine.*

Colin knew this meant he was his own. No one owned him. He wasn't sure if the hole was real.

He stood, tucked in his shirt and decided what to do. Say nothing, that was for sure.

He made his way back to the Toyota and his mates Stu and Mal. Colin had never met anyone who needed water as badly as Stu.

'How does it look, cob?' asked Stu.

Colin shook his head. 'Keep goin'.'

He was in charge here. He wasn't alone. There was a second one of him, now, riding with him. A stronger Col. Long ago he was waiting for himself in a place that stank of ashes. Some things had to be left alone until people were ready for them.

If this friendship was real he would bring Stuart up here and he would find the water, no worries.

'LOOK AT THIS ONE,' SAID MAL FITCH, bouncing around in the middle in the Toyota. He passed over another photo from the bundle he had that had been taken by the old-time water man, Gunner Fitch.

Colin needed only to glance at them. 'Uh huh.' Two rocks like a goat's ears. A prickly bush with a cave mouth behind it. A black dog standing on a car. He recognised every place from their drive around these hills. Soon he would return to them.

'Who's the lady?'

'She's my mother, Rosan.'

Colin brought his ring finger to his mouth, and began tapping his teeth with the metal. There was so much more than water here he almost shitted himself with joy.

'She's dead,' said Mal.

'Stop!' Col yelled.

Stu jammed the brakes on, throwing them all against the windscreen.

Colin leaned out of the cab, pointing ahead with his skinny arm.

'What is it, mate?' They'd begun talking to each other coaxingly — Mal encouraged it, picking up on atmospheres, fitting in, adjusting roles, directing voices. He couldn't help it.

'I dunno, pal,' said Stuart.

'I do, but,' said Mal. 'It's my turn now, buddy boy.'

Staring up at Mal through the meagre tussocks was the oval eye of the tin torch. The other two were silent. Mal climbed down from the truck and went over to fetch it. As he picked it up, the batteries slid out, leaving the case empty in his hand. The batteries banged his toes on landing and disappeared into the grass. Mal ran his fingers along the ridged length of the case. The metal felt flimsy. It was choked with spiderwebs and rust. Mal felt stupid about crying, but he cried. He'd forgotten the ivory button for instant on and the small tin slide as perfect as a miniature barge for keeping it on.

ON A TIN CHIMNEY ABOVE the men's quarters kitchen a sentinel cockatoo raised its yellow crest and stared around, dragging out a painful screech.

The water drillers slept through it on the verandah on their wire-sprung camp beds. Erwin Schmidt lay on his back wearing a dirt-stained singlet and old blue underpants, his hands folded over his protruding stomach, snoring while the early sun melted the surrounding hills and shone against his twitching eyelids and into his brain, giving him a dream of cactus beds, furry spikes, dry stones. The sun in the sky throbbed like a birth-swell but Erwin's life was always jammed in the breech like a too-big baby's. Back at Rocky Springs a plastic pipe ran from the roof of his house into a stone cistern blasted from the quartz rocks of the Gideon Ranges. At any time there were twenty-four thousand gallons of water trapped in the rock to balance against the dryness of Rocky Springs with its goat herds and biblical hills — water like a bank balance gathering increase because barely touched, small deletions from it made to dampen the lips and swab the neck, larger contributions dribbling in from rare passing thunderstorms and dewy nights, always dampest under a full moon. The water in the rock was all Erwin wanted. It held him on a long leash. He could go a long way out from there, with the knowledge of water away behind him. He had come all the way here, to Croppdale, the most easterly distance they had ever come, and still he felt he hadn't left home.

He narrowed his eyes.

A naked woman crossed the dusty road. A strong sad voice sang 'Misty Blue'. He closed his eyes. Not his.

KURT WOLPERS PARTED THE LIDS of a throbbing eye. They'd drunk the two cartons last night.

The woman went past the end of his bed and, thinking he was asleep, her grey-eyed glance fell across him. She was a slight, well-made woman, titsy with supple shoulders, freckled back, straight spine, narrow waist, good hips. Kurt's eye ran down the cleft of her arse all the way to where her footprints left a trace of her. He wanted his bare hand on the small of that back, and guiding the woman around to see him, he wanted to look into her face. *You shouldn't show yourself to a man on first waking if you don't want him to loose an arrow in your direction, lady.* Kurt Wolpers was hard as a hammer under his dirty quilt.

She walked from the shower enclosure down the road, placing her feet deliberately, swayingly in the dust, long-toed capable feet and good ankles. She tripped. Recovered. Then she was gone. Soapy water ran away from the shower enclosure and stopped gurgling. Before it disappeared Kurt Wolpers swung from his bed, hauled his trousers on, went over there, caught the intensity of a life into his nostrils, hungrily taking it all in, the trampled flowers, the artificial chemicals refined to make the perfume of the soap bar she used, and all the different places she had stepped on the shower cement after getting out from under the water, showing as wet footmarks as if a dozen women had stood there in a circle, not just one. His. This was enough. Runaway water glistened on chips of mica in the sand and turned the ground dark as he looked.

Kurt Wolpers went over to the drilling rig and reached up into the toolbox for a spanner as long as his arm. He sprang onto the back of the ramshackle old truck, and balanced himself barefoot on a stack of sun-hot drill pipes. They made a rolling, grinding noise as he danced on them. He was outlined against the sky where Erwin could have seen him if he had wanted to, or anyone else if they wished, because Kurt Wolpers didn't try to hide what he was doing. On his lips was a faint nauseated sneer. He arched like a spring in the effort required to twist bolt heads from the main holding plate, his sinews and tendons taut. The nuts were as big as his fists; each one as it came off had to be knocked out of the mouth of the spanner with a jarring clang. The woman was watching — he knew that: those tricky grey eyes (he could feel them making him proud) peering through a crevice of the half-wall of the rubble-strewn dairy.

SHE WAS TOWELLING HER HAIR and combing it out, first one side and then the other, in long, flat strips. When she had done with combing she gathered it back, and twisted rubber bands to make a ponytail. By the time she had finished, the water driller was down on the ground burying the nuts in the dirt and walking away from the truck, back to the showers, already working on cleaning himself up.

She thought of a man she had summoned up from a crack in a pavement like a weed. Lachlan

Strong the drover. Was this water driller him? It was laughable.

What had made Ida's *Prosperity* right for its audience was expressed by Mal Fitch in the programme notes. 'This is a play that doesn't happen on the stage but in your heads, in your blood and fingertips and in your genitals if that can be said.' Mal had brilliantly slowed the action, abandoning slabs of Ida's lovingly worded text and lingering over a gesture, a turned head, a rolled eye. From the action of lighting a fire, kneading a damper, peeling a garter from a shapely ankle, there came the rattle of thunder. The songs were obscure folk songs, and snatches of Shakespeare reworked, and over-obvious bush ballads given a mournful twist by that newly-favoured performer of Mal's, Yvette Danielsen, dressed as a boy playing the electric violin, making it sound as if pain was just beautiful, as if you weren't anyone unless you had it, feelings of longing fashioned in jagged tin. So many elements were discordant in this piece but they worked in favour of an effect.

Lachlan Strong the drover came to the campsite where he was only to stay the night, the squatter giving his permission for that, but in the night he cut the fences and his sheep mingled with the owner's stock and he stayed. You could smell the ash, the filth, the independent existence of him. Ida had forced him into being out of a sense of rejection and uselessness. She remembered the lover of her fourteenth year who had never touched her, barely spoken to her, hardly even looked at her. Lachlan Strong's genesis was when Ida had gone outside after a fight with Mal, and she had imagined him up from a split in the pavement of a side lane. He arrived like a weed, bent over, swaying in a warm night wind redolent of deceit. *Oh yes, you. You are a man.* He didn't come out right in the play. How could such stillness, such silence, be portrayed? Instead a rangy, bearded, sarcastic bushman was broken against the intense violining of Midge to become the lover of her dreams. The actors moved around the stage as if drugged. 'If you think you are slow, slow down,' Mal would shout.

What Mal shovelled out of himself entered the play. Here at Croppdale all his old magnetism was gone, his basking lizard-like sexuality was gone, and Mal Fitch was just an ageing bloke, unable to locate again what it had been between them. Either something else would gather and be ready for his next play and Ida wouldn't be there, or else Mal would stay slung in this Croppdale mood, which she had never found in him before. She looked at a programme note for *Prosperity* that had been left out in the weather. It was yellowed and curled in the sun, grit rustling the pages. Subtleties were leached from the photo of Mal, his face reduced to eye sockets in a charred, undifferentiated head. It was hard to tell who this was, whether it was Mal at all. It was more like a man who was much younger than Mal when he died — the overpowering presence in Mal's life, his father.

Carbon Head

K URT WOLPERS GRABBED COLIN BYRON by the upper
arm when he came back from the hills in the
white-hot morning.

'What's the story, Col?'

'See up along that line of rocks above the river
there?'

'Yep,' Kurt squinted.

'That's where we went. It's dry. Not even a thimbleful of cat's piss for yers.'

In response to this statement, Kurt smacked Colin
across the face. It wasn't unexpected. Colin clutched his

mouth and glared at Kurt through sullen hot tears. Kurt was wearing a Hawaiian shirt printed with bananas and musical martini glasses, that danced like skeletons when he swung, and a pair of clean-washed jeans tight as a joke. His knuckles had calluses from barking on steel. His burgundy cowboy boots, smeared with yellow Dubbin, were soaking in the sun on the splintery tankstand timbers.

Colin concentrated on them while a few drops of blood trickled from his cut lip. 'You'll pay for this,' from the corner of his mouth.

Kurt pushed Colin into the showers, telling him to clean himself up and think harder about water. Colin didn't want a shower — the nozzle only dribbled. He did his best, though, thinking of his next move, changing into clean clothes, then stepping through a hole in the side wall. He limped up to the main house where Stuart D'Inglis had said come and have breakfast. Kurt wouldn't follow him in that direction. He knew Colin didn't like homesteads anywhere he went, and besides, more importantly, wasn't welcome in them, was regarded as a stinking rat by decent people. But Colin had made a friendship with a tall, miserable bloke who was way above him in life but showed kindness. Stu didn't know who he was — most people didn't. He would ask Stu if he could live in the house, sleep in a cupboard under the stairs or on a dog rug, in a woodbox, anywhere. And Stu would say, Yes, why not, sport? And that Mal Fitch, he reckoned, would frown at him in that smiling way he had, realising he had unfinished business with Col. Divining wasn't a gift people asked for, it wasn't about tricks, it came through them. They were seeing that together. Diviners didn't need show: they were sun and moon combined. The world busted open in front of their faces.

I am the metal of kings whose rule on earth has ended. The words came to Colin when Kurt belted him. *I am the metal of kings.* Take that. It jarred the roots of Colin's bones and made him think of mineshafts in the hills. Some of the diggings were like thrones sunk against hillsides. Others were like hallways leading into the mountain. Definitely he was home here, and would die here if anyone tried to take him away.

Colin twisted the snake ring on the fourth finger of his left hand. Bits of scale came away, leaving a burning green stain. He ran his fingers along the hot sides of the truck, noticing what Kurt had done for tomcat reasons and told nobody about — loosened the bolts on the holding plate to prevent any drilling. Colin could see where the nuts were buried — he'd have to be as blind as fat-eyed Erwin not to: a hump in the ground holding iron, a hump for a hump, as Kurt might say, hitching his balls and shaking his crotch about.

Erwin Schmidt came round the corner and kneed Colin in the backside, accusing him of losing the nuts.

'Dumb animal!'

'What would you know?'

Colin was sick of it all. They thought they used him as they chose. They were wrong. *Listen to me. I don't have all the time in the world as you might think. I don't spend forever in time. My returns are never infinite. When things tarnish I will gladly be gone. Then you will know me.*

This was him. Things were coming to Colin now. He was getting the hang of his life. The ring, the truck, the radiator cap. He went to the truck and with a sharp nail scratched eyeballs into the silver-frosted blanks of the divining emblem. Then he stood back and attempted to polish the little guy with the sleeve of his shirt. *Give him a go.* He'd always hated him. *Apply the heat, warm the bugger's blood.* But he was already hot, and torn flannel didn't make anything brighter. Bits of paint flaked off, the rusty divining wire snapped in the bunched fists. Colin cringed as he looked around for Erwin and Kurt, expecting another hiding. All he saw was Mal Fitch watching him from the verandah of the homestead. A leg broke at the hip, an arm, then the feet snapped, leaving the radiator cap with a rough stump, like a broken tooth. He stuffed the pieces in his pocket and walked away.

A shadow behind him, composed of linden leaves and the broken parts of an old potato digger, was the image of a man reclining on his back, a hat pulled over his eyes, smoking a thin cigarette, watching. A slight breeze stirred, and the shadow forming the hat brim flipped up from the two wavering sun patches making the eyes. Stuart's old duck-hunting retriever, Ted, came up to the tree's edge and stood pointing, nose to tail aligned, forepaw bent stiffly and trustingly. Ted stood motionless for fully five minutes, asking, *Bring me a duck*. When a puff of breeze reversed, a curl of dust lashed around the illusion, and the dog unfroze, snapped at a fly, lurched off.

IN THE OLD DAYS, Jim D'Inglis and his brother Kelvin would wake at dawn. Whispering in the dark, they'd begin planning their games. They headed out into the paddocks surprising the nocturnal life still active — foxes, mopokes on telephone poles, wombats lurching across paddocks in the strengthening between-light. It was here poor Kel had become stuck, in the borderland of day. When the brothers were small — this came back to Jim as he steadied himself, boots dangling over the side of the well, ready to go in — Kel had seen a man emerging from the house, striding across the yards, and scaling the rocks above the home compound with limbs of smoke while owls hooted and the morning star shone through the branches of cliffside kurrajongs.

What made Kel so absurd was the way he elaborated — like saying the man had put his hands to his head, roared in anger, then twisted his head off, jamming it into a split in the rock.

That had been more than fifty years ago. Jim and the rest, their father included, had smiled at Kel even beyond his death. But each day of his work on the old well Jim went deeper into a Kel-inspired feeling. It seemed to Jim now that Kel had lived his life with naked devotion, exposed to his worst fears whatever the odds. Kel had been the strange brother, all right. But who was the strangest, really? Jim saw the tendency coming down through Stuart. Georgina asked Jim to recognise that he himself had caused suffering, always deflecting pain from himself. He'd never given anything up, even for love. It was Georgina who had sacrificed, when Jim went off to save the world, when she had made her decision and married Kel, to give Ida a father.

Today, when Jim was down past the rim-stones of the shaft, the bright morning glare filtered to a blue, shadowed beauty that intoxicated him. He jammed his boots on the opposite wall and savoured the feeling. The work was taking care of itself. After endless bucketing, mud and sludge drained of its own accord. The old stone that was jammed in the throat of the shaft moved jerkily downwards, grinding and growling. It had this effect: it was a moon with gravity pull passing under. Night was still down there, the stars shining in drips of springwater on cool-sweating granite chunks. Jim felt the wrong way round. He wanted his head in those stars. He wanted to soar in the well-depths. This was how Kel had lived his life. Once he'd crossed over he never came back. He'd chosen to be mad. All those trips to Kenmore and murderous brain-damaging volts of ECT hadn't discouraged him. He'd just dropped his head and kept on coming until the fearsome, inevitable night of his death. The scouring of the well was happening right through Jim. He had returned to Croppdale making conscious choices, mending his life with Georgina, settling in at the cottage, confronting Stuart — never dreaming it was something else he needed. A catastrophe? 'I'll die in the well,' he thought, feeling excitement and dread.

KEITH WIENCKE WAS LOST. He shouldered his way through whippy gums growing thickly on the southern ridge above Croppdale. He couldn't see ahead more than a few metres at a time. This wasn't how he'd imagined it was going to be. He'd come the wrong way. After leaving Alec Hooper he thought he'd be getting it easy, walking along sandbanks and making his way along an open, rocky riverbed, smooth going with a deep pool for swimming. It was all state forest beyond Croppdale — he could camp anywhere, no one would move him on.

Instead he was on this crazy ridge. It was like being stuck inside a cauliflower.

Branches grew straight from lumpy roots, fanned out, crossing each other. He'd never seen anything like it. Lift one away from in front of you and it sprang back to clamp you from behind. The bark was white, smooth as bone. If you wanted to imprison a bloke you couldn't do better than this. He felt that Alec Hooper knew this hell was here and had put him up into it by giving wrong directions.

His bag tore and the sound grated his teeth. A twig snapped not far behind him. When he turned around to look a stick poked him in the eye. 'Shit!' His voice smothered. He shuffled a few paces more, then caught a boot and unbalanced, falling forward with his chest flat on the next clump, his rifle jamming between the sticks, the barrel jabbing up under his chin. Bad luck if it went off. He wriggled upright. Then went down on his knees and crawled, ants in his mouth, sticks scraping his chest, rifle and carry bag dragging behind him. It was a wallaby tunnel he was in with dry shit showing the way.

At last he emerged into bright daylight, torn and bleeding. He stood on a bare boulder jutting out above the whole of Croppdale. He'd come round one-eighty degrees. A glint of windscreen showed where Alec Hooper's ute was parked in the heath beyond the cliff edge. So Alec was still out here. The dry river was under his feet and on the other side of the wide valley was another ridge the height of this one, only it was bare of trees and pitted with old diggings. Keith Wiencke opened a Mr Juicy and while draining it thought about his problem. He'd taken the wrong ridge, all right. 'That *there* ridge, mate,' Hooper had emphasised, 'will drop you down where you want to be. You won't even have to throw in a line when you get there. Just feel around under the stones and tickle yourself a trout, eh, with your little finger, eh?' What was going on here? What was so special about a little finger? A conversation with Alec Hooper broke up a bloke's thoughts. He looked at it to check. Nothing, it was just smaller, like every- one's. He didn't know why this was aggravating. But it was. It was the story of his life. The more Keith Wiencke thought about something, thought of getting it, of why it was suitable for him, the further it shrank away. Say that piece of older skirt he fancied. Say them cool fingers touching when they shook hands. *Say* that name again.

He sat on the gritty rock with sweat coming from his arms like white blood. Ida. She didn't make him feel good the same way any more. Through Alec Hooper, as a matter of fact, she enraged him. He'd like to give her the bullet.

He lined up the rifle scope and raked it around the valley to see if he could spot anyone. Fatty and Skinny the water men were still visible. Woolly-headed Mal Fitch from the room opposite at the Cri crossed the yards carrying luggage. A black dog followed him. Keith Wiencke didn't like Mal Fitch. The nights he ran the bar he was moody, always on the hammer with boozers who wanted free drinks because Tutter Fitch was always smashed and supplied them. Mal Fitch was up himself the way he talked. Plummy. Mrs Tutter when she'd had a skinful told everyone that she and this Mal used to have it off in the upstairs corridor. Charming.

Whoa, and there she was, the looker, working like a demon chipping stone blocks and fitting them into a wall. Keith Wiencke focused hard, trying to improve her definition. She rucked up her T-shirt and wiped her face. He lay on his stomach and wriggled further into the ground. No feeling. He wanted to see the beads of perspiration on her upper lip. Couldn't do that. It would be easy to loose off a round. Flick the safety and finger the tit. Hey. You. This way. Squeeze. Pow.

Think sweet last thoughts about Alec Hooper, why don't you?

He blinked his eyes to lose their blur, shifted the scope around, focused on a rooftop, a treetop, a TV aerial, a cliff. This was no good. Up there on the cliff something caught his eye and he swivelled back. He couldn't believe it, suddenly. Fear clawed his guts. A face looked straight back at him, staring from the cliffs above the homestead there. Glistening black. Dead centre in the scope, a man's face in daylight.

Keith Wiencke looked again. He was wrong. It wasn't a face. But the terror wouldn't leave him. There must have been a fire there years ago, among those ferns and bushes and trees. It was a burnt stump, with ears, a forehead, a grinning mouth all twisted in a shout. *See*? it seemed to say. *This is burnt up anger. What fucking use*? He ran his hands down his rifle and knew why Alec Hooper had placed it back in his hands. What fucking use.

THE OTHER DAY IN THE HOTEL Keith Wiencke had gone into the office and waited while Betty Kingling untangled the cord from around her wrist and handed him the receiver. 'It's for you, love.' He leaned against the glass window of the office and looked out into the foyer. Alec Hooper had drifted past. Harry Frawtell had glared at him while on the way through to the dining room with a beer and a tomato juice. 'Light yer tail.' Old Mal Fitch in his black trousers and on his small feet went gliding past as if he didn't exist. There was breathing on the other end of the line. It was Rebecca, his ex-wife. Keith Wiencke stood up straighter. His heartbeat quadrupled its thump. His mouth felt dry. Love was a gun to the head and he couldn't take it. Why did it mean having things shoved on you?

'I've got Benjamin here. It's his birthday, remember?' The airless glass and plywood booth of the hotel's phone box had been like a coffin.

'Bennie?' No answer. Just the purr and chuckle of the STD line, which maybe was all a small boy hundreds of kilometres away needed from a father.

'Are you playing with a typewriter, Dad?' the small voice asked.

A whisper came through the phone. It was all Keith Wiencke could concentrate on. It wasn't a child. No. It was the whisper of his ex-wife's knees and elbows against herself as she bent to help their son. Her cool flesh like silk in the heat. She had never known what she had. Never rated it. The hot-eyed brethren panted after her. He hated to say they could have her, but he forced himself to say it: *they could have her*.

When he tried to remember what his son looked like he hadn't been able to. 'Keith, are you there?' Rebecca insisted at the other end of the line. 'Say something. Are you *drunk*?'

Boxed in like that, with the landlady listening on her extension line in the hotel office, he was trapped. Things he felt about Rebecca he caught hold of in his mind and turned back inside himself. He changed the angle of his shoulder against the glass because people could see him as they walked through the foyer: it was no place for tears.

'Speak,' he heard Rebecca ordering.

Keith moved the receiver to his other ear and leaned his forehead against the smudged glass. A small, distant, nasal howl came at him, disembodied from his life. Keith shouted into the phone, 'I'll come and get you'.

Then he hung up, and leant back on the glass of the booth, feeling alive for a change. He hadn't known how he would get there, though. Or what he'd do when he did.

A TWIG SNAPPED IN THE growth behind him. He kept his neck twisted round till it ached, trying to see if anyone was there. Then he put the rifle aside and lit a smoke. It was nothing, that snap. Just a wallaby limping through the maze.

Then after a while Keith Wiencke unloaded the rifle and unscrewed the telescopic sight. He emptied the magazine and trickled the cartridges one after another over the gritty lip of the drop. They scraped like beetle casings as they disappeared and dropped free. Even this wasn't enough to get through to the feeling he had now. So he unpacked his carry bag and threw away his other two packets of shells. Something else was needed. He took the rifle by the barrel, two thousand dollars worth of armament, spun it around his head, and let go. The weapon went spinning, reflecting light, winking and planing until it curved from view in the valley of the Upper Cropp.

When Keith Wiencke looked back at the charred head, the light had changed, the shadows weren't the same. There was nothing there. 'Fuck you!' he yelled, making his throat raw. He understood what he had just done about as much as he would understand a fish crawling from the ocean, crossing the land, getting up on its haunches and finding speech.

'Fuck you!' echoed over Croppdale.

All he knew now was that he was sleepy. He made a pillow of his pack and shut his eyes, the summer breezes of Croppdale ruffling his hair. The sun burnt him and dehydrated him and he began dying.

WILLIAM D'INGLIS CAME TO A DECISION that morning as he descended the stairs from the attic bedroom, lurching and croaking, calling for Stu: 'Tie, jacket, cane!'

He'd been three days without stirring from his room. It felt like a lifetime. He wanted to get the taste of life back into his mouth.

He wanted Stu to adjust the polished knot of his Klippel silk with patient fingers — this century-old man whose dress habits were unchanged since the time Gunner Fitch cursed him. He wanted to lean on the cane he had last seen rolling down the verandah roof in the direction of a crow, and he wanted to take a deep clean breath for a change. He wanted his son Jimmy to check whether he'd taken his medication too many times by mistake. He seemed to have been munching pills since daylight. He'd rarely done anything in his life that couldn't be traded, embraced, or swallowed. Now he had gut-ache of the spirit.

Memories returned to him with the hiss, glide, and crash of metal. Claws on tin. Loosening machine parts. Flap of drive belts in antiquated milling wheels. Events from years ago were more important to him than yesterday as he stood at the top of the attic stairs.

It was on this spot that he had summoned his strength and delivered himself of a blow that had taken out Gunner Fitch's gold tooth in '39. His virility was at a peak then. When he gathered the tooth from the floor it still had shreds of salmon-pink flesh attached. *Most* satisfactory. But the gold of the filling was shaped like a smooth-fitting smile in the enamel. It mocked him as it lay in a tray of shell-casing with other dated trinkets. After that day, he and Rosan had lived a time suitable to lovers. Neither had known guilt. But the Gunner was a cunning ghost. He was in that ring of snakes, only ever getting brighter in William D'Inglis's consideration. What had been left undone? *I promise I'll bring them snakes right out of you, mate. So you look them in the eye or you won't have no peace, let me tell you.* After a good few years Rosan wanted to change the terms of a liaison that had been deftly settled as far as William was concerned on a dusty mattress that day in his men's quarters. There were two types of women in his estimation, those who worked on a man and those who played the game. Rosan changed from the latter to the former over the years. He didn't like it. She had a habit of unoriginality he believed was evidence of a certain mental weakness. She copied passages from books in her childish scrawl, and sent them to him anonymously: *One who loves you sends you this, wishing you the happiness that she will never have, unless you give it to her. I am ashamed, ashamed indeed, to reveal my name, but if you ask what I require of you, I should like to plead my cause. You can have evidence of my wounded heart by looking at my pale cheeks, my thinness, the expression of my face, my eyes, so often wet with tears. My sighs, that have no apparent cause, tell the same tale, my frequent touchings, as perhaps you have noticed, can be felt to be different.*

They were always anonymous, these notes, but he knew who they were from. Behind their hints of unwelcome moral action (i.e. marriage) he felt the interfering hand of Gunner Fitch clutching beyond the grave. But for the Gunner there was no grave, was there, just the military convention of one, because reduced to atoms he could be anywhere at any one time, the bastard. He drifted the world on favourable winds, and only caring for the Gunner's dog had withheld the horrors from William D'Inglis.

MEN USED TO SAY THAT Gunner Fitch was the most callous soldier they knew. After demobilisation, rumours went round about what he'd done in the war. Returned men kept quiet about such stuff, and Bill D'Inglis defended him for years — until Gunner made that move on Peg MacPriam that predated Bill's liaison with Rosan. Then their relations blew sky-high. Then Bill let it out: Gunner was a man who spat on dead mates' faces. One was a lanky musical kid from Logan's Reef with wrist bones like golf balls, Josh Kingling. He'd been sixteen when he died. He never complained, always fought cheerfully, foul-mouthed and cavalier, and when he perished in the big freeze of '17 Gunner Fitch drank water from the pond where he lay staring, frozen eyeballs rolled upwards.

When Peg left him and the boys, and William D'Inglis met Gunner Fitch on Picnic Race Day in '39, and desired Rosan, their fates were truly bound. Gunner hammered it home the night he came calling. His ache would always be in the little faces of the golden snakes, in their useless venom, in the hollow mountain, in the howl of the dog lost there in the hills. A vision appeared in William D'Inglis's catnaps even now, Rosan at her loveliest, slender arms wrapped in sinuous copperheads, the snarling black dog at her feet. 'Leave me alone,' she demanded.

'It's too bloody late.' Then at the end: 'I'm not yours'.

Until this time, his affair with Rosan had gone smoothly. Things went along in a fine arrangement of mutual understanding. Only at the end was there bitterness. It coincided with the time William D'Inglis had been able to keep the dog fed. Home at Croppdale after nights in her bed he'd wade across the river with a bucket of liver and heart. He'd be out in the frost till dawn, some nights, until the shadow came in, limping and baulking. He was never allowed to touch her. She'd snap those dirty yellow fangs. This continued from 1940 till 1955, when those kids found her, when Alec Hooper brought her right into the house in his arms. When he struck Ida in his anger. When he sent the boy to the mill.

Soon after, a two-hundred-pound bag of flour had snapped his neck, and he'd been in a brace for seventy-two months. He couldn't ever again turn his head without pain. Car travel annoyed him. The day of Rosan Fitch's funeral he sat on the verandah at Croppdale dosed on painkillers and glad to be finished with them all.

But always in dreams the surly Gunner returned, waving his divining rods, pencilling his graph paper, winking his gold tooth, twirling his bloody snakes. He led the way down ladders, down hairpin bends on mountain roads, down railway zigzags and through endless Logan's Loops. He seemed to want to lead William D'Inglis downwards for a reason that was never clear. Love had only been the gateway to this. At the end of all the gyrations there was always a sheet of water.

A voice echoed over the rocks backing Croppdale homestead: *Fuck you!*

William D'Inglis drew a crackly breath and licked his dry lips. The person he thought had never mattered was the son. A hard boy to charm. He had gone away, melted into the background of town life, both famed and reviled as was the pattern among those who left the country and made good in the city. As if in a rumour William D'Inglis was conscious of an association between Mal Fitch and Ida — with her there was always 'someone in the background'. The Gunner had always said that if he had a son he'd name him after one of the two boys from the Reef who'd died in the big freeze of '17. Their names were ... one came to him — Mal — and the other was ... Josh.

'*Josh?*' he croaked out the side window.

Josh Kingling. Josh had lain under water. So this was the idea. To die and to raise the dead.

A YOUNG MAN REACHED LOGAN'S REEF after hitch-
hiking all night. Now he was heading away from the
town on the Croppdale road. After a month of Sydney party-going culminating in Christmas Day
human pyramids on Bondi Beach he'd been diagnosed with sunstroke, heartstrain and a damaged
liver. He was almost twenty-one years old. His hazy
plan had been to surprise his mother before Christmas, but the idea was lost in a boozy round. Blinking
in this harsh Australian light, with a nasal Pommy
accent, he claimed to be Aussie by birth, asking down
the main street of Logan's Reef for the road to Croppdale Farm, fooling no one about his origins. Who ever
called it a 'Farm'? Who spoke like this? Only a true
D'Inglis if ever there was one. They cultivated the
plum. And another thing. People went to a great deal
of trouble showing him the way, and he didn't
bother to thank them. That particular tendency ran
in the family too.

Now he's sticking his thumb out on the shadeless,
devastated roadside where ringbarked trees are
aligned like matches spilt from matchboxes. A lovely
young woman stops her car, it's Rennie Logan, she's
taken a day off school in a spate of decision-making
to drive out to Croppdale and tell Stuart D'Inglis face
to face that their engagement, stupendously stupid
concept, is off.

'Hop in.' She thumps the accelerator and they're away. She peels off a webbed driving glove and they shake hands across the gear shift — all is clear, she identifies him instantly: he's a D'Inglis.

'*Guy*. Yes, we've all heard about you for years.'

His aim, he said, was to reach his mother for his birthday. His twenty-first in a few days' time. 'That's nice,' said Rennie. It *was* nice. She drove along feeling happier than she'd felt before. Or maybe ever. She told him about this road — how Sir Dusty D'Inglis broke his neck here leaping logs on a hunter, but lived to be ninety-nine. 'Your great-grandfather William's just beaten that record. Apparently he broke his neck too — a feud of some kind, is the story. Now he's a hundred. My grade four kids all wrote cards to him. He sent them money for ice blocks. I thought that was sweet.'

No response this time. Guy D'Inglis was asleep against the passenger window. Sometimes a shadow blotted the car, and over the whine of her engine Rennie Logan heard a carping flutter. She craned her neck and caught a glimpse of Harry Frawtell's hang-glider. She couldn't believe it. He was following her. She drove her glitter-blue Mazda with the frowning skill of a rally driver. On the updrafts of the escarpment the hang-glider swooped and soared, cutting corners and diving across the sandy wastes of the meandering Cropp. Mostly it stayed in her blind spot, gaining height. She reached the great ugly Croppdale entrance, and it was still there. She found the lichened rock and the key crumbed with dry soil, wiped it on her jeans, opened the padlock, slipped free the heavy chain, swung the gate, and went through. Only then did Guy D'Inglis yawn awake. His cheekbones were so fine that the light seemed to shine through them, and under his look of exhaustion there was an impression of tireless honesty. An appalling lifelong tension broke for Rennie Logan when she looked at him. She heard that flapping again, scanned the sky, saw nothing. Then came a long silence, a rush of air through the treetops, and finally the uncanny scream of a fox whistle. There it was. Weaving and banking. A rainbow sailfish. 'Absolutely amazing,' said Guy D'Inglis, who watched till the shape contracted behind the trees.

There was a feeling then of strained breathing in the heat-crackling silence. Scalps prickled. As they went round the car their hands touched. They drew back. An indefinable barrier of shyness came down. In the sky, drawn up in a thermal, Harry Frawtell in his hang-glider sack dangled from the rainbow-coloured wing like a grub in a moth casing. He spat his fox whistle from his mouth; it hung by a string around his neck, slapping his chest in the buffets.

Higher and higher he worked, trying to see everything.

Back in the car Rennie Logan had one hand on the steering wheel, another on the ignition key. She didn't want to move yet. She told Guy about Cropp-dale. There was something dried up about the place, she warned him. Frozen in time. As she spoke all she could see in her mind were rusting potato diggers and fossilised crowns, sea urchins and long worms, yellow bones, rusting name plates on old dog collars, and names written in mortar.

'Hmm,' was all his response.

'Oh, but the river is beautiful,' she said.

Impulsively, Rennie Logan reached over to Guy D'Inglis, cupped her hand at the back of his sweaty pale neck, brought his head close to hers and kissed him long and gently.

'I just had to do that,' she said as she released her hold, put the car in gear, and got moving again.

Guy D'Inglis leaned against the side door and looked at her as they jolted along. 'Who are you really?'

'Who are you?'

They would have time to find out.

ALEC HOOPER HAD LEARNT THIS about Keith Wiencke in the time he'd known him: he was a sleepwalker — he didn't connect up. After watching from the scrub and seeing him throw his rifle away and fall asleep, Alec moved down along the ridge a short distance. He didn't have explanations for this but considered what he had seen. Like it wasn't an illusion. Otherwise what had happened? It was as if a spell was cast, and the bloke'd had no choice but to obey. He'd better keep an eye on him now.

In the time Alec had spent offsiding for this Wiencke at the wheat dump he'd learnt what there was to know. Wiencke had arrived from the West only six weeks before with nothing besides a change of clothes, a carton of cigarettes, an armload of reading matter to keep him occupied at night, and a belief, he said, that this was where he would straighten a buggered-up life. He looked angry when he told Alec things. His life was the fault of someone else. He couldn't quite say who. A young wife who'd got religion? He said he was going to make some big changes, though. And Logan's Reef was the place. Then he would get his small son from his ex and start over again.

'You can try what you want,' Alec warned him, 'but Reefers don't change. The atmosphere ain't right.'

Keith Wiencke replied that he knew it was easy to like small towns in the time you had — around six weeks — before everyone knew your business better than you did. Alec agreed with him on that point. It came out that Wiencke had been an alco in the town he came from. His missus had kicked him out and so on. Such a familiar story Alec switched off. The Criterion Hotel was a test of strength for him with the noisy bar and the boozy life and underage drinkers an arm's reach away. He'd stand at the bar downing a lemon squash. Then he'd go up to his room and smoke for hours in the window in the dark. Alec saw him up there when he left for home, looking down into the darkened hotel yard, and across towards the lights of the trotting paceway. He saw Mal Fitch at a window too — mirrors of each other in the dark, young and old.

Alec's last day at the wheat dump, Friday, was a scorcher. Squalls, dust, dry lightning. He took his last walk around the pile. The wind howled but everything held. The dump was ten metres high, three hundred metres long. The tarp was tied down by nylon ropes and old tractor tyres. Along the gutters a stream of mice ran, ignoring him. He shouldered the door of the storeshed and locked up. Other blokes would knock off what they could at this point in their careers. Fuel, rope, stationery, poison, anything.

The place reeked of rodent-destroying chemicals and the mice on the shelves were so crazed with hunger they sat looking at him as they chewed the labels from bulk tins of Racumin. Life had to be about something more than this, mates, Alec told them.

He met Keith Wiencke at the gate. They set off for the pub together, heads down against flying grit. Scabby dogs went for their heels. There was deep water in the pools of the Upper Cropp, round Croppdale, said Alec. It was much cooler up there, by as much as ten degrees. 'That's for me.' Wiencke had punched Alec on the arm. 'Take me up there — I'll bring me gun.' He wanted to pack an esky and go patrolling the back roads right then.

'It mightn't be what you think it is,' said Alec. 'It never was.'

TAKING A BOX OF MATCHES and a twist of newspaper from his pocket, Doc Jim lit a taper. When it flamed, he leaned over the drop of the well, opened his fingers, and away it went, floating, lighting the side walls as it sank, five, ten, twenty metres of jagged granite blocks briefly visible until the taper landed softly, where it flared, proving the air was clear down there, that a breeze, somehow, was coming from underneath, fanning the flames, sighing upwards, sending flecks of ash into Jim's hair.

He balanced a moment on the last rung, knowing that if the rope broke he was lost. Georgina had said last night that she'd had enough tension, she would not come looking for him if he slipped or was gassed — that his determination to reach the base of the well was just upsetting to her, nothing more than that, a fetish unrelated to their real problem, water. His manic enthusiasm resisted the clear flow of her love for him lately. For her, now, there would be no more coming down to the well with a folding stool and watching him from under a sun umbrella as he brought up interesting life on the tip of his spade. No. She stayed in bed these mornings, face to the wall, drinking lemon tea, rereading her Georgette Heyer collection with fierce concentration. If Jim was serious about the water problem, she said, he would get a tanker from town, or the two of them could move to town, shifting into one of the many unoccupied cottages in Logan's Reef until Stuart came to his senses. But Jim's action in the face of Georgina's concerns was as stubborn as any idealism that had driven him in the past.

What arose, then, in the column of the well, in the soft light under the early morning paddocks, was a thick, smooth, implacable brown sludge. Up it wallowed under Jim D'Inglis's bootsoles. There wasn't time for Jim to give it any thought. He wasn't alarmed. This was his moment of absolute risk. It seemed beautifully appropriate, whatever it was — like a drug. Over a smooth velvety unblemished surface Jim hovered, his boots balanced on the lowest rung of the ladder, his body twisted over the fall, arms out like a diver's. Maybe it was well gas, this vacuous stuff, inviting Jim to flick himself in. Maybe it was only what it looked like, a thick, hypnotic mud released by altering pressures in the byways of the disturbed spring, something in geomorphology clogging the senses. It didn't matter. It was compelling.

Kel's legacy. What was it? The impossibility of understanding without total immersion.

Jim D'Inglis threw wide his arms and plunged into the well, palms narrowly grazing the rough walls, chest taut, wet bootsoles briefly shining before the darkness swallowed him.

SCENE: VERANDAH OF CROPPDALE HOMESTEAD, as featured in architectural classics as yet unwritten, *Raw*

Built Houses of Australia and *Stone Walls Before Federation*.

Mal loved the dump. He sat on the terrace in the early sun, tinkering with the torch he'd found in the grass, cleaning out the internal rust with a wire bottlebrush. Croppdale spoke to him. He was in love with an austere, unexpectedly messy place. He'd always resisted tracking out to Croppdale. Yet through resistance he'd spent a lifetime coming. Croppdale was a props store for life in the open air. The show? *The Return of Gunner Fitch*. Mal looked around warily, feeling self-conscious and worried about Ida's reaction seeing him here like this. She'd smile, catching him out in another pretension, saying, What was he play-acting now? Who? Old Sir Magnus with his tradition of late breakfasts on the flagstones — a sly ambition of Mal's since the time he'd let her fall on her head?

Mal kept his face turned away from the front door of the homestead, waiting for Stuart to get his grandfather dressed. He didn't want his reunion with William D'Inglis to be too sudden. He'd moved up to the house and settled into a room waiting for the old man to take his time over him. Stage experience slowed time, made him ready. Mal wanted to let this meeting sink in, keeping the old man attentive for the moment of recognition. Don't rush it. Mal wanted a spectator, so dreamed him up in the dry, buzzy heat — who else but the Gunner, with his charts of the Upper Cropp, the Gunner waiting attentively on the landowner before departing for his death. *Just before you go, Dad*, Mal flicked over his shoulder, *Get a load of this one. Your boy.*

Two circles scraped in the cement foundations of the terrace caught Mal's eye. They were childish impressions of enormous eyes, the clumsy shape of a dog, paws like boxing gloves, tail coiled like a scorpion's. It was the Dog With Eyes Like Saucers from his childhood stories. At that moment Mal could barely bring himself to look round to the door of the house, where he heard the sound of voices and a shuffling slippered step. He knew what would happen next — all years reduced to one, Mal aged around seven, a soft floury voice telling him things to make him tense, to make him never want to grow up for the impossibility of it happening, an impression of sweat in the wind as a door opened rudely, without invitation, an impression of slickered sandy arm-hair wet from the rain, and the reek of dog in the room, wooden curtain rings ripped back, a bedtime story told, a slobbery goodnight kiss conveying indifference.

LURKING AROUND THE BACK OF Croppdale homestead, Colin Byron heard the name hissed from an
upper side window.

'Josh!'

Nobody there. He put his palms against the gritty
wall and kept himself calm.

The voice in his head came back: *Rust on the
plough, gold pitted and worn, canvas shredded, photos
faded and torn, an old truck sinking into the earth.* He
made words with a rhythm to stave off a fit. Getting
a pattern going made the fit slide away, packing
itself up, no longer sizzling around the edges of his
vision like white fire. The voice inside him chat-
tered on like the Diamond T when she stopped,
spoke like the rumble of the road when the road
ended, whispered like the air trapped in a mountain, moaned like a chained hound, tapped like a
gold ring on a tooth. Keep it going, Col. *I cannot
arrange anything except what I manage in life, the truck I
drive, the rocks I roll, the ring I wear. I am desire that burns
in life and wants to be true.*

Otherwise his fits were explosions. He chucked
one outside the Night Train and knew that the
person who reached for his hand would be glorious.
Nobody did, and one in particular made an evil
sneer. He would pay with his understanding.
Another time he detonated when he was pushed

from a ute speeding past the well derrick he'd seen poking above sandhills. A trayload of shooters had said they didn't want a loony in their vehicle. They said they'd tell someone where he was, but no one ever came. He'd needed the drilling truck and there it was, the knobbly derrick visible over a rise. Colin left with Erwin and Kurt the next day in a thunderstorm. The storm had exploded on his behalf. Then, framing these events of his life, he met Stu D'Inglis and passed under the gate of Croppdale.

Colin Byron moved along the side wall of the homestead, idly loosening sheets of mortar with his fingertips. The crust shattered at his feet. Small crowns were cemented on the stones. They were worn and sad, and Colin couldn't move them. He saw a dog drawn with a stick, and looked up from it and met Mal Fitch's eyes. They smiled at each other. Dried moss was in the grooves. The letters K·E·L· and J·I·M· Behind the house he came to a deep-set window of thick reflecting glass with bubbles and streaks in it like stretched toffee. He tried to see inside, cupping his hands, pressing the twin cartilages of his nose to the cold barrier. Words rained down on him as sooty bush bees flew round his face from a hole in the lintel. The bees tickled Colin's ears. They hung on his head like a smoky crown. They made him dark in daylight — 'Josh,' he smiled, delighted with himself.

From inside the house, on the other side of the thick window-glass, an old man stared into the face of Colin Byron.

'Who are you?' his voice trembled.

'Josh!'

Colin Byron held the snake ring against the glass, tip, tap, where it was magnified for the watcher. A small crust of chemical stain flaked from the scales, making them brighter. Colin looked over his shoulder at the shadows playing around the old potato digger, where a fat-leafed tree rippled in the heat waves, and currawongs rat-tatted on the lids of forty-four-gallon drums, where a spilt sack of Lucky Dog attracted them.

The old man stared and his eyes bulged.

Josh is my true name, born of a spark fired in an old truck in 1967. I sizzled to earth out west somewhere. The night I was born the sky flickered red in the afterglow. It gave me my carroty colour. My mother, I don't know who she was, she placed me on a bed of cold ashes and went outside and never come back. I arrived here with two no-hopers — a lazy man and a self-lover.

'Trespasser!'

People think they know this earth — they live on it all their lives but they've never been under it. Wake up to yerself, old boy.

WILLIAM D'INGLIS EMERGED ONTO THE verandah of the homestead waving a stick, shuffling his slippers, snapping his false teeth in. He saw Mal Fitch and exclaimed: 'I fought that father of yours — he took my ring — he tried to put the wind up me. I *resisted*. He was a bloody thief.'

'Sir —' Mal heard himself stutter, cursing himself for an onrush of old-fashioned respect and fear. He wanted to say that Gunner Fitch never took anything. He wanted to say that Gunner brought things out in people. But what did he know? He could only talk about himself, of what was inside himself. Here was William D'Inglis in a reek of old fur, dusty, pelt-rolled, tedious odours. He knew that all right.

'He carried grease balls in his handkerchief. They called him Filth.'

William D'Inglis wore green corduroy trousers and a hairy tweed sportscoat, overlarge on his wasted bony shoulders. Century-old man looked no older than frail seventy, thought Mal. William D'Inglis, it seemed, went to the trouble of knotting a tie while living alone. Gunner would be the same if he had lived, a centenarian, still wearing his black suit and homburg, no doubt. It was unnatural, thought Mal, stubborn to live so long and dress as if you were about to leave for a meeting of the shire council and not for eternity.

'Your father came back.'

Close like this, peering testily at Mal, the old man stank of other things. Dirty laundry. His breathing like tide-suck. The amazing remembered thickness of Bay Rum.

'We fought.'

'I am Malcolm — remember?'

No flicker of recognition, that is, no surprise: he was known.

'Malcolm. Mal. Bring — me — a — cigar.'

'Are you sure you —?'

'Just get it, sonny.' William D'Inglis stared, his eyeline passing over Mal's shoulder to the corner of the house, where Colin Byron stood leaning on a post, gazing at his knuckles.

'*Arrgh!*' growled William D'Inglis, flicking his hands dismissively at the skinny water intruder as if he didn't really believe he was standing there, as if he were a lifelong irritation, a ghost.

AT THE OLD DAIRY IDA turned around to select another stone for her wall, and found that the lithe water driller Kurt who'd been watching her naked had come silently around the corner of the ruin. In his chapped fists he held the next stone ready for her, a box-shaped chiselled limestone block, holding it easily in one hand whereas she had needed two, and even then had staggered under the weight.

'Thank you.'

'This should be about the right size, I think.' His upper lip curled. Women made him sarcastic as hell, it seemed. Every time Ida turned around he was still there, passing another stone from the pile, always well-chosen.

'Do you normally just impose yourself on people?' Ida asked.

His answer was a sneer that said he did, that it often advantaged him, and if it didn't, so what?

His silences made her nervously sociable.

'You've done stonework before?'

'Yeah, I've done most things, lady.'

Sorry she asked. She let him get on with it. He unbuttoned his shirt and tied it around his head like a turban. The sun shone on his brown, sweat-streaked back and glinted off the gold chain he wore around his neck. The name Davinia shattered a heart tattooed across his right breast.

'The name is Kurt,' he pointed at himself as if in a crowd.

'Davinia broke your heart, did she?'

'That's *her* heart, I reckon.'

Well, thought Ida. Poor woman. Then she thought, he is too old, too crude, too arrogant, too stupid — but welcome anyway, Lachlan Strong the Drover. In return for a kindness she would wash any old traveller's greasy moleskins on the banks of the Condamine. Except this Kurt didn't even want to know what her name was.

She sat in the shade, head back on a tattered cushion, and thought, what if there was no Mal, no family, no anyone else, and this man was the last on earth? Who is he — my death? Well, if he tried what he was thinking, breathing hard with a whistling ferocity, and looking down the length of her like hot fat seeking a fire, she would overarm him with a river stone within reach here, talcum-smooth and weighty. Life to the end.

Shading her eyes, Ida saw Mal on the terrace with her grandfather, both men puffing on cigars and sending up smoke signals in the crystalline air. She couldn't ever remember Mal smoking a cigar. It was just like him — grabbing any available pretension to achieve definition. This morning it made Ida smile. There was relief around the idea of Mal being here. He'd overflown her into a family connection — a strange one for Croppdale: peaceful. A feeling was gone that had emanated from Mal and hovered around Ida in some fashion since the day she'd realised, at the age of eleven, that she wasn't ill any more, that she'd gone (as she later learned) into remission.

Kurt Wolpers saw that smile and worked harder, deciding it was for him. The sweat ran off his smooth muscles like bars and notes of music as he huskily whistled her tune, 'Misty Blue', to convey what he meant: heartbreak, longing, and the matter of a slow slippery fuck later — how about it?

THERE WAS A DREAM IDA HAD. Every element in it was real. She was on a platform at Logan's Reef station, trying to catch a train home to Croppdale. Mal was the conductor and wouldn't let her on. When she protested he pulled out a flare gun and shot her. A white disc the size of an all-day sucker flew into her, filling her with a warm, sickly light. It was the same feeling she'd had when she went to hospital as a girl for her barium meal X-rays. Then she had seemed to glow with unnatural heat. After so many tests the doctors came in scratching their heads, saying there must have been a miracle, or a mistake — the cancer wasn't anywhere in her, she was free of it all. That was when she was eleven. In the dream Mal was trying to kill her, but weirdly the shot enabled her to get up and catch the train, which went somewhere else altogether, into Logan's Loop, so seductive, then out again and along past the mill, into a different part of the countryside. After the shooting Mal didn't appear on the train; he stayed on the platform and she looked back at him through a sooty window, watching him watching her.

Lying back on her cushions in the shade in the heat, the next thing Ida knew was an all-too-familiar swarm of black spots in front of her eyes, and a sensation of rushing, nauseating release, as if she were flying from a height. She'd fainted or fallen asleep. When she rubbed her eyes the water driller was leaning over her, shaking her by the shoulders. 'Miss?'

She pushed him away in alarm, looked around for that stupid waterworn stone, and sat up straight. No, don't be hysterical, Ida. He wasn't trying anything on. She'd only frightened him into kindness.

'You're sick.' His dry, dusty hand was at her elbow as he helped her to her feet.

'I feel awful,' said Ida. 'Will you drive me somewhere?'

'Name it.'

He took her hand and, so unlike himself it was strange, led her considerately, tenderly, to her car.

OFTEN ABOVE THE CROPP RIVER GORGE, where he launched his hang-glider, Harry Frawtell would swoop low over lovers bedded on the casuarina needles of the forest. It was a great thing to tongue his fox whistle there as he rushed over, looking back over his shoulder as he climbed, seeing the bloke with his pants round his ankles scanning the sky in the wrong bloody direction and looking confused. He'd earned a name for himself as an airborne sleaze, but he wasn't. He was on the lookout for someone. He'd once seen Stuart D'Inglis there, and he'd circled back, needing to know whether Rennie Logan was with him. She wasn't. Turned out it was just Stuart and his dog eating a takeaway before heading home to the farm.

'I don't bloody believe it,' Harry muttered to himself this time. Because here on the glittering sandy reaches of the Upper Cropp where he was at work weaving intricate infinity signs in the silvery southerly updrafts, he saw, from a thousand feet, his love Rennie Logan in the arms of a stranger. They were hard at it. Some kid. *Who the fuck*, groaned Harry Frawtell as he put the nose down, built up speed and banked, couldn't identify the bloke, and was washed in sadness, then slipped his fox whistle onto his tongue and caught an updraft, the agony of an impaled rabbit coming through the tin whistle matching his state of mind. Beat after beat he made against the steep bare slopes where the southerly wind poured its strength. Away, high above the ridgetops, he flew the steepest, tightest spirals he'd ever attempted, and found himself looking straight down into an old shadowed mineshaft, where a pool of water glowed beautifully blue at the bottom of the day.

'I don't bloody believe it!' he shouted, as the rainbow wingtips lost contact with the air, and the glider hesitated, then stalled in a ghastly fashion, flapped, jolted, and then Harry Frawtell just let himself go, plummeting heavily and pushing the useless craft away into a different part of sky, giving all his thought to aiming at the pool of narrow water underneath, where he planned a neat diving entry and an equally impressive resurfacing.

ERWIN SCHMIDT KNEW THAT COLIN BYRON had lied about the water. He could smell it here himself, for crying out loud. All over these goddamn hills. After his breakfast he set off walking in the thin, burning upland air, following a rusty water pipe. It was the direction he'd seen Kurt driving the woman in her small car. Swift worker. He made Erwin fret. They'd had much trouble in the past, husbands wielding lengths of pipe, women following them from town to town — all that kind of thing, including enquiries by police about carnal knowledge, accusations that were later withdrawn. A mate was a mate, though. Had Erwin stood by his mate and never breathed a word to Davinia? Too right he had.

Car tracks and the water pipe crossed the river between drooping willow trees, where the rusty water pipe hung suspended, hinged on joints of radiator hose. Then it dropped to the ground again, looped over gullies, angled between rocks. Erwin plodded stoically along in his thongs. At the end of the last straight the tracks turned towards an old wooden cottage in a bare paddock. The cottage had roses around it. Kind of pretty in the dry. The blue car was parked at the front. Erwin loped past curiously, then circled back. Kurt was into it with her already, he supposed. Erwin didn't like to pry. This time it would be a world record, though.

But then from out in the paddock Kurt appeared, holding the elbow of a man who was covered in mud, with weed stuck in his hair, a man staggering, almost falling over. He looked half-drowned, but how could that be so, in a drought?

WITH A SPONGE AND A jug of warm water Georgina cleaned sticky brown mud from Jim D'Inglis's age-ing, freckled back and wiped green slime from his shivery limbs. 'What happened?' she insisted. He shook his head. Couldn't say. He'd fallen, that was all, and then made his way up again in a surge of rising water, floating to the surface where Kurt Wolpers had found him semiconscious. Georgina refrained from saying I told you so. Jim said it was all over from start to finish in about a minute.

'Wait until Stuart hears about this,' said Georgina tightly. The extremes he'd driven them to.

Jim closed his eyes and tipped his head back against the rotting bathroom wall. He'd fallen into a daylight dream. He was standing again at the base of the well, on the curved top surface of the boulder where — it seemed — he'd landed on his knees after diving into the muck. Leeches came at him through the debris. The light was blue down there. He hadn't been afraid. At the far end of the lake of soft blue water was an icy-pale ledge, a platform. Stalagmites reached up, forming a mound of white, a kind of below-ground hilltop. A voice echoingly called, 'I don't bloody believe it!' Then there was a loud thump. Jim blinked, and where there had only been whiteness, the shape of a man was spread-eagled. He was absolutely motionless, feet together, arms spread wide. The light down there was sourceless. A strong breeze touched Jim's face. A sound came at him through the hollow bones of the mountain. It was organ music, a sound created by a surge of water slamming into him, taking him up again, it seemed, where he woke floating in the well, his arms flailing, his mouth choked with weed, that hand reaching out for him.

'Jim.' Georgina shook his shoulders. 'There's something wrong with Ida. Go in and see her, please. And Jim,' she warned, 'don't give me anything about not being allowed to do this, none of your phone me a real doctor this time. Just help.'

IN THE HAUNTED LONELY DEPTHS of Storm Wilde, a glistening whale homed with a shudder, vomiting ambergris. She gathered the shivering treasure into her pale hands. It was her life. She cried out in delight.

'Ida? What is it?'

Jim sat at her bedside for a long time before she replied. She looked at him hazily, thinking he'd been soaked in a downpour.

She whispered, 'Oh, I'm sick again'.

'Again?'

She took his hand and played with his fingers the way she would have as a child, when he had never been there, but had always been away doing good for strangers.

'I'm sick the way I was when I was a girl. When I was dying.'

Nocturnal

THE MAN IS A BAT. Before he spreads his dark coat-
tails and flies, he stands with his head in the hole
of a cliff and worries it pleasurably, as if extracting
nectar. He reaches an arm into the hole. Now he's a
rabbiter getting out a nest of kittens. But no. What
emerges is a long tin torch, heavy with batteries.

As he straightens himself, sheets of carbon blackness pour from his shoulders. He stamps his feet. We
hear the crack of bones. My God, now, look at this
long face, how high the forehead, for he wears no hat
for once, a sooty line above his eyebrows, his

baldness a dirty, dented half-shone billycan. Flap, smack, roar, he's launched in a spiral of light — coming round in a long smiling circuit, Colin Byron and Mal Fitch joining him, one clicking teeth, the other playing spoons.

Then with arms around each other's shoulders, they descend a hieroglyph taken from a railway tunnel, Logan's Loop, gliding over themselves and under, the father and his boy upside down, right-angling, left-angling, dangling at speed and humming 'Danny Boy' together. Mal knows who the Gunner is through this, where he goes from here, what is to be done about him. *You cunning old bastard*, he grins. *Welcome*.

The process working its way through Mal is a familiar pattern of emotions. Down at Whale Belly Players it's always reverse the clock. Get down to the level of connection. Smoke out an emotion and hold it low.

The gloomy, skinny, long-dead diviner tosses the torch to Mal, who stamps on it, folds it over, reduces it to a wad of tin. Then he spits on it and watches it rust into the dirt. The graphite cores, pulverised, dispersed, are caught by the wind and blow around the world.

A wagtail trills in the silence. On his narrow bed Mal Fitch raises himself on an elbow, and leans

wonderingly against the window-glass of the Croppdale bedroom where he lies. He rubs his eyes and
yawns. For the last few moments he follows a shape
down from the crowded starriness above, feeling the
ground whisper as the Gunner totteringly laughs on
landing. The pleasure in this man Mal never knew is
so intense that he knows he will never lose him. For
this is his father, who strides off over the hills, humming an old air. For this is the arrival Mal has been
awaiting all his life. For this is Mal himself.

Above them, Colin Byron spreads his arms, cruci-
form in the night sky. A piece of metal clatters on the
roof iron and bounces into an unused chimney,
where it tinkles downwards between sooty old
bricks, bedding itself in cold ash. Fires flare in the
house, fed by cords of yellow box and fiercely-
burning blackwood trunks hot enough to melt gold.

IN THE COTTAGE NEAR THE overflowing well there is
no place for lust. It feels itself bruised and beaten, low
and confused. Kurt Wolpers excuses himself from
the household and retires to a clump of tussocks on
the old mined hill, where he tries to recover his self-
respect from a dangerous near miss. A woman so ill it

made him want her more. She looked at him like death. He frightened himself out of it.

He dreams he's on a bluff above the dark water of a rocky gorge, breathing hard after plenty of scrub bashing, looking down into the water, a fifteen-foot dive. Deep black water, with rock shelves intruding everywhere. Dangerous water. He dives in. Take me out of this shithouse life. He doesn't die, though. He ends up speeding along the final straight to Gideon Hills, coils of golden dust flying up, the flat of his hand banging the horn to announce his arrival.

It's not too late. Dora, get on the blower. Tell Davinia. We're back. Me and the fat stuff.

ERWIN IS IN THE SAME DREAM as Kurt. Here is his house — that strange brick dwelling sitting on an outcrop of rock, with a system of downpipes leading from the iron roof to a water tank dug from rock. Away in the distance are the swells and humps of blue granite ranges with the biblical name.

A shadow loops and undulates across the boulders behind the house, exaggerating the shape of a woman in a loose print frock. Dear old Dora — gardening by the light of the moon. This is what Dora calls rearranging plastic pots of cactus. Gardening. Thousands of kilometres away, her husband Erwin sits smoking a cigarette and drinking a stubby of beer, a big man wearing baggy trousers and a white singlet. The time is way after midnight. He wants to be gardening too.

No complaints. They can be here or there, they can be anywhere as long as one or the other of them doesn't die. They don't speak as a rule. They are contented with each other as a rule. If the night, the rock, the silvery silence chose this moment to absorb them into its peace, they would go without a murmur. Go together. They would say goodbye to time that has had its play with them.

IN IDA'S DREAMS KELVIN is the one who is dying, and calls out as he did in life for Doc Jim, who boils oil in a saucepan and, using a funnel, pours it in Kelvin's ear. Why Jim does murder is not clear. He doesn't want money. He doesn't want property. He says he wants peace, he says he wants love, has never wanted anything else, but Stuart is dancing around like a crazed mantis denouncing the long-buried love Jim has for Georgina. 'Peace is impossible. Love has already been given.' Ida must find a solution for Stuart: he is where this ends, this pain of hers, for there is love in Stuart he wants to strangle. Struggling panicky from the mattress, she must find a cure for his pain. Arms reach out towards her, voices chorus love. She can hear but her brother cannot. It isn't true that nobody cares. Call Mal. He can no longer hurt me. Doc Jim holds her hand again and she is calm. There must be somebody to balance Stuart out. Find that someone and let her know who.

OUT IN THE DARK Stuart D'Inglis and Colin Byron are climbing along starlit cliffs, hand over helping hand. They are looking for a nest of baby possums. In the house under their feet the old man cries out in nightmare, thin and piping. The sound megaphones through an empty chimney and surges against the rockface.

Stuart and Colin Byron enter the house. 'You can doss in with me, sport.' Male voices talking in undertones.

Colin has lost his ring. 'It just slipped off me finger.' He feels foggy in the head.

'You're a careless bugger. When?'

'It was when you grabbed me.'

'Did I grab you?'

'You fell. I caught you.'

'That's bullshit.'

Stuart lies awake staring at the ceiling. He fell, all right. But from where? There is a young woman in Logan's Reef more beautiful than anyone could ever imagine. She has a long black braid of hair hanging straight between her shoulder blades, and eyes the depth of coalsacks. She walks with the grace of an African dancer and speaks with the voice of an angel. She is a kindergarten teacher. Her name is Rennie Logan. On hot afternoons she waits at the Logan's Reef War Memorial Pool with her classes, and gazes longingly up the road to Croppdale, where she waits for Stuart to appear. He has to be frank with himself, though. There is something Rennie withholds. He cannot define what it is. What he thought was outside Croppdale threatening its boundaries has somehow flipped over and is inside here. Love has no greater gift to offer than acceptance. Fear replaces anger in Stuart D'Inglis and helplessly he begins crying in the unquestioning presence of Colin Byron.

Colin Byron gets him a glass of water and sits on the edge of the bed just to be with him.

'She's right, mate,' he consoles.

AT AROUND TWO IN THE MORNING Mal Fitch brushes past Colin Byron in the hall of the homestead — 'G'night' — and goes to the kitchen, where from a brass tap sticking through the wall he draws himself a glass of rust-flaked water. He remembers how it was in the old shop: water glitteringly pure taken from a tap like this one. Mal drinks. His glass swirls with specks of metal and mosquito wrigglers. It offers sour refreshment. Not bad.

Thirst slaked, Mal sleeps again — head on his arms on the zinc covering of the kitchen table. Sleeps like a child. He no longer has any urge to find the potbellied figure on the radiator cap and ask him questions. In the old playtext that Ida pulled from his shelf round the time of *Prosperity*, Mal had read: *There's no vocabulary for love within a family, love that's lived in but not looked at, love within the light of which all else is seen, the love within which all other love finds speech. This love is silent.*

Silent, but Croppdale lends its closing image to stand for speech.

Croppdale. It would do Mal. It always had — if only he'd seen it. He is totally changed at Croppdale, and the thing about change is it shows you who you were all along. It brings you to yourself — that is all. You dance in the birthplace of your soul. Emotions fall through time, seeking purchase. Invisible, they snag. If they are attached to objects, these things stay bright until they're found and brought up, exposed to the air of recognition. Mal has learnt at least this. Everything around him is crumbly and flaking, his love, his anxiety, his career. He's through.

He wakes and yawns and stretches in the mouse-scratchy darkness of the kitchen. His hands above his head plough through granules of carbon black.

Jim softly taps him on the shoulder and Mal jumps. 'Ida wants you. Come.'

IN THE ATTIC BEDROOM ABOVE Mal's head the old man folds his hands across his chest, exhales a last breath, and begins walking. Energy flows into him, a clean, crystalline strength, as from the steady flow of unrestricted water. He's outside and across the river before he knows what's happening. Looking back, the homestead is under floodwater, a great, sparkling, steady flow.

Out in the dark another figure joins him: Gunner Fitch with his suitcoat thrown back over his shoulder, and Nell the limping black dog bounding along ahead of them, showing the way.

Up on the ridge where the Chinese mineshafts are,

a woman is dancing. They are both sick with love for her, these two. Now they will have to let her be. Rosan, Rosan — what have we done to your life and to our own? Such longing stays with them. She has tight blonde curls and a lovely, wide-foreheaded face. Her squared-off tongue-tip touches her lower lip with youthful concentration, a habit she passed on to her boy Mal. She wears a print dress and grey silk stockings, and impractical shoes for the place she is in, light dancing pumps that skip among shimmering snakes that nip at her shapely ankles. Out along the dangerous ridgetops she moves. There are sleepers on the ground, generations of the living, including strangers and half-familiar faces: an English boy who looks like Ida in the arms of a beautiful young woman who is a relation of Rosan's, Rennie — she and Rosan they have the same wide honest forehead — and Ida too is there, attended by sleeping Mal, who's anchored like a rotund boat to his snores, and Doc Jim too, he's asleep guarding Ida from the ravages of her passage, clutching his African walking stick, lying full-length on the ground like a scrawny shepherd in a symbolic painting. Ida, look, has her observant grey eyes open. She's watching Rosan. Oh, see, there's a kind of bar of shade about halfway up Rosan's body and she dances out of it, higher and higher into the light which is milky yellow, half-sunlight, half-moonlight, and she joins her hands above her head, and Ida leaps up and goes with her, step by step, movement by movement.

Gunner Fitch makes a casual arm gesture. Back among the men water spews from the ground in a gush, delivering a man from the inside of the mountain. He spins in the air and slams into the branches of a fallen tree, where he gets his balance, and smiles with an air of faint grievance. This is mill manager Harry Frawtell. Gunner Fitch then snaps his fingers. Out of the shadows on either side of Harry Frawtell come Mal and Josh, the foul young soldiers who raped women and knocked gold teeth out of the mouths of friend and foe in the mud before they died in the big freeze of '17.

Then Gunner isn't there and none of them are there.

COLIN BYRON SLEEPS, THE HAIR standing up on the back of his head, his thumb hooked in his mouth — and while he sleeps, he pulls on his trousers, pads barefooted through the house, gets out to the verandah where his boots are, and sniffs the air. Nobody there, but *somewhere*.

A strange feeling of being under water and yet being able to breathe, his movements unimpeded by any pressure.

'Wait,' calls Stu. 'I'll come with you.'

They go on foot. The river is wide at this point, flowing smoothly as if down a weir. Colin gets the truck, removes the wheels, loads them on the back, and they cross the river using the rig like a barge. Stuart uses a crowbar to make a rudder. On the other side they restore the wheels and drive up into the hills, where they set the truck alight and push it down a shaft. Down there it burns for a long time, giving off a rosy reflected light like the pre-dawn sun below the horizon.

Stuart will take water to the cottage in the morning.

THE TRUCK IS WRECKED and the ring is gone. The broken figure on the radiator cap is in a hundred pieces. The metal of the zinc eye is peeled back, revealing a tender living organ, wet, marbled, jellied white. The eye of Malcolm Fitch watching Ida D'Inglis peacefully sleeping. No other. Out in the dirt ants shoulder aside divining wires from their path.

Rainbow rags of hang-glider wings are torn, scattered as pollen. The body of Harry Frawtell, a good angry man, lies split open at the ribcage on a high rock, with a fox tearing at his liver.

Georgina shows Guy D'Inglis into Ida's bedroom. When she wakes he will be the first person she sees. Rennie Logan rests a loving hand on Guy's shoulder. Like Mal, she feels she has lived at Croppdale all her life, no matter how brief her stay here.

UP ALONG THE RIDGETOPS it is cool. There one man rests on a bed of bracken — Alec Hooper. He is watchful. Another is near death from heatstroke — Keith Wiencke. No matter how hard he tries he won't be allowed to die. He will come through this. He's too bloody imperfect to be allowed to shuffle off yet. While Alec Hooper dips a rag in a canister of water and trickles it over Wiencke's blistered lips, the younger man hallucinates, making a speech to a three year old boy on a plastic two-way radio: 'I am your father. Wait for me.'

Alec Hooper remembers how it was on the Cropp River that time with Ida. They boiled the billy on the sand. Wattle-blossom floated on the surface of the pool. They swam the tired horses there. Slicked manes and dark eyes in the evening light, strong necks and smooth wet backs sending out ripples. How do you escape from such love? It isn't real. The horses emerged from the water crusted with golden bloom like ceremonial coats. Alec Hooper weeps remembering, his chest heaving like a tangle of barbed wire.

NEXT WINTER THE RING of snakes passes from Cropp-dale homestead in a scuttle of ash. Tread on it crossing the yard in your boots and it will crush to powder. A gust of wind and it's gone.

Roger McDonald
Slipstream

**'I bored a hole in the air for the first time.
I did something first. They hate that here.'**

Roy Hilman was a famous aviator and Australian hero. A
pilot in the Great War, a stunt flier in early Hollywood, a
trans-Pacific pioneer and a national celebrity, Hilman was
a man drawn upwards by dogged, dazzling ambition.
Seemingly unbreakable, idolised by a nation, he was also
menaced by shadows.

Roger McDonald puts this Roy Hilman of popular legend
and official biography into human perspective in
Slipstream, a richly perceptive, many-layered exploration
of the tensions between reality and illusion in the life of a
man who was also a myth.

In the foreground of the novel are the people closest to
Hilman: his wife Olga, seduced by the velocity of flight and
the man who controlled it; Charles Coulter, Hilman's
sponsor, abandoned by Olga for the man he backed
financially; Claude McKechnie, Hilman's official
biographer, a young man in search of an idol; Leonard
Baxter, who braves public outrage and sacrifices his
career for the love of another man's wife. All are bound
together by intrigue and colliding emotions, their complex
responses to Hilman coloured by their own dreams and
desires.

Against a background of business, politics and flying, this
absorbing novel examines the price of fame as it is
expressed in the life of Roy Hilman, a figure whose
haunting power is inseparable from the pure fascination of
flight itself.

Roger McDonald
Shearers' Motel

**Another shed coming up on the horizon... a low,
wide roof of galvanised iron the only landmark in a
million square miles of flatness and glare.**

Into the hard-living world of travelling shearers in the
Australian outback comes acclaimed writer Roger
McDonald, driving an old truck rattling with cooking gear.
He has abandoned writing for a time and found work as a
cook for a team of New Zealand shearers travelling
through New South Wales, South Australia and Victoria. He
is determined to find a sense of belonging: somehow to
join his life with the landscape, the places and the people
he meets along the way.

Shearers' Motel is the record of that quest, of its triumphs
and its failures — a story told with a heartfelt sense of the
profundity of ordinary lives.

Written with an insider's affection and familiarity sharpened
by an outsider's perception, this moving account of
working life in a classic Australian industry gives a new
twist to a long tradition of outback travel writing. It confirms
Roger McDonald as one of our finest and most lyrical
chroniclers of the land.

'Roger McDonald uses language with the precision of a
diamond cutter.'
US PUBLISHERS WEEKLY

Roger McDonald
Shearers' Motel

'A wonderfully sensual account of a year spent cooking for Maori shearers in outback Australia. Roger McDonald is exploring his own hopes and frustrations as well as the lives and landscape around him. An ingeniously conceived and brilliantly constructed work presented with great literary skill.'
JUDGES' REPORT, C.U.B. BANJO AWARDS, 1993

'A triumph of stylish, thoughtful writing... one of the best books I have read for a long time.'
ROBIN LUCAS, THE BRISBANE REVIEW

'A masterpiece of observation, portraiture and landscape painting.'
ALAN GOULD, THE CANBERRA TIMES

'*Shearers' Motel* is a joy to read. It could be enjoyed for its language alone, which is evocative, descriptive and precise. Lovers of poetry can revel in its imagery. Those familiar with the Australian outback can relate to its graphic reality. Those who do not know the Australian environment can be assured that they are faced with as true a description as the written word will allow.'
MARGARET DEAVES, THE NEWCASTLE HERALD

'*Shearers' Motel* is not like any other Australian novel, either in form or in content. McDonald has taken great risks in achieving it, both as a man and as a writer. He has been valiantly successful.'
GEOFFREY DUTTON, AUSTRALIAN BOOK REVIEW

'The observation, the humane sympathy, and not least the writing in *Shearers' Motel* convince me I can trust Roger McDonald to explain the beauty and the bastardry of the bush to me.'
DON ANDERSON, THE SYDNEY MORNING HERALD

Outside Time

TWO-THIRTY IN THE MORNING and he found himself wide awake. It was the second week of shearing at Gograndli Station. He went outside. Everything was changed from the stark, negative impressions of daytime. Bright moonlight shone between buildings. The deadly nightshade in the walkway outside the kitchen door had a silvery stiffness. Cobwebs shone in shadows. Windows were blank. The galvanised roofing of the shearers' quarters seemed frosted. Fretworked tree shadows in the yards and the holding paddocks were transparent as air. There did not seem to be any trees nearby when the sun was at its height. Now they declared themselves, a spectral forest. Back across the river no light shone from Gograndli homestead. The tension of the waking world was relaxed. Wagtails and magpies stirred, ducks whooshed overhead, emus stalked the salt-bush plain with emerald eyes. Dark shapes of night stood separate from each other in a gathering ground-mist. The red gums on the riverbank were stately, the coolabahs on the floodplain shifted informally closer. Now they joined ranks with everything. A spirit breathed.

He walked around the huts and stood over the old dump with its shattered glass, ruptured water tank, and rusted motor parts, his bootlaces dragging in the dirt, his beltless trousers held up by one hand. Generations of broken beer bottles shone in piles as he pissed on them.

Over his shoulder were the huts. Inside the huts were a dozen sleepers. He had the feeling that nothing on earth could wake them at this hour. They were felled in rows, two by two, arranged on metal beds, their heads against the back wall and their feet pointing towards the doors. They were all the same now, felled into the stillness between the noisy movements of their lives. The depth of night had dropped them like a scythe, their wakefulness mown by a blade of silvery photons whetted on moonrock.

At four he woke again. There was a different quality to the light. The moon was low, angled through the louvres on the ruined wash-house wall. Its light no longer called to mind comparisons with day, reversals of familiarity, pale images and recompenses of waking reality. Now a magnetic lowness was in the air. A mood of violent attraction and unaccustomed dread had him sitting up, throwing back his sleeping bag, sitting on the steps of his room and lacing his boots. Shadows were elongated, prowlike, fixed, clawed, slammed, hooked on the ground. It was the dream hour, a time bewildering to consciousness. He lit the fire in the stove and stared at the flames. Outside a visual gravity tugged the mind lower than ever it went. Suicide hour. Death hour. Hour of departure. From here to the edge of the world wasn't far. It lay past a steep, eroded cliffline north of the river's meander, where the wagtails and magpies went silent, and only sheep bleated, lost souls endlessly stressed, asking what next. Out from that edge stars would declare themselves after moonset. Another hour and the sky would lighten, galah- and corella-pink would flush the east, morning sun like a trumpet blast would stream down the plain, etching the shoddy coolabahs and the mournfully decaying red gums in pitiless light.

But not yet. There was still this cold, brooding stillness of the low-angled moonlight. He passed along the row between the huts with an armload of wood. Inky shadows stood at the shearers' doors. Their dogs chained to the stumps watched him, and went back to sleep. Sadie was asleep on her sack. He made a mug of tea and sat on the mess-room steps and waited. This was his time.

Momentum

CAL CAME INTO THE KITCHEN, half-smiling, angling sideways, staring at the food table with a disdainful twist to his thick, wide lips. He was a physical force come to a standstill. The floor seemed to dip in the direction of Cal like a weatherboard whirlpool. Others milled around while he made up his mind what he wanted.

'I don't care, Cookie,' he shrugged, transferring food to his plate with a blunt wrist action. Pumpkin, peas, mashed potato, mutton. What did it matter? Burgers and chips were Cal's soul food, beer and Jack Daniel's his spiritual refreshment. Fights were his glory.

He watched Cal trudge around the spread, getting his share of tinned fruit, UHT cream (crushing the carton in his fist), red jelly. 'Anything else?' No reply. The others pressing behind him expressed their usual exhausted truculence — 'This looks good' — 'What's this here shit?' — 'Pile it on, Cookie' — but Cal made him afraid. There was nothing compromised about him. The first time, when he asked him his full name, his eyes cannoned in slow motion towards the questioner. Then he looked down. 'Calvin.' The utterance was like the drop of steel into the innards of a pinball machine. It held Cal's attention while he wallowed in introspection. The name rolled, tumbled, slipped from his tongue. 'Calvin' — said with an extra, unneeded movement of the lips, a foam of spittle at the corner of the mouth, as if between the 'l' and the 'v' there was something else, a chomp, a rip, a delectation of strangeness. Then he raised his head again, as if coming up from the depths of water, shedding a weight. Something echoed back into his brain as he met another set of eyes. 'Calvin.'

Watching Calvin eat, he imagined him gnawing on human bones and spitting gristle to the dust. He thought if there came a night when graves opened and the dead walked, Calvin would be there.

One day at Gograndli Station Cal became animated. 'What's dis? Dis any good, Cookie?' He was in a good mood. It was corned leg there on the table — a different colour. Something had touched him, an incident in the shed, a word of praise or blame or aggression, a letter from home? He poked the mottled pink and brown of the meat with serving tongs. Back in New Zealand Cal's uncle was a famous Maori orator. The family kept an eye on him. The overseer was Cal's cousin. The others were animated, light-hearted or grave, having the full range of experience to play with. But Calvin seemed to have wrestled potential to a standstill — crushed it with inexorable strength. He only moved fast when he ran for a cold beer, or raced to the showers before the hot water went. Then his run was like a heavy trot, a topple, a lumber. Other times he dragged his toes in the dust.

One Sunday morning at Gograndli Sadie went crazy following new smells. She tracked splashes of blood. He walked up from where he was camped on the river and saw a shadow in the meat house. A freshly killed sheep had been put there the night before. Now it had a companion, a smaller, darker double. He went up to the gauze and saw it was a wild pig. Its chest had been cleaved open and the guts taken out. His dirtied butcher's knife hung where the last knife stroke had finished. Dried mud caked the pig's grey, mottled bristles. A jellied mass of ruby-red blood lay splashed on the cement.

He learned what had happened. Cal and the classer and the shed hands had driven to Ivanhoe to go to the pub. Coming home their headlights had caught a sucking pig on the rain-spattered track. The classer set his dog to it. The dog cornered the pig in a culvert. Someone found a screwdriver in the glove box and ran out into the dark, and drove it into the pig's brain.

On Monday while he prepared the pork there was a battle going on in the shed over Cal's attitudes. From what he could gather Winston Didale wanted Cal sacked. He shore in a dream, he had seen it himself in the few minutes before smoko, when he took the sandwich boxes over and lingered a minute, assessing the scene before going back to fetch the tea billies. 'Cal is lazy,' said Harold. Straightening his back from his work Cal had the preoccupied, distanced look of a man about to do something immediate, particular. The same wide spread of gravity that ripped galaxies apart focused on insignificant Calvin. Where was the knife, the pigsticker, the gun? Cal had all the time in the world as he lowered his handpiece and unclenched the cramp in his fingers. The grower stood beside the wool table with his arms folded over his skinny chest, his mind full of the implications of a few cents here and there, the hocks not taken off cleanly, the national disaster of second cuts (where the sheep were left striped with unusable wool). While Cal rotated his gaze, work structures shattered. They were bullshit to Cal — the collapsing and re-assembling pattern of the camp; the administrative needs of the contractor, the one who looked after him, Harold; the wants of the grower; the paperwork; the food orders; getting the wool away. *Pah*.

Harold took Cal aside and spoke a few stern,

whispered words. 'It grieves me to see you with these attitudes, brother.' Cal dropped his chin. Okay, he'd surrender his handpiece and work the wool board instead. Why de fuck not.

Calvin was no longer a shearer. He was a rousie now, what he had been since the age of seven and younger. What he had been since the mothers strung their baby baskets above the wool tables, bringing them into this life. There he went tripping along in his Adidas with a millet broom held loosely between the fingers of one hand, skirting, getting the shit separated from the bellies, armloading fleeces down to the end of the shed where the owner still kept an eye on him. That owner — who was he? No shape or form that Calvin could see.

One day this same Calvin would take up the knife inside himself and he would carve. One day he would cut his image inside the house at the inland town where he lived with his unwedded wife and his new, beautiful daughter with her tiny brown limbs, her smokily glowing skin, her blue water-pool eyes and her lovely dark-petalled lips. Calvin would find himself holding her and chuckling with a deep, bewildered delight, and then he would go outside and think for a minute, and then he would come inside again and get started. Stubbies would smash on the walls. Upturned, the record player would shatter. The TV and the video would crash. Then Calvin would come to Harold's house and take the twin-cab ute. He would drive for five hundred kilometres with his foot to the floor, take apart a shop in one of those towns over the border there, because something was needed for his child, something that no one would let him have, and turn around again and come back to the Western Division, listening to police calls on the UHF scanner, feeling himself slow down, tire, sink back red-eyed, satisfied, ready for the handcuffs and the time ahead when he would contemplate against the blankness of a cell wall what ever it was that appealed to him, locked him in, held him down, made him do what he did, made him who he was. Calvin.